T0123201

TABLE FIVE

TABLE FIVE

SALLY LONG

TABLE FIVE

iUniverse books may be ordered through booksellers or by contacting:

iUniverse
1663 Liberty Drive
Bloomington, IN 47403
www.iuniverse.com
1-800-Authors (1-800-288-4677)

ISBN: 978-1-5320-1146-7 (sc)
ISBN: 978-1-5320-1147-4 (e)

Library of Congress Control Number: 2016919168

Print information available on the last page.

iUniverse rev. date: 11/29/2016

Special thanks to Earley Engineering, the Peacock group, Prairie Lane Tech, David Nelson Exquisite Jewelry, Rich the Sandwich Guy, Sco-Ped Financial and Stephen B. Rubens. Cover design by S. B. Rubens. Cover photography by Diane M. Earley. Thanks also to Georgia from Alaska for suggesting I write a book named *Table Five*.

CONTENTS

PROLOGUE

M y attention was diverted from the rolling Czechoslovakian countryside when Fred's hand twitched on top of my thigh. Seated next to me, mouth agape, his slender yet muscular frame looked like a slouching statue. I could see him breathing so I knew he wasn't dead, just asleep. I touched the uncut diamond nugget through his pants pocket, causing him to stir. Asleep or not, he was hypersensitive to the rock. The hypnotic cadence of steel train wheels can bring that sleepy feeling. I slipped a paper cup of green tea from his hand and drained the last splash, then put a napkin in it. At least he wasn't snoring.

With its thick, red-vinyl bench seats and chrome grab bars, the train was anything but high-speed and certainly not modern. But it was clean, and when you were on a Czech passenger train, the decor made it difficult to ascertain in which decade it was built.

As I gazed once again out the window, the countryside appeared timeless; it could have been World War II, World War I, or before the railroad tracks on which we rode had even been forged. At mid-autumn, my eyes drank in each breathtaking acre of spectacular color. The previous thirty-six hours had been tense, and I was just starting to relax.

We had left Pardubice shortly after sunrise, bleary-eyed from our late and celebratory last night there. I had woken with a bit of a sour stomach due to the large meal and excessive tannin in the red Czech table wine. Apricot preserves spread thick on wheat flatbread and watered—down, super-strong Czech coffee in the morning had settled me as well as could be expected.

Fred had insisted we visit Pardubice, a leg of the trip I had questioned, but he convinced me it was important due to the plot that had unfolded throughout the preceding months. Our trip from New York to Switzerland, the Czech Republic, Antwerp, then Italy and back home was going by in a blink.

Our departure from Pardubice felt more like an escape. I had come to believe we were lucky our throats hadn't been slit. The cast of characters we had met seemed to have emerged from some Cold War spy novel. But I'm a Nebraska farm girl, not the cloak-and-dagger type ducking around corners running from pock-faced guys with eye patches and four-inch cheek scars. After all that, watching the European landscape created a sense of security; yet it was a false one, as I'd not only just escaped Pardubice but was still involved in a bloody and bizarre unsolved double-death case in New York.

Antwerp, our next destination, was potentially as dangerous as Pardubice. There was no doubt we'd encounter people in Antwerp who were aware of the diamond also. We would continue playing tourists, an illusion we had attempted to maintain.

Catching the smiling conductor before he spoke, I put a shush finger to my lips and pulled our tickets from Fred's breast pocket for validation. I returned the smile, then glanced at Fred and back through the coach window. The rhythm of steel wheels was getting to me also, as my eyes closed for a short nap before the train's connection in Prague. As my circuits shut down, there was one last fleeting thought: *I still don't want to get married* ...

BOOTS TO HEELS

Although I'm originally from a farm in Touhy, Nebraska, west of Omaha, I'm anything but a tomboy farm girl. I currently live close to the East Coast. My driver's license reads Agatha Lantana. I've been saddled with Aggie most of my life, but Agatha was just as bad. I thought it clever to turn my name around and have been going by Lantana ever since I left the Midwest four years ago.

I grew up in Touhy, did all the right things, did well in school, dated cute boys and could really rock a pair of tight jeans, although I always wished I had a C cup. I was never prom queen, but by all accounts, people would comment that I was pretty; both my parents were good-looking, and my light brown hair was a contrast complement to my blue-gray eyes. If I ever got full of myself or my looks, however, my three brothers could knock me off my glamour box in a second. My revenge was outrunning them on and off the field with my shapely legs. Also, Dad was proud that I was pretty good at baseball.

I locked into a great guy named Tom and got married when I was twenty-six.

Like so many girls in the middle of nowhere, however, I felt I was missing something. Maybe I just didn't want to end up looking like my aunts and the other moms, a worn-out Daisy Duke at forty. My mom would always be Mom, always pretty to me at forty or 140. Yet I'd see old pictures of my aunts or my friends' moms and the way they'd aged—the way it looked like life was passing, or had passed, them by.

It seemed to me, particularly in the Midwest, that women are supposed to be patient and let babies occupy their bodies for the better part of a year. This can happen as many times as you choose, or it'll just happen because you think it's supposed to. I did want kids, or perhaps in some instinctual and maternal way, I thought I was supposed to have them. You think you can do better raising a child than your parents or friends. Your kids are going to be different than all the other little troublemakers running around. This or that won't happen to you and your kids.

After a miscarriage and the depression that followed, I caught Tom cheating. That wasn't the entire reason I decided to divorce and flit away, but it was the impetus to shift and Tom wasn't totally at fault. Things change in people's lives all the time; it happens to all types of people, all over the world. Hell, I cheated on Tom once when we were going steady in high school, not a *full* sexual cheat but heady for high school. To be honest, after we were married, I knew I wasn't providing all of his needs. Through a lot of soul–searching, I wondered how many people were really happy in their long-term relationships. I guess my parents seemed to make it work. Yoko was robbed of John, but they had separated also—would they still have been together now?

Dad's parents lived close by and played the perfect stereotypical grandparents, stepping right from the television screen of a Waltons' episode. Except they weren't actors; they were human. My grandfather was a cheater; he worked in sales for John Deere and was "on the road" a lot. He was a kind-looking old man, usually in his blue-gray bib overalls until he left for his sales calls wearing his starched white shirt and wide brown tie.

My Gram Agatha—yes, I'm her namesake—knew. It was the worst-kept secret in the whole county. I was in seventh grade and caught her crying on a Tuesday afternoon after school. A little over five feet tall, her salt-and-pepper hair in a permanent bun, her slim frame belied her wiry toughness. It was easy for me to ask in my innocent schoolgirl way why she didn't do something about it. She told me she wasn't going to change horse's mid-stream. As a depression-era child, she clung to that perceived marriage ideal and security factor. She ended up a widow anyway, never getting what she wanted—someone to grow old with.

I had a special affinity and affection for my gram. Maybe because she was a throwback to a different time, the way she talked, what she'd been through, how she made me feel. I suppose a lot of grams are like that, wise with years, but not disciplinarians. Disciplinarians are what parents are for, and my Gram Agatha loved pulling a good one over on my parents or keeping a secret with me.

When I was a little girl, I asked her what the universal "no" symbol meant. She explained the bar through the circle, like on a no smoking sign, meant you shouldn't do that; it was bad and against the rules. So, in my still rudimentary language, I would see a circle and bar sign, look around, point, and excitedly exclaim, "Circle bar! Circle bar!" Gram thought that was clever and incredibly cute. Much later, when she met one of my first dates at the house, I later asked her what she thought of him.

She cried, "Circle bar! Circle bar!"

I just loved Gram.

With broad shoulders, a blockish jaw, and his oak brown hair, my dad was my superhero—still is. Late one summer night, when I was twelve years old, I went outside with our malamute-shepherd mix Shep and wandered farther from the farmhouse than I was supposed to. We were used to the plaintive cries of coyotes in the distance. If you've never heard these creatures, their howl is what I imagine tortured babies would sound like. Suddenly a pack of coyotes appeared from the edge of the cornfield.

There were about four or five, and Shep sensed them several seconds before I saw the first one. I was petrified. They were very organized and aggressive as three lunged at Shep. He valiantly began his defense, going into full-fight mode. My little-girl scream was probably higher and louder than the cacophony of the fight scene. The cowardly pack members took turns shooting in and out, biting at Shep and then retreating as a second and third would rush in. A shotgun blast shocked us all as Dad came running toward us, blasting a second shot skyward. I scrambled toward Dad as Shep bravely continued his defense. Dad triggered a third shot leveled at the pack; the pattern loosely spread behind Shep, as one coyote fell and stray buckshot pelted two others. The pack slithered like ghosts back into the cornfield as Dad pulled his .22 caliber revolver from his waistband and shot the downed coyote in the head.

We made our way back to the farmhouse. As we reached the light, I raced into my mother's arms; she was waiting on the porch, ready to assess the damage to Shep, limping behind us, his face covered in blood. She quickly checked me over as we went for a pail of warm water, peroxide, and an armful of rags. The coyotes had torn most of Shep's left ear off, the tip of his tail was gone and bleeding, and his right foreleg had been punctured. Mom cleaned the wounds as I held and comforted Shep. She dressed the injuries with salve and long, gauze bandages.

Dad and I sat up the rest of the night, with Shep wrapped in an old blanket on the floor in front of us. I woke up on the floor about dawn, with a pillow under my head and a blanket over me. Mom was sitting in her chair; I guess Dad had gone to bed only an hour before.

As his only daughter, I didn't realize, until I was older, the effort he put into our relationship, compared with those of my three crazy brothers. He seemed to know where the balance was in nurturing my feminine side but making sure I wouldn't get shoved around by my siblings and, in turn, by men later in life. Sure, I was Mom's pride and joy as the only daughter, but she was also proud of Dad because of his extra efforts. I will always remember life lessons he taught me. I learned how to work for, and save, a dollar, and I'd started a rainy-day nest-egg fund long before I left home. After leaving, I met lots of men and didn't fall prey to the considerable list of helpful guys more interested in my "rear" than my "ca-reer."

Dad would occasionally refer to the coyote story as it related to life lessons. Dad taught me also not to confuse generosity with sincerity. He was a TV sitcom junkie using analogies and characters from Andy Griffith, Jackie Gleason, Dick Van Dyke, and the rest of those actors. It drove me a little crazy, but overall he got the point across.

I wanted something different out of life, even if I didn't know what it was. It wasn't any single event that pushed me. Lots of women dream of striking out independently yet never act on their dream. Is it fear of the unknown that makes them hang out and fall into that familiar familial mold? Maybe I didn't like who I was becoming or visualizing my middle-age spread in a photograph twenty years from then if I'd stayed complacent in Touhy. Perhaps I knew down deep that what I wanted wasn't there. It was a little early for a midlife crisis, and getting old with someone wasn't yet on my long-term horizon. The move just seemed right ... and I was pushing thirty.

I traded my jeans and boots for skirts and CFM shoes and made it to Chicago after a three-month gig at a fancy restaurant in Des Moines. I had been a waitress in Touhy and was now landing jobs at some high-end restaurants. Owners and managers seemed to like my combination of wholesome Midwest girl mixed with coquettish persona and realized I had business savvy also. I kept the jeans in my wardrobe and Agatha on my driver's license but began going by Lantana, which I pronounced Lahn-tah-nah, in essence re-creating myself. I shunned "Lonna" and "Lonnie"; I *became* Lantana. My demeanor, the way I spoke, and the way I carried myself—all were Lantana. My real dream was to have a restaurant of my own one day. My fantasy was to operate a bistro in Europe. Hey, dream big, right?

Through a series of connections, happenstance deals, and plain dumb luck, the next couple of years had me in Indianapolis, Cleveland, Pittsburg, and ultimately New York

State. Other than a few fill-ins, I was always in the food and beverage business.

New York wasn't exactly a cold call for me. I had worked for a guy named Rich in Pennsylvania, near Pittsburg. He owned and operated three popular submarine sandwich stores called "Big Mouth's Hungry Hobo" in the university areas. Rich was a husky Italian guy with thick black hair, who sold a lot of subs. An innovator and marketing master he handcrafted his subs with custom mixed seasonings. Incredibly gregarious, Rich's businesses did very well, but paradoxically, never showed much profit. Every night at close, while I was doing the books or ordering product, Rich was scooping an onion-permeated hand into the registers on his nightly rounds. I decided to move on when he began adjusting the numbers in *my* books, ultimately being presented to the IRS. Rich worked a gambling book on every sport that involved a ball. We split on good terms, having learned many tidbits of wisdom, and he turned me on to my next restaurateur.

Giovanni was near Schenectady, New York, and guess what? He owned an Italian place. No need to guess again; it was called Giovanni's. It was a tidy place with character, in a strip mall, well established, with a good, mostly word-of-mouth local following and a delicious authentic Italian menu. By luck I landed the job with a phone call, and had enough savings to get through if it didn't work out. The first time I met Giovanni, it was love at first sight; for him. He was a bit full of himself, with a ladies' man persona; I don't think I'd ever encountered a guy so blatant with his intentions. I swear I thought he was going to shake my boobs instead of my hand when I met him, B-cup or not. I didn't last long, or should I say he didn't. So this was New York, or at least my first New Yorker.

I had talked a few times with Sherry, a shirttail relative in Albany, New York, to check things out in her area; she helped me get a line on an efficiency apartment. I loaded up my green Corolla, which I called Carlita, but before pointing it east, I stopped at Giovanni's for my final check. Against my better judgment, I gave Giovanni a hug, although I had a clenched fist within a rabbit's punch of his crotch. He gave me my check and a veal Parmesan sandwich to go, and I hit the interstate.

I settled into the tiny apartment for a few days and was getting acclimated when Sherry came over. Years would pass between our meetings, and although she always looked older than her years, she maintained her skinny frame and ruler-straight blond hair. From fifteen to twenty-five to thirty-five years old, the poor girl always looked like she had been rode hard and put up wet, as my uncle Verge would say.

When we met, her first words were, "What a dump."

She was right, but the place was what I'd expected—cheap—and it would suffice until I became a bit more established. Sherry and I were never very close; she showed me around and gave me information, like where to go and where not to go. We had something to eat and a few drinks and never talked again.

I was bartending in a sports bar earning an hourly wage, and the tips were good, really good. I had bartended before but always in restaurants. Waxing philosophical, I remembered how old thirty-three had seemed to me when I was twenty-one. How my perspective had changed! How generous these lonely married, single, or divorced men were just to receive a smile and pleasant conversation with their beer. They weren't flirty or dirty, just nice guys in a sad sort of way. I felt Troy, New York, had some potential for me. Troy was adjacent to Albany, neither of which was New York City, but they were good-sized metropolitan areas. I found a decent apartment with a one-year lease and kept bartending, but I hadn't lost sight of my goal of getting a foothold in a nice restaurant.

I was perusing the electronics want ads on the couch one afternoon and laid my head back. Closing my eyes, I contemplated how good a cosmo would taste. I had just enough Stoli left in the freezer. Hmm, that was one option—I'd already had one interview that day—but responsibility was trying to get the best of me. I should have strapped back into my uncomfortable push-up bra and my only Jimmy Choos and, at almost 4:00 p.m., checked out the new sushi restaurant downtown for a job. Part of my indecision was based on the thought, *it'll be the same old crap*. I was overqualified as a waitress and not interested in screwing the boss for the hostess job, especially since five-foot Asians weren't my type.

Somehow the drink still sounded better. It might have sounded better, but my savings were tickling my predetermined yellow zone. *Got it*, I thought; *put on the costume, go to the sushi place, and if I don't like the prospects, hang out and have a drink*. I love it when a plan comes together. The plan, my situation, and my life were about to change dramatically.

LA VENTANA

I stepped into the elevator in the Ivanhoe, a commercial building in downtown Troy, and pushed the button for the top floor, where the Soo Soo Sushi House was located. The doors opened on seven, and a cute couple in their early twenties got in. The guy was good-looking, but the girl was an absolute knockout, in tight jeans and an equally tight T-shirt showing off her considerable assets. He pushed the button for the twelfth floor and got out when the doors opened; she stayed in. I looked at her and said, "Wow, I thought you guys were together."

She replied, "I wish—he was hot. I guess we're both going to the top floor."

Next, the eighteenth-floor elevator doors opened, and three guys were standing there, also early to mid-twenties, wearing Dockers and pullovers and smelling like stale beer cans. I thought their eyes were going to pop out of their heads when they saw little Ms. Hot Stuff. I just had a bad vibe, grabbed Hot Stuff by the elbow, and said, "Our floor, Sue. 'Scuse us!"

We brushed past them and turned immediately down the hall. The elevator door closed, separating us from them. Ms. Hot Stuff appeared befuddled as I said, "That just didn't look good, hon." She slowly nodded in agreement, and I pushed the button for another car.

Waiting for the elevator, I noticed a restaurant on eighteen, La Ventana. I wished Hot Stuff good luck, advised her to be careful, and told her I was going to check out this place. It looked posh and polished, and this description isn't from just another hayseed from Nebraska. The entrance hardware was polished brass from floor to ceiling, attached to thick glass doors perfectly weighted to open effortlessly. Just inside, a modern chandelier hung, dripping with crystal pendants. Past the hostess podium and prominently positioned center stage in the dining room, in front of a large panoramic window, was a table I would come to know as Table Five. Troy wasn't New York City by any means, but I found out La Ventana, table five, and Abel, the owner, had a reputation, and at least here, you had arrived if seated at T-5. Looking around, it crossed my mind this was the type of establishment I dreamed of operating myself. *Start here and conquer Europe next*, I laughed to myself.

The whole place appeared so inviting, the sushi place could wait. Apparently Arrogant Abel, owner and chief jerk, I soon learned, had pissed off his hostess Jessica so badly she walked out after tossing a white wine on him less than an hour before I had shown up. Jessica later mockingly quipped she wished it had been a burgundy to ruin his *"Pierre Cardin K-Mart"* shirt. Abel was clearly in a dither and a fix; he haphazardly pointed me to the bar, thinking I was there for a drink. I briefly explained I was actually a hostess looking for employment, and he decided to give me a try for the dinner crowd—on the spot! Squeezing into the uncomfortable bra and heels and applying my L'Oréal instead of the cheap makeup had paid off—and I didn't even need a C cup.

I met Jessica when she came back to the restaurant to pick up her check and some belongings. This would be the first of many conversations with Jess, later becoming good friends. We couldn't talk in the restaurant but quickly exchanged numbers and I met her for drinks a few days later. Depending upon our schedules, we would meet for a drink or even a quick cup of coffee during the day if things were slow at our places. We got to know each other well. She had quickly gotten another job downtown, albeit bartending, the position she originally had started with at La Ventana. She harbored no resentment toward me, as she'd had it with Abel, his personality and general MO. She became invaluable to me with behind-the-scenes info on the operation and an education on the idiosyncratic Abel. She told me about his rip-off games played with the staff, the purveyors, and the customers. Some I knew; some were very innovative.

Through our various conversations I explained I was understandably nervous my first day. I had needed help and, looking around, couldn't find Abel. After seating a large party, I flew back to his office to find him with his head on his desk. I freaked—this was a major red flag! I didn't know if he was drunk, just had a stroke, or was dead. He shook it off saying he had a headache, came out long enough to solve my problem and instruct me on a few things, and disappeared again.

Jessica said he suffered from headaches, sometimes so bad they were incapacitating.

"Migraines, Jess?"

She replied, "Yes, I guess so."

As our friendship developed there was no subject off limits. It was clear she enjoyed sex very much—and provided me considerable details that, some of which, were filed in the "too much information" department. She explained she could tolerate Abel's stable of sex mates, herself included, "As long as there was a condom, but I got sick of empty promises, bonuses did not come with the bone."

I liked Jess and believed her to be honest in the business operation, but she was certainly optioned with a different moral constitution and vocabulary than me. She didn't feel the hostess pay scale was adequate compensation for the job she did, let alone additional duties performed that she did not consider enjoyable. As she put it, Arrogant Abel (AA) just wasn't that good standing, sitting, above or below the covers. It wasn't that he was small; apparently he just didn't know what to do with the "pink invader," his proud name for his member. Jessica had her own names for it, at least as colorful and hilariously demeaning to poor Abel.

Jessica, originally from Detroit, was, as you can imagine from my description, a little rough around the edges. She was tough, from a broken home; I sensed she had been knocked around more than she let on. I thought it was commendable, with her lifestyle, that she didn't have children. Jess had been at the restaurant for about two years, becoming a hostess after bartending. She was thirty-four, a year older than me, and Abel was forty-four. He had owned and operated La Ventana for about nine years. He had told her he'd worked at or managed different restaurants from Southern California through the Bay Area, worked in Denver, and was now in Troy. Having looked around La Ventana, I said, "Abel must have one hell of a good relationship with his commercial banker or very rich parents to put a place like this together at thirty-five years of age."

Jess could only say Abel seemed to have a lot of money but never spoke of any relatives, parents, ex-wives, or where his money had come from. Her intimate relationship with him had nothing to do with intimacy. He never shared anything of his personal life. She had nothing good to say about his manners, his ethics, or his personality. Yet she could find no fault when it came to his business acumen, his handling of customers, and overall intelligence. She didn't know if he was fluent in any other languages, but he seemed to understand and hold his own, perhaps stiltedly, in conversations besides English, ranging from Czech and Polish to Spanish.

Abel immediately recognized my value and kept me on as hostess. This was perfect because I didn't have to waste months proving myself for the job; I began with a salary instead of an hourly wage, and I didn't have to grovel for tips. I anticipated him hitting on me, and it didn't take long for the flirts to start. I agreed with Jessica: AA was a very competent and talented restaurateur and could do anything in his store, including cook. This was good because you, and more importantly he, never knew who he was going to piss off next, like the high-strung chef from Chile who wasn't about to take crap from anyone, let alone a mini-megalomaniac named Abel. He stormed out of the kitchen after Abel criticized him once too often for too much or too little salt in the soup.

Abel then hired a Chef Jorge, though Sergio was the current chef and had been for some time. Jessica related that Sergio arrived one day supposedly from a merchant marine ship. A paperwork dispute with immigration forced him to disappear into the streets of New York; he found his way to Troy and into the restaurant to put in an application. He coincidentally was walking in while Jorge, the aforementioned chef, was storming out, giving Abel the finger in three languages. This was probably due to Abel complaining that Jorge's porridge was either too hot or cold, but never just right.

Between a rock and a foreigner, Abel hired Sergio, like me, on the spot. After the lunch crowd that day, Sergio got a legal pad and, in a methodical way, inventoried long- and short-term supplies and scrutinized the spice selection. He took two busboys that Abel trusted with $1000 cash and left for an hour and a half, coming back in a taxicab carrying the equivalent of four shopping carts worth of food, the receipt, and change. He returned with an array of vegetables and delightfully fresh sea bass, tilapia, orange roughy and eel, prime beef, lamb, and capon. He commenced to prepare several dishes exquisitely. He'd been at La Ventana ever since.

I presumed La Ventana would be another stepping-stone in my career. Yet in a short amount of time, it appeared more interesting than other places across the country where I had worked, and I decided to stay awhile. By the same token, I knew I'd get totally burned out on Abel, his antics, and this gig too. In the back of my mind, I'd always thought I'd have my own business by forty. Thanks to my parent's genetics, I hoped I'd still be slender, decent–looking, and have some zip left, as my gram would say. I never slept with Abel and didn't plan to, not that he didn't continually try with flirtation and innuendo. Besides my Midwest and Catholic scruples, I never found him attractive in the least.

THE CAST AND CREW

Having been in the food industry for a long time, I recognized restaurants were as different as they were the same. It wasn't long before I had a good handle on any place I worked. The Ventana operation was no different. It's easy to connect with the purveyors when you know their language. The delivery guys are even better, and it's easy to be nice and give them a wink; throwing a sandwich together for them pays huge dividends. They would do just about anything I asked—not so much when Abel would ask.

This rapport did not escape Abel as he continued to give me more responsibility. I had a minor in accounting and knew my way around multiple electronic cash registers. More on that later. When I was into my second year, it seemed Arrogant Abel was more than willing to ramp up my tasks and responsibility, because it allowed him the opportunity to play the role he played best and thrived on, Mr. Big Shot. I think he also continued to believe at some point he'd be able to hike my skirt up on a booth after close and put another notch in his little black

(menu) book. But that wasn't going to happen, not that I let
him know. I could stroke his ego all day with him believing I
would stroke something else later.

As the seasons changed, along with help and assistant
chefs, AA relied on me more and more for the business of his
store. Mind you, I'm good with the books, but I never play or
juggle with the numbers, especially books and numbers that
I'm going to sign off on. He would reward my expertise with
an unrecorded cash bonus or vacuum-packed high-end product
like lobster, beef tenderloin, or wine. He also gifted product
close to expiration or wine that didn't sell very well. This ended
up going out the back door and to the trunk of Carlita. Much
of it did not make it to my apartment, though. I'm a good cook
but usually didn't have time, energy, or inclination to fix food
so I gave most of the goodies away to Jessica, friends I had met,
busboys who helped me, or oldster neighbors in my apartment
complex. Something always gnawed at me, though, about Abel's
generosity, which I found hard to believe. I just didn't trust
Arrogant Abel.

Of course the holidays were a big deal for La Ventana
and AA, as he was high on dollar signs when drink and meal
specials were the norm and cash was plentiful. AA could make
people feel they were special—people and their wallets.

There were the "holiday regulars," as Abel called them, who
came for Thanksgiving, Christmas, or Easter. AA was great at
hosting a birthday, bar mitzvah, or anniversary too. La Ventana
had two banquet rooms, A and B, off the main dining room
to accommodate special affairs. The rooms were decorated
differently than the main dining room. Room B was stark
and businesslike with bland cream-colored vinyl wallpaper and
muted beige commercial carpet. Simple round banquet tables

with white cloths were surrounded with stackable gold metal chairs covered in black vinyl. The room was used for small receptions, business luncheons and so forth.

Room A was decorated for the younger, mover-shaker, decadent crowd that wanted privacy to snort coke and get dirty with someone in the private restrooms or booths. The room was done in tasteful gray hounds tooth carpet, rich burgundy wallpaper, and modern brushed stainless steel light fixtures that were dimmable. Although the wall art was fake, it was elegantly done, with colorful abstract pieces highlighted with mini halogen spots. Abel catered fully to the power struck and rich. I never saw so much wasted food, since many patrons were high on cocaine or some other mood elevator and not hungry. But that was okay; there were plenty of to-go containers, the tab was always paid, and the bar bill was a stairway to heaven.

I called banquet room A the playpen, as I had walked in on some very bizarre behavior, some rivaling anything you could see on the Internet. There had been something for everyone— girl on girl, boy on girl, boys on girl. I have to admit sometimes it was titillating to me also, although the time I walked in on just two guys doing something, I wasn't sure whether to look or spin around and shriek. I looked.

None of this was illegal. Abel pointed out these acts were not being performed for money—that we knew of—but had someone with higher moral standards than a pornographer walked in, there might have been a problem.

Abel certainly didn't promote the activity, but the restaurant could be very busy and we had no sex police on staff to monitor naughty behavior. A private party was private. By the time someone would tip off Abel as to illicit action transpiring in the playpen, he could only take necessary precautions, be it for the security of the room or diversion, depending upon who might be snooping around. Abel was reluctant to ask anyone to leave or to disrupt these blatant sexual dalliances. Depending upon how wild and loud things got, occasionally it was necessary to intervene. If you didn't know, there are some wild things that go on in bars, restaurants, and public places in general. Forget about "This is Vegas"; stuff happens everywhere and lots of times right under your nose.

When Abel was playing his big-shot role, he'd bring his own potential scores into the playpen if there were a party going on. Not necessarily during a sex romp, since he would never expose himself to that liability. Before any wild stuff began, Abel would bring in a "date" to show off and show her off. Especially if there was someone there of notoriety—a sports celebrity or someone with local cred or clout. One time Abel was courting a salacious salesperson, ostensibly to buy wine. The wine was too expensive for Abel's profit margin. But *she* wasn't too expensive for Abel. Perhaps in an effort to fast-forward his own playtime with visual foreplay, he took his date into a playpen party just as things were getting exciting. It didn't take her long to figure out she wasn't there to help Abel inventory the wine before they headed for his office.

After a few months on the job, I knew fairly well the cast of characters that were La Ventana. Abel had nicknames for everyone.

The Hipster and Dipster would proudly promenade in for Table Five. The Hipster had an array of women he would manipulate and, with luck, some who would manipulate him. As far as I was concerned, most were escorts. Whoever was the Hipster's date of the day, Abel would label the Dipster du jour. They might have been dippy, but they weren't dumb. I'm sure they were likely getting more tips and trinkets than just the status of dining at Table Five. It was no surprise the Hipster's modus operandi was cash and plenty of it. His pockets oozed C-notes like a toothpaste tube on the counter, half-squeezed with the cap off. Judging from the Hipster's usual arm candy, his date would be using the entire tube. The Hipster wasn't bad-looking, but that certainly wasn't enough to hook some of the high-end ornamentation he was bedding down if he didn't have a fat wallet. The schmo dressed like Al Bundy.

On one particular night after long waits between cocktails, appetizers, wine, and the main course, no one was sure at what point the Hipster had been manipulated beneath Table Five. AA claimed ignorance. Everyone knew better, especially the female cleaning crew, some of whom were no strangers to Arrogant Abel's own behavior.

Prestigious Table Five didn't come cheap. There was always a reserved sign on T-5 whether it was reserved or not. Abel mentioned to me this device was a psychological factor that enhanced the aura that was T-5. Insiders knew it was not always booked. Some people tipped me, while others would order a particular bottle of wine from Abel to be seated at the illustrious table. Abel rarely let strangers have it, even if it were a busy night. If it were not reserved, he would hold it for the right type of customer, beautiful or affluent-looking people. It overlooked the Hudson River from the eighteenth floor through a panoramic window—therefore, the name La Ventana, Spanish for "the window."

The main dining room was done in understated elegance, with neutral carpet and tall, gloss-black ceramic urns lipped in gold and placed on half walls, breaking up the space among the apricot and turquoise linen-covered tables and booth tops. Rich, rust-colored, leather-like upholstery was attached to heavy chairs with faceted brass-headed nails. The chairs were so heavy they begged for gentlemen to pull them out for their companions, while I watched other less-intelligent men let women struggle with them. The Spanish name and theme tied into the featured South American cuisine, prepared by our well-heeled chefs. We were known for chefs who were able to prepare chef's specials or catch-of-the-day-type dishes found that day in the markets. There were always fantastic Latin items on the menu. Sergio made specialty fish in exotic sauces with flavor-complementing dishes. Admittedly it was all delicious.

I don't know if we were under the radar compared to New York City, but our share of bad behavior came in spurts. And so it went with covers—that's restaurantese for the number people or plates of food served and, after dinner the group typically walked out a couple of C-notes lighter after the exorbitant liquor bill. I never caught AA in the act, but Jessica had told me he would swap cheaper booze into expensive labeled bottles, and likewise with wine bottles that were already open. Sometimes he would defraud someone with wine pricing; he would chuckle and say, "I'm the last guy with the pen!" as he fondled the bill. Lots of patrons were so smashed they didn't know the difference and didn't care.

The list went on with Abel and his customer nicknames—Robert the Repeater, Barnyard, and Beer-Can Bob. Whether the names were kind, mean, flattering, or discriminatory, there was no mistaking who you were talking about when they came in. It was important to be discreet with the nicknames. We were careful not to use the plethora of names in front of busboys, servers, or heaven forbid, another customer. These customers weren't exclusive to T-5, but after a while, you knew who wanted to be where—or where Abel wanted a customer to be. For example, we would always put Dander at booth two because it did not have direct light shining on the table as the snow fell from his mop of hair. Or Rain Man, aka Robert the Repeater, who wasn't so much a savant; he just repeated everything you said at least once. When asked, "Robert, would you like an appetizer tonight?" Robert would say, "Would like an appetizer tonight? No."

Troy Roy was with the Troy Fire Department, a fireman and EMT most noted for his penchant for running into burning buildings. He had been reassigned from hazard duty after a burning beam fell on him in a warehouse fire. AA, apparently a sitcom TV fan also, called one sweet old lady Lovey, as in Mrs. Howell from *Gilligan's Island*, when she hobbled in with her ingrate niece and nephew. Always with a reservation, she proudly took the helm of Table Five, as AA would fawn over her, pulling her chair out, turning up his volume just enough because she was hard of hearing, and pedaling routinely the most expensive dish on the menu. The young relatives didn't care; there would be enough money to go around after Lovey paid the check, and she would ultimately leave her wealth to the ingrates after *she* checked out.

Sometimes I busted AA trying to grab cash from Lovey's table to pocket a portion of an incredibly large tip before the servers got there to pick it up. As a former waitress, that really pissed me off. Abel knew how to work everyone. He knew who was loaded or connected, who could be beneficial to him and who to stay away from, for example, someone selling benefit tickets. Table Five was showcased to make a big deal of dining at it, but it was really. Abel was a showman if anything, with a gift of gab his own, knowing how to treat beautiful women, little kids (with rich parents), and oldsters. From that standpoint I admired him and his theatrical handling of the clientele.

Every so often, always with a reservation and fanfare, there was a little dark-skinned Jewish man with a goatee that would come in dressed as a yacht captain with cap and ascot. His name was Stu, or Stuie to his pals. Abel nicknamed him the Rabbi. He would use a stupid Brit accent, but it sounded more as if he were from Minnesota. Apparently, he had pockets oozing money also, because the glitter-laden hood ornaments that accompanied him didn't seem to care if he was whispering romantic Shakespeare or, "Yah, dah Minn-ah-soe-dah Twins are gonna win."

I didn't care either; I played him up like the international playboy *he wasn't*. He always tipped the hostess, as Jessica put it, a Hamilton. He seemed to have money to burn and would talk about being an oil refinery magnate. Nobody believed him, but tip or not, I liked him; he had a boyish charm and was funny.

After the Hipster-Dipster episode, when the Hipster had a reservation, Abel would quickly put a short tablecloth on T-5. The Hipster might have dressed like a throwback, but he wasn't dumb. After the short cloth swap, he preferred a booth. Abel joked he would put a night vision camera under the table. Initially I thought that his reasoning was strictly perversion, but Arrogant Abel later suggested it might be useful as blackmail at some point. I wasn't sure if that was a joke or he was serious. Abel, always the entrepreneur.

Fred

The uncomfortable Barbie clothes occasionally had their advantages. Sometimes it was a game for me too; other times I was lonely and just uncomfortable. You likely have your own idea of the flirting and hookups that occur in restaurants and bars. Having worked as a bartender, waitress, and hostess halfway across the United States, I consider myself a bit of an expert in this department of reading people and their flirting. Depending upon your gender, geographic area, and which side of the bar you sit, you have your own perception and your own experiences.

Through every walk of life, from the beefy farm boys of the Midwest, the college kids in the college towns, GQ businessmen and beyond, there is as wide a cross-section and mix as anywhere. There are the crass and rude end of the spectrum right through and including the overly nice, almost apologetic Romeo types attempting an end through means of soft-spokenness and body language. Although I believe it's the same for men, in what I call the flirting dance, I can only offer a spin on my own experience. I have witnessed some crass and rude women's performances with bartenders and waiters, but generally that involves being overserved.

I find it interesting that there are absolute lines of delineation between the flirter's approach to a female bartender versus a server versus a hostess. A bartender gets the worst type of flirt. I think it's because bartenders, by necessity, serve alcohol; the bar patron is drinking, and his inhibitions are lower than those of the dinner guest. But if a Roman Catholic nun had a part-time job as a bartender, she would still be perceived as easy. Waitresses might be working to finish a PhD in specialized medicine, but the perception is they are lower class and barely made it out of seventh grade. Hostesses, on the other hand, are hit on least, as they are viewed as already having their PhD or are the owner's wife or girlfriend. So if you're the hostess and interested in a patron (who's not with a woman) and it is not going to interfere with the business at hand, it will be up to you to make the effort.

Fred had been coming to Chez Neo, the bar inside La Ventana, for some time, never with a date but by himself or with one or two male friends. I estimated almost immediately that he was interested in me. Although I was used to beefy farm boys, Fred was a good-looking, dark-complected guy, slim but with a nice build and about my age. I had dated a few times as I traversed the country, but only because I had been asked out, and hadn't had sex in forever. I didn't know where I was going to land and felt I didn't have time for a relationship anyway. I found Fred attractive, but I worked a lot of hours, and dating does take time. The only thing I couldn't figure out was why he didn't call himself Fredrick or F. Charles (if Charles was his middle name) and then his last name. Perhaps he was more comfortable with Fred than I was with Aggie.

I don't consider myself attracted to a particular type of guy; it's the whole package that attracts me—head, heart, and body. Fred started coming in for drinks by himself, usually with a *Wall Street Journal* tucked under his arm, and always sought me out to say hello. He asked enough off-and-on questions of the bartender that it was clear he was there for me. He quipped that I was Ms. Lantana from La Ventana—clever. We began chatting, which meant I was also finding some excuse to engage with him. He was intelligent, which makes a man more attractive, and the rest was a natural progression.

Maybe the turning point was one night when his conversation fell flat and he rebounded with an old joke. "A priest, a rabbi, and a black minister come into a bar, and the bartender says …" It was so corny, and I had heard variations of it scores of times over the years, but I burst into laughter. I caught Fred by such surprise he began laughing also, and I decided to go out with him. I never did hear his punch line.

Fred, originally from the Chicago area, had moved around major cities and had been a commodities broker with a couple of firms. He had won and lost everything at least twice, as he put it, but had gained maturity and experience through his hard knocks. How could you not? He seemed to know a little about everything, but not in a braggadocios way, and was now trading stocks for himself and a handful of clients. He still dabbled in commodities, currencies mostly, and would do quick plays with pounds, yen, euros, or dollars. He would take a "pop" jumping in and out of markets so quickly I never understood how it worked. He had never been married and didn't have any children, or so he said.

He practiced what was called "range trading" and claimed he was pretty good at it. He had worked on the exchange trading floor in Chicago and said it was so crooked he had to leave. I didn't think he had any reason to lie about it, but it was still too early to buy into the entire story. He explained that unlike investing in stocks that you typically keep for a longer time, commodities were extremely volatile.

"These markets take no prisoners," he said.

He was quite passionate about it. He followed trends and algorithms and explained how so many people get attached to a play or stock and continue riding it down like gamblers on a bad streak. They think it will turn around and end up losing it all. "The market has a personality and plays with your emotions like a beautiful woman. You've got to be extremely cold to win," he told me. I asked if that was so with women also. He didn't answer that one.

He carried himself confidently, and the smile on his face told me he did okay for himself with the markets. With my women's intuition, Fred seemed like a good guy to have on your side. He was a good guy too. He had little to say about his family in general but never spoke positively about his father. I later found out his father had been an inside trader and thief and actually ripped off his own son, Fred. Nice. This seemed to have a profound effect on Fred's integrity in his own business dealings. That's why he had left the exchange floor.

Fred began coming in more regularly. He had several conversations with Abel, and surprisingly, Abel warmed up to him. This was unusual for Abel, so they must have been talking money, and Fred perhaps gave Abel a beneficial tip. Fred was never a pest in the restaurant and, as time went on, was actually helpful in that he would see little things in and around the restaurant and just do them, whether it was tending to a physical thing like grabbing a box of product that was mistakenly delivered to the front door or follow-up signing for the delivery in Chez Neo if I was distracted. It was cute when I'd see him, unobserved, casually straighten a table setting or a lamp in one fluid movement as he walked by. I started looking forward to seeing him come in.

I liked that he wouldn't get in my hair and left well before closing. I'd sit at the bar with him if it was slow, and we'd kiss before he left. He took it slow, which I kind of liked too, but I found myself wanting more. It was about this time that he asked me out to dinner. Anyone who wants to tie up with a

manager working restaurant hours must be special to start with.
I'm typically beat by close, and it's usually after ten. He knew
this and asked anyway. I told him I could really go for a Papa's
Tapas gyro deluxe and a bottle of Roditys Greek rose but likely
didn't have the energy after work. It was a hike to Papa's from
our store, I'd be too dressed up, and so on. I picked a night, and
he claimed we'd have a snack close by and then he'd walk me
to Carlita the Corolla. I had just closed out the Chez registers
when he walked in with a sack from Papa's Tapas and a bottle of
chilled Roditys and said he had reserved Table Five—the sign
was on it! I don't think I'd had so much fun in a year. I took
him home and fucked him like I hoped he'd never been fucked.

Obviously we'd become comfortable with each other, and
I managed to break free a bit more. Like the song, he knew
all the right places ... but he didn't need any pills. Sometimes
I questioned if Fred's performance meant he *was* taking an
enhancement pill. We were by all means compatible in that
department, and the boy could wear me out. Fred and I
were never at a loss for conversation, whether it be politics,
the weather, or the restaurant. We'd also joke about what a
character Abel was, not necessarily a good character and that
karma would someday catch up with him, or at least an STD.

My schedule was hectic and weekends were usually at the
store, but Fred and I managed a few weekday getaways. There
was always too much activity on the weekends, and AA would
flip out if I wasn't there, handling everything, including fanning
Table Five's customers with attentiveness.

The months passed, and I became more involved with Fred.
He didn't live too far from me, and we spent quite a bit of time
at each other's apartments. Sometimes I couldn't believe my
good luck. Fred didn't want to be attached at the hip, didn't

seem to mind my long hours, and took good care of me from my perspective—and the sex was great.

I had long been out of the little efficiency and was in a cute two-bedroom in a nice complex on the east end. It was safe and clean, with decent neighbors, up to code, and very hip. The apartment was modern, with nice appliances, and the only thing that didn't work was the icemaker. I giggled when I saw the old lever-style tin ice trays at a dollar store one day and bought two. They reminded me of Grandma Agatha's old Frigidaire and drinking Kool-Aid at her house as a little girl in the humid Nebraska summertime. It just made me feel good anytime I used them.

Fred and I spent plenty of nights closing the restaurant together. He wasn't a barfly nor did he have his own bar stool, but he did have a presence that I appreciated. Abel took more of a liking to him, and although Fred got some free drinks here and there, he was also beneficial in keeping a watchful eye on the operation and patrons. The drinks paid off also in some contacts he made relative to his financial work. Abel recognized Fred was bringing in his own customers, not just for drinks but dinners too. Through various conversations, Abel began questioning Fred about commodity scams and unscrupulous trading tactics. Fred told Abel straight out that some of the antics he proposed were a good way to get arrested. I didn't ask; I didn't want to know. Fred delicately evaded the questioning, trying not to piss off Abel. After all, it was Abel's place, and we'd be cutting our collective noses off to spite our faces if we angered him. Fred couldn't believe Abel could contrive some bait-and-switch maneuvers that had such entertainment value inasmuch as, in Fred's mind, they were impossible. This occasionally made Abel the brunt of our jokes. Perhaps we were jealous Abel was so successful, yet such a jerk. Or is that what you needed to be successful?

Kellogg

Fred stayed busy trading commodities and frequenting the Chez Neo several nights a week, many times just popping in for a quick drink or to say hello. When he was there, he would inconspicuously watch the register and neutralize the occasional overserved patron. Some days in the restaurant business are typically light with customers. That's why you see specials, two for one's, discounts and so on. There's an old restaurant joke that some weekdays are weak days. I took off early on a *weakday* Tuesday afternoon as Abel stayed at the store to do bookwork and liquor inventory. I was in my apartment with the remnants of a three dollar glass of wine Abel would have sold for nine dollars. Beginning the second year of my apartment lease, as we entered fall, it was beginning to cool off earlier in the day. Relaxing on my couch with a *Vanity Fair* and comforter over me, I was in heaven. I was feeling a little sleepy and sexy and hoped Fred might come over to *relax* also. It wouldn't be unusual for him to come in with a bundle of goodies under his arm and prepare a great meal later.

Suddenly he appeared at the door, wearing his secret agent shabby raincoat that only came out during downpours. I gave him a wry smile, thinking he might have stripped in the hall and was going to flash me. When I told him that, he said he suspected the Nose, Mrs. Hannity, across the hall was hoping for the same thing while poking her proboscis out the door. More climactic than that, he opened the coat, fully clothed, to proudly display a dingy gray oversize rodent. This was the ugliest rat-hamster terrier mix I'd ever seen. "What ... is *that*?" I asked not too calmly.

He soberly explained it was, in fact, some sort of rat-hamster terrier mix; he'd always wanted a dog, claimed it wouldn't be any trouble for us, and told me some lie as to it following him home.

I, in a tone slightly elevated from the last, exclaimed, "Trouble for *us*?" I'd dealt with and fended off every come-on and sales pitch imaginable and never buckled. The last thing I would fall for would be, "I'll take care of the dog, and you won't have to do anything."

But I often missed the dogs at the farm and had mentioned that to Fred. Most were outside dogs, but we always had one house dog/watchdog that was part of the family, like Shep. This mutt was supposedly housebroken, apparently a city dweller already, and would relieve himself in the corner of the five-by-eleven-foot balcony, in a litter box no less. "What's his name?" I asked.

That was up in the air, but Fred wanted it to be a masculine name, a bit of a pun on ferocity versus size.

I suggested, since he went in a cat box, "How 'bout 'Little Big Man Pussy Dog'?" My burst of laughter was cut short with looks from Fred and the mutt. I didn't know who was more emasculated. I decided to drop that name; I didn't want the little guy, or Fred, to develop an inferiority complex.

Fred needed to run some errands, and now fully awake, I decided to take a jog and see if Tiny Tim could keep up. I figured he couldn't, but he'd be no problem to carry when he ran out of steam. We hit the park with a makeshift leash, and no sooner did we encounter other pets and owners than Muttsy made a flying leap to mount a large female collie. Clamping onto her haunches with his forelegs, he gyrated wildly before falling to the ground. This was much to everyone's surprise, chagrin, and embarrassment, especially mine. What could I do? It was obvious the little sex offender was with me. I was sure Fred would be proud of his protégé. The little guy was fired up by then and kept up just fine for our run.

Once back at the apartment, I poured myself a bowl of cornflakes as a snack and ran water for a shower. I walked by the kitchen door and caught the mongrel up on the table face-down in my cereal! I screamed, "Get outta there—Kellogg!" Kellogg, huh, that's it! If the worst was going to be teaching him to eat from his own dish instead of mine on the table, I guessed it wouldn't be so bad.

I played with him the rest of the afternoon but not before we went out for some cheap bowls, a comb, and dog shampoo to clean him up in the kitchen sink. I estimated he was about two years old and did surprisingly well with basic commands learned from somewhere. He turned out to be a quick study and most importantly wasn't a yapper. It didn't take long for curiosity to get the best of the Nose. Mrs. Hannity came tapping at my door, and Kellogg barked—what a bonus, a watchdog! Pets were allowed in the building, so that wasn't an issue with the Nose. The more we hung out, the more I enjoyed Kellogg's quirky personality. He didn't eat much, used the litter box as claimed, and I was done rationalizing his ownership.

I texted Fred and told him I had good news and bad news. He immediately called back wanting only the good news. I told him we could keep the lousy mutt. Fred arrived a while later, curious as to what the bad news was. Kellogg walked out from behind the couch with a splendid new look, all cleaned up, combed out, a silly pink bow on top of his head, and bright red toenails! Rather than being humiliated, he appeared proud.

Kellogg adapted quickly between stays at both apartments. At home the farm dogs were never allowed in our beds. You never knew if they had just left the chicken coop or pigpen with who knows what squeezed between their toes. If they raced down the hallway and leaped into your bed, it could be ugly. Out of habit I tried keeping Kellogg from my bed, but he had an uncanny way of sneaking up sometime during the night. Some mornings he could scare the daylights out of me, somehow getting under the covers and shocking me before I was fully awake.

JET

On a chilly overcast morning later that same fall, I was already on edge when Fred came into La Ventana with a kid wrapped in rags, looking like he was fresh from a refugee camp, except with some meat on his bones. One busboy hadn't shown up, and in two hours, I had a business lunch for twenty-five stockbrokers and bankers in banquet room B. Chef Sergio was prepping chicken breasts and fettuccine Florentine, but my tilapia filets had yet to arrive. I didn't know what Fred was up to, so I gave him "the look" and exclaimed, "What?" I could see this coming from a half mile away. The last thing I needed was another shaggy stray in my life.

I got, "What?" back.

"Fred, I've got my hands full, and Nick didn't show again. I don't have time to deal with anyone. I've got to make do to get through this luncheon."

"This is Joseph. He can fill in for Nick *right now*. Joseph is point-and-shoot; turn him loose with the other guys," said Fred.

I gave a dismissive wave of my hand and flew back to the office and computer. Several minutes later, I passed banquet room B; Joseph looked like a blur against the other two guys, all three engaged in conversation. It appeared his rapid movements were actually motivating the setup process. The fish arrived, and the luncheon went fine. Joe helped with the teardown; I paid him cash and got his phone number.

Later I apologized and thanked Fred, getting the backstory on our new helper. Apparently Fred had run across Joe a number of times in the downtown district as he raced in and out of various businesses, doing part-time work and odd jobs. Fred would make small talk with him as he was unloading a truck or washing windows and was impressed with his industrious nature. In between one of these jobs, Fred asked if Joseph wanted to get a doughnut. Give the kid a gold star! He said no, he wanted a cheeseburger. Fred was impressed again with the kid requesting exactly what he wanted. Fred took him to the Hut down the street and bought him a double with Swiss and jalapeno onion rings.

Joseph had come from Italy with his grandmother at age ten. Fluent in Italian, he fine-tuned his English and had graduated from high school. He was now making ends meet while he was looking for steady work. He and his grandmother, Alba, lived in an apartment in old downtown. They landed in Troy from Senerchia, Italy, because several relatives lived in the area, and it was decided Joseph would have better opportunities leaving his Italian hamlet and becoming Americanized. He would also have the benefit of growing up with a wide variety of younger relatives other than Grandma. Naturally there was a sad story behind the fact that his parents had divorced. I related a bit because his situation was like that of a close cousin of mine, who had become a mess after his parents split.

The next time I saw Joe, he was very presentable, in a clean shirt and jeans. I put him on as a part-timer. He was a-nice looking young guy, unquestionably Italian, with rounded features and deeply set eyes, black straight hair, and olive-toned skin. I asked Joseph Tratorio if he liked being called Joe or Joey.

"I actually prefer Joseph, not Joe or Joey," he explained.

Fred was right; the kid spoke his mind. I liked him already; maybe Joey to him was like my Aggie thing. He was fitted off the rack in a busboy uniform, and we watched him zip circles around everyone. Always upbeat and in good humor, this contagious demeanor and personality rubbed off on not only the busboys, but the rest of us. I was logging his name in for payroll and thought, *Joseph Enzo Tratorio, J-E-T. He flies around this place like a jet.* I suggested JET to him, and he smiled at the new moniker.

Abel initially didn't trust him, thinking he was stealing, even though nothing was missing. Fred kept an eye on him, checking booze and other product and even left some cash out. JET returned the cash to Abel or me. Of course Abel tried to pocket the money that I had to wrestle back to reimburse Fred. We had a policy that any cash found or busboy table tips was put in a jar in the kitchen and split among the busboys once a month. Unlike servers, who have assigned tables in a section of the restaurant, the busboys bus whatever tables are dirty. After a busy brunch, JET told me he was about to clean up T-5 and noticed a twenty dollar bill *under* it. He could have picked it up and put it in the kitchen tip jar but told me he was tired of being baited with cash! He let another boy do the job and came back to find the twenty gone. He wouldn't tell me who, but I had seen Nick clearing the table. Fred claimed he did not plant *that* cash but bluffed Nick into admitting he took it. I printed Nick's last check and let him go, saying nothing about the twenty. That afternoon Abel was puffed up telling me he had finally caught JET stealing. I told AA what had happened, and *he* was out the twenty! That was the end of ethical testing for JET.

Abel relented and, I think, realized what a gold mine we had in the kid. JET could and would do anything without complaining—plunge a plugged toilet or help Lovey to her Bentley. He seemed to be the proverbial dying breed of young person. He was stronger than he looked too; he could wield fully loaded dinner carts or jerk half barrels of Heineken off the two-wheeler, slinging them into the cooler beneath the bar.

I had already given JET more hours now that Nick was gone and, as time went on, gave him more responsibility, along with a dollar above minimum wage for his efforts. He was performing what I considered managerial tasks. He was sharp as a pinprick for his age, and I liked him. I was a little too young to be his mother, but I couldn't help thinking of JET as the kid I never had, and I didn't have to go through all the crap of raising him. I wanted to take care of him or at least give him the opportunity to make good. I suppose part of my maternal concern was recognizing what a good kid he was, taking care of his grandmother suffering from rheumatoid arthritis. My grandmother suffered also. I missed having my family around, and many times JET and Grandma Alba reminded me of one of my brothers and Gram Agatha.

My sentiment paid big dividends for the Tratorios as they were eating much better than some, with takeout containers of untouched leftovers that went home with JET. He rode his bicycle most days and parked it inside the back door from the alley, unless it was very bad out and he hoofed it. Other times Fred took JET home or picked him up in his manure-brown Ford Taurus when it was storming or really cold. JET had become my right hand in the past months as he intrinsically understood the operation, or maybe he understood and anticipated me. He was a quick study. If it wasn't for the JET nickname, he could have been Radar to my Col. Potter on *MASH*.

Daleka

Abel was rarely without a "date," whether he met women in the restaurant or hobnobbing at other establishments. Some of Abel's girls gave the impression of incredibly transparent bimbos, yet were crafty in their own right, knowing immediately what his intentions were, how to game play, and how to benefit. Other women's sixth sense was not as finely tuned to figure out the endgame. I'm sure they still got it in the end.

Abel bantered his bull and spouted about New York celebrities he knew that he really didn't while pouring mislabeled wine down his victim's throat.

I would hear variations of, "Honey, let me open this cabernet; it's a hundred-eighty bucks a bottle, but I can't think of anyone I would rather share it with," while he was surely thinking, "Wonder what color your panties are? Wonder if they're silk?"

Bimbos usually bought the rap—why else would they be there? Intellectual conversation with Abel? There were some sly girls that occasionally slid beneath Abel's radar. I would tip him off to a potential troublemaker or maybe even a blackmailer. I might notice a subtle tan line on a ring finger that he hadn't, or see a woman madly texting before she even made it into the ladies room. I didn't care if an irate husband beat the crap out of Abel, but I didn't want the staff or myself catching a stray bullet from some jealous wild man.

One day, a group—not sure if they were female bodybuilders or muscle-bound drag queens—came in during lunch and innocently asked for T-5, which happened to be open. Three of the four had Eastern European accents. I had never seen Abel so enamored. Maybe he'd been beaten up by an eighth-grade girl basketball player when he was in sixth and liked it, or maybe she was in sixth and he was in eighth! At any rate, he was smitten with one of the girls and pulled up an extra chair to T-5 to chat with her and the muscular entourage. After he introduced himself, she claimed her name was Daleka. I have to admit, if I was in a heavy part of town by myself, I would want these girls as backup. Daleka seemed to be closest to another woman named Bora. I wondered what their sexual preferences were, as Bora was somewhat more feminine yet still had a "get out of my way or I'll knock you down" demeanor.

They all kept coming back, usually within a somewhat scheduled lunch hour, indicating they were working girls. But likewise they didn't come in at the same time when they did come in. So what? It was a little game I played figuring out the roles of the clientele, especially these girls. Whatever the fascination, Abel would give them T-5 if available, chat it up, and sometimes offer free dessert.

As time went on, Daleka came in by herself or sometimes with Bora later in the day to sip wine in the bar with Abel's company. I did my best to check Daleka out to see if she was a he. I shook hands, checking out grip and size, scrutinized her Adam's apple, and noticed how flat the front of her skirt or slacks was. Of course if she *were* a he, I presume the package would be securely strapped down. Nothing definitive. She was attractive in a rugged sort of way. A round yet broad face, with a strong jaw but pouty, sensuous lips that always glistened with fresh gloss. Jet-black hair was cut in a pageboy to complete the bowling ball look. But it didn't actually look bad on her. Considering her build, she carried herself lightly. I don't know much about sex changes or hormone treatment, but short of inspecting her face with a magnifying glass, it didn't look as if she had a beard. She and Bora dressed between casual and edgy and always had funky rings, necklaces, and earrings. The jewelry was oversize costume stuff, probably cubic zirconium, which they thought was chic—or maybe it was a Euro thing.

Within a few months, Abel and Daleka had become an item. Out of character for Abel, he had left his usual hood ornaments on their hoods and took to parking in Daleka's garage or at booth four, an intermediate stop to the office. B-4 was a bit more reserved, darker, and private compared to T-5, where the entire intent was to see and be seen. Plus, true love or not, AA wasn't about to use Table Five for any reason other than making money. T-5 was just too valuable from a profit standpoint. The concept of love was also out of character for Abel, so I was curious as to whether this relationship was anything more than superficial. I'm not sure Abel knew how to spell love. For that matter, I'm not sure love was in his vocabulary.

Many times the two looked as if they were having a business meeting, both with small notepads that would appear and disappear, in addition to talking into their smartphones as if taking audio notes. Daleka seemed thoroughly engaged regardless of the activity. I continued to be fascinated as to what the attraction was between these two odd ducks. Thinking about her baseball mitt hands, I both cringed and delighted at the thought of the pink invader being at her mercy. Likewise, even though Abel considered himself a gift to the opposite gender, I had heard enough from Jessica and related gossip from other "dates" to know that Abel couldn't find a G-spot with a GPS. Ultimately I thought Daleka, who was young enough to be Abel's daughter, was in this for the status, connections to other clubs, food, wine, or lines of coke that Abel probably had access to—even if he didn't use.

PDA and clandestine behaviors and activities continued to escalate with AA and Daleka. I knew they were drinking and, at this point, was not so sure they weren't doing drugs of some kind. Guttural sounds emanated from Abel's office, and sometimes I thought someone was getting hurt. I envisioned, if there was pain involved, it would be on Abel's end. His voice either contracted or expanded to a lower or higher octave depending upon what I could only imagine was happening to the pink invader.

There was an eight-by-eight-inch window toward the top center of Abel's office door, with tinted mirror film. Abel, apparently never good with a straightedge, cut it short and installed it leaving a small gap along one side that allowed you to peek through. You would think he knew about it, but perhaps he thought no one else did, or maybe he thought he was invisible. Late one night I did peek, and he wasn't invisible, nor was Daleka. I grabbed my mouth to avoid shrieking, not from horror but from laughter. Abel was dressed like the dance hall gal at the Long Branch Saloon from a sixties Technicolor western. He was in a ridiculous black pantyhose getup with red lace. The invader was generously positioned, or padded, for maximum bulge beneath the panties and framed with gaudy red lace. I looked away just as quickly. I didn't want to think about those two wallowing on Abel's desktop.

It wasn't Halloween, so I could only presume they *must* be doing drugs. No one slithers into a creepy costume like that just on alcohol, or do they? What was driving this action? The groaning and squealing got so loud one evening as the restaurant got busy that I kicked the office door as I was walking by. It squelched the audible ecstasy.

Some days Abel's mood was bearlike. I knew how to handle him but would give the staff a heads-up to stay out of his way. I attributed this behavior to a slow dollar day, a hangover, a possible spat with Daleka, or him just being a greedy, self-centered, unhappy prick. I still found no evidence of drug use or addiction. There was no weight gain or loss, no super-blips in the revenue stream, no sick days, just business as usual. We never talked about his relationship with Daleka or if that's why he was a grouch. Once I had considered his ego had been deflated because I would not allow myself to be one of his conquests. Maintaining my distance, I reasoned, was a tactical move, inasmuch as I was trusted to handle any La Ventana ripple or tsunami. As far as I was concerned, our relationship needed to stay businesslike. Even if I found Abel attractive, I wouldn't cheat on Fred—not my style. Finally, I thought I was becoming egocentric, thinking I could have that great an impact on Abel's mood swings.

I had walked into his office a few times to find him with his head on the desk or him lying on the leather couch by the window. Asked what was wrong, he would simply say he had a headache. He refused aspirin or ibuprofen; he told me "no" when I asked if it was a migraine and if he wanted something stronger. The headaches seemed more frequent the longer I was at La Ventana.

One afternoon I hurried into the office, not realizing Abel was there. It was dark, and the curtains were drawn. Abel was on the couch but with a cold rag over his eyes. He stirred and asked who was there. He sighed as I identified myself and asked me to come over to the couch. As I passed his desk, I saw a syringe. *Holy crap!* I thought. But instead of any evidence of a street drug, there was an insulated wrapper labeled "Sumatriptan."

I stood over him, and he could feel my presence. He sighed again heavily, holding out his left hand. Apprehensively I took it in mine as he asked me to sit down.

He lay speechless for several moments and then spoke barely above a whisper. "Did you see the needle?"

"Uh-huh."

"I do suffer from migraines. That's the drug I take. This is a bad one. Ya know, I know I'm a little rough on our people sometimes. I want you to know you're a good girl and ... why are you so nice to me?"

The words left my lips before I realized I had even said it. "So, you are human?"

He tried to smile, but I think even that was painful. I didn't think I could ever show sympathy for AA, but I did. He told me Table Five was reserved for some big shots at seven-thirty; he hadn't put it in the book because he planned on entertaining, but now he wouldn't be able to do it. No special pricing, but ultimate service. I squeezed his hand gently, laying it back down by his side, and walked out, silently closing the door.

BRUNCH

JET and the staff made out well on brunch days and not just from tips. After brunch there were plenty of leftovers and carry-outs, and everyone appreciated the feast. Unfortunately for Abel, there were many items he couldn't sell on Monday as they wouldn't be fresh enough to serve, plus much of it was not regular menu fare. Giving away the equivalent of dollars irritated Abel. I attempted to bring the bright side of this to his attention. Not only did he take a tax deduction on unused brunch food but, not that he cared, he could enhance his big-shot role by showing generosity to the employees. I suggested he even donate desserts, bakery items, and appetizers to the retirement home up the street.

As the boys were breaking down tables one afternoon, JET talked about treating some relatives and his Grandma Alba, known also as Nonna Bella, to brunch. This would, however, mean he'd have to take off work on Sunday, and we counted on his efficiency on brunch day. We picked a date, and he and the boys stayed late on a Saturday night to set up after striking dinner service.

We decided to free up Table Five for the Tratorio clan to enhance the red carpet treatment, and JET came in with a new shirt and pressed jeans. I didn't expect Alba to show up in a washed-out sundress but likewise didn't expect her in smart slacks, a colorful chartreuse blouse, a splash of makeup, and obvious attention having been paid to her salt-and-pepper hair. I imagined Nonna Bella, literally meaning "good grandma," had the stallions snorting and stomping their hooves back in the day. I suggested comping their meal, but Fred astutely pointed out that this was JET's time to shine and we shouldn't take anything away from him being the man, and breadwinner, of the house and proudly receiving the check, scrutinizing it, and pulling out a roll to pay for the entire family. Fred smacked that one out of the park. When all was said and done, we couldn't tell who was more proud, JET or Nonna Bella. The beverage waitress bought into the entire affair and treated the table, and especially JET, like VIPs.

Somewhere between the Waldorf salad, slices of smoked Gouda, and iced prawns, Daleka and Bora sashayed in. Flamethrowers appeared in Grandma Alba's eyes. The girls wouldn't have stood a chance dressed in asbestos. Almost uncontrollably, she pointed a rheumatoid crooked index finger at Daleka and mumbled something in Italian. Uncle Tony gently pulled her wrist down and redirected her attention back to the party. Apparently the combination of Daleka's countenance and accent sent Nonna Bella over the edge.

We later found out it gave her a flashback of an internment camp during World War II when, as a little girl, young women detainees were given special privileges to boss others around.

Special privileges to girls with a cute figure, be they Jews, Poles, Italians, or Czechs. This was done for sexual favors, depending upon how attractive they were. The Nazis not only had them act as personal maids and slept with them; they were told they would get preferential treatment and transferred if they spied on activities of the other inmates. The Nazis indeed kept their word, treating them better and sending them to another camp, except later they were murdered like anyone else when they became pregnant or their usefulness had otherwise expired.

To divert Nonna's attention, JET asked if she'd like to visit the kitchen and meet Sergio, our chef, if he weren't too busy. She was ecstatic at the privilege. I hoped Sergio wouldn't be too busy, but most of the heavy lifting had been done, and at that point, all that was required was keeping up with management and presentation of prepared food as empty serving trays came back. JET came back out alone, and many minutes later, there was muffled laughter and howling, as if a separate party were in full swing in the kitchen. Apparently, one was. Nonna Bella and Chef Sergio had become fast friends and were already concocting something with flour, eggs, sugar, cinnamon, cocoa, banana, lemon, and the kitchen sink, while a helper was modifying biscuit or pizza dough into pastry shells. I walked away before I either got yelled at or something blew up.

A bakery tray came out twenty minutes later, full of petit fours and mini-turnovers. They were colorful and shiny, with powdered sugar sprinkled modestly around the confections, completing the masterpieces. Upon sampling, they were exquisite. Grandma Alba and Sergio were fast friends and kindred chefs. Sergio was particularly interested in Alba's pasta sauces, which I'm sure were not based on anything Ragu had to offer.

Part of the mutual camaraderie was the fact that Sergio was from Barcelona originally and Nonna had spent time between Gibraltar and Barcelona. Sergio said he was growing weary of the United States and was ready to go back to Spain. The more they talked, Nonna explained she longed for her country also. Everyone had another glass of champagne, including JET, who I knew was doing some sneaking.

Nonna Bella invited me over for dinner the following Wednesday, which was typically a slow day. I accepted graciously but wondered if she'd remember come Monday afternoon.

Nonetheless on Wednesday, I went to Grandma Alba's apartment in an old section on East Seventh Street, a forgotten area of the ever deteriorating central business district that had been so full of life a few decades before. There was a reputable ethnic mix with enough good people to keep an eye out for Alba and vice versa. Even if Alba didn't have a snub-nosed .357 tucked under her apron, you sensed she could probably drop a thug at ten yards with a deftly thrown iron skillet flung like a professional Frisbee player.

I arrived at six thirty sharp and was met with an addictive aroma of baked chicken, tomatoes, and garlic long before I'd made it to the door. The apartment was, as expected, hospital clean, with its1960s yellow-topped Formica and chrome kitchen table set and her Italian china pulled out for just such an occasion. I brought a gift bottle of sipping sherry and placed it on the table. Black-and-white family photographs in thin antique silver frames were scattered about. There were many photos from Salerno, much larger than the smaller village of Senerchia, where Alba was raised and still had family. She and JET emigrated from Senerchia, coming stateside when his parents separated, unable to raise the boy. They probably divorced, but Roman Catholic Italians rarely speak of such things.

A wedding picture of Alba and Antonio hung on the sparse living room wall above a doily-armed well-worn couch. Next to it was Nonna's chair and her little end table, perfectly organized with a big-button phone, TV remote, foot warmer, and Bible. JET went out as we settled down to a cup of coffee in the living room. Alba's eyes twinkled when I mentioned Antonio. It was clear she was still deeply in love with him and missed her country and her relatives, but the collective opinion was that Joseph should come to the States for several reasons, not the least of which was the American opportunity. She did, however, speak of going back to Italy. There were enough relatives here to spread a sheltering wing and keep track of Alba and JET until that time. I sensed Alba was just as keen to the fact she might never get back home. JET's father was Alba's son, and short of great detail, the problem was with JET's mother, who drank too much, was loose with her money, probably had an affair, and so on. Of course, this was Alba speaking about *her* son, and frankly, it was none of my business either way.

Antonio was a metal fabricator who worked in a lamp shop, creating elaborate brass and bronze ceiling fixtures and table lamps, one of which sat on an end table in the living room. Alba worked part-time in a bakery and restaurant after their son, Richie, grew older. Antonio had had a stroke about ten years ago, went downhill quickly, and became a full-time job for Alba as caretaker.

I sincerely told her that she and Richie had done a great job raising Joseph, and I admired him and his work ethic very much. She beamed at the compliment. It was a lovely evening, with no complaints about red table wine with chicken.

CHEZ NEO

If I could write songs and play piano, I could top Billy Joel's hit "Piano Man." My signature song would be called "Chez Neo," and it would tell a bittersweet story of bar customers also. Chez Neo was the lounge just inside the front door entrance to the right, designed to get in and out unnoticed from the restaurant. It was built out in modern décor, dark enough to hide in certain areas if, perhaps, your liaisons were covert—or show your availability under sexy LED mini-spots in the center. The lights also illuminated black and chrome high-top tables. The bar was much the same: lustrous ebony with comfy stools and a huge mirror behind, showcasing the high-end selection of twinkling booze bottles. If you didn't know, just as there is a salty snack on the bar so you drink more, there's a mirror facing customers because people love to look at themselves. Additional spots shone tastefully down on reproductions of classic modern art by Pollack, Picasso, Dali, and Warhol in chrome surrounds.

There were a few regulars but no real barflies to pollute the atmosphere. The customers arrived at their habit-formed hours like any bar. The class of people and their costumes changed yet remained the same. On any given night, there was an array of vodka-soaked, well-dressed businessmen dreading going home; perhaps a stray, high-end hooker, some hard to identify as such, some not so difficult; and other people just checking the place out. The most unsavory were three younger guys pushing the unwritten dress code. Yes, the leering guys from the elevator on the first day. Apparently they each had only one pair of Dockers and a selection of nice pullovers in an attempt to pick up women who were assuredly out of their league. Sometimes they'd get boisterous or vulgar, and Fred or Abel would have to hush them. But they'd drop $100 in booze and tips in a couple of hours and be on their way. Abel debated the inconvenience with the cash register, but the cash register always won. Fred called them the "Chez Playboys," or "Chez Plays" for short. Chez was pronounced "Chay," of course.

My favorite customer by far was Za ("Zah"). Originally from Communist Romania, Za immigrated here in the early 1960s after having been shuffled around Yugoslavia, Poland, and even western Russia. She was fourteen when she had come home from school one afternoon to find her alcoholic father hanging in the bathroom. Judging from her stories and calculating the time frame, I placed her at about seventy, and if I look like that at seventy, I'll be content with my B cup. She was stone-cold cool and reminded me of Veronica Lake, the 1940s movie star sex symbol. Za was a slender cat exuding a sexual presence in dresses she rarely wore twice. I attributed the couture to the two African American men that courted her individually. I wondered if there was any connection between the two; I never asked, and she never offered. One drove a 7 Series BMW, the other a gold-trimmed AMG Mercedes; both cars were black onyx, deep like a placid ocean beneath a midnight moon. To keep the guys straight in my mind, I named them "Mercedes" and "Series 7."

Za's signature drink was an Absolut dirty martini with a blue cheese stuffed olive. She sipped it with a sidecar of seltzer through thin lips, her face as wrinkle free as a saucer of heavy cream on a counter. She sat quietly at a tall top along the back wall, surveying all with eyes of wisdom. I would join her any chance I could, just to hear her sultry accent. She saw Daleka through the Chez entrance one night and started an almost imperceptible growl, shaking her head slowly. I glanced over my shoulder and back at Za, who was arching an eyebrow.

Za stared into her martini and said in a low voice, "She walks in shadows."

One Thursday night Abel appeared to be salivating as he waited for Daleka, and I was still trying to figure out the "there's more to this" attraction. AA was always plotting something, and in his mind, always thought he was pushing the envelope. Abel pushing the envelope usually ended with him having a paper cut. As far as I was concerned, this new toy was no different.

Za had a different impression and said, "Age matters little in events of the heart. In love the old are like the giddy teenager, but with more stories to tell."

I replied with a quote of my own: "In lust, the old perv is giddy when being physically abused by someone half his age."

Suddenly there was a cacophonous commotion in the kitchen. Sergio was screaming, and pots were clanging.

After another quick series of pan-banging racket, Sergio came careening out of the kitchen screaming, "*Fire!*"

Not known for tact under fire, pun intended, Abel barked at me to keep the patrons calm. His yelling did little to reinforce maintaining a Zen atmosphere in the restaurant. Apparently there was a grease fire raging. The NSF hood fire extinguishing system was plugged with grease due to Abel's shoddy maintenance. A bright yellow-blue fire was in full bloom. JET grabbed a fifteen-pound ABC fire extinguisher and shut down the blaze, along with about six hundred and fifty retail dollars' worth of dinners and fancy sauces. Sergio was spewing profanity in Spanish. My immediate thought was, where are we going to get another chef at this hour? Even Abel can't recover this quickly. Sergio finished his tantrum, and thankfully, went back into the kitchen. JET thought Abel would fire him or at least scream at him for ruining the food and making the kitchen look like Christmas morning covered in snow, but Abel realized he didn't have any choice. By rights, the kid actually saved the kitchen.

Troy Roy, our off-duty fire department EMT, had already radioed the TFD, but Fred had gotten to him, shortcutting the cavalry seconds before they mounted up with sirens shrieking in response to the in-house automatic alarm in the kitchen. I thanked Roy for not pulling an ax from his hat and taking down walls. The epitome of heroic cool, he had calmly put his scotch down and was ready to treat smoke victims or go into action with whatever was needed.

Daleka had just come in and, acting like an entitled gangster's moll, was all over me with questions, which I had no time to answer. Fred was fielding customers' concerns, and somehow, between a round of free drinks—Fred's idea—and me suggesting offering customers a coupon for a buy one, get one free dinner for their inconvenience, we got through it. I had already been laying groundwork for a raise, and this seemed a good opportunity. Before I even asked, the raise was in my check as the following day was payday.

SHORTCUT

O n a Wednesday night after ten o'clock, dinner service was over, the books were balanced, and I was beat. Fred hadn't been around that day. Chez Neo wasn't busy, so I instructed the bartender and JET to perform the closing protocol and clean up a bit, then JET would check the lights and lock up. On my feet all day, I just wanted to get home to a hot shower, climb into bed with a cup of decaf tea, and read until I fell asleep, which I knew wouldn't take long. In the parking garage about twenty feet from aging but trusty Carlita, I remembered the document I created with new passwords. I'd need it before I left for work in the morning. Crap. Typically I wouldn't cut down the alley at night, but I was too tired to follow my usual route. I entered the side that runs the entire block. About halfway down the alley, there is a "T" splitting the block and emptying a few doors from the building's entrance and lobby. As I rounded the corner, I almost collided with the Chez Playboys.

We surprised each other. They were more than half drunk, and before I could diffuse anything with a salutation, the first came out with something vulgar. I didn't like them anyway, never had anything to do with them, and therefore didn't know their names. "Hi, guys, Fred's waiting for me upstairs," which I thought was pretty clever in a split second except ...

"Naw, Fred hasn't been there all night," said one. "Naw, baby, you're going the wrong way."

Another followed quickly with, "No, she's taking a shortcut the *right* way. She's coming to see us!"

With only one flickering halogen light at the junction of the alley, there were plenty of shadows and reflections. I didn't know if I saw a blade, a gun, or a redneck belt buckle peeking out from the first asshole's waistband, but whatever it was, I knew it couldn't be good. The back two were chuckling, with one guy picking at his crotch.

A dozen thoughts flashed through my mind in milliseconds. Fred, Touhy, Nebraska, an unpleasant sexual experience in my teens, and the .32 caliber Jetfire Beretta pistol my brother Chad had given me, which was safely tucked in my jewelry box in my apartment. Even my pepper spray was not in the too-small purse I was carrying. Then a splash of humor crossed my mind. I'm fucked—no, that was their idea. Kellogg as a Great Dane. Rape class, where you're supposed to have the calm to wet yourself and repulse your attacker(s). Or the best: Daleka and the muscle squad there to kick some ass for my rescue. At close to ten years older than these jerks, I could probably still outrun them had I changed into my tennis shoes, but I still had on my pumps. My tight skirt prevented me from punting at least one pair of balls, which would have allowed me some satisfaction.

One last try. "Okay you guys have a good night, and we'll see you tomorrow."

That resulted in greater laughter from the two in back.

The first one said, "We all checked out how fine you were first time we saw you. We even talk about it." As he stepped forward, he exhaled. "We're jus' kinda funnin' around. Why don't ya lighten up a little, Lanny?"

"*Fuck you!*" I growled through gritted teeth. I felt as if the coyotes were coming out of the cornfield. As quickly as the words left my lips, a blurred backhand swept up and caught my right cheekbone and temple. Stunned, my vision became a checkerboard of stars. Trying to keep my balance, I felt a hand grab the bottom of my skirt. Was this to prevent me from falling or just save them time? The blow was too hard. I started falling, the seam of the skirt ripped, and I went down hard on my left side to the concrete, gravel, and garbage. A buzzing started in my right ear and then became a drone. Was I going into shock? Maybe that would be good if I passed out and didn't have to deal with this.

The drone increased. It became a rumble and was getting louder, like a train. I imagined the fifteen-yard Allied Waste dumpster in the alley accelerating toward us. No, I wasn't imagining. As the jerks spun around, it was too late; the dumpster slammed into the back two, knocking one down and the other off-balance. The drone had taken over my hearing, and from the ground my distorted vision caught the slow-motion blur of a wooden vegetable crate fly from the dumpster top and blindside the off-balance guy at terminal velocity across his head. The crate swung around in a figure eight motion, catching number two in the shoulder as he was attempting to raise his arms—defensively or aggressively, I didn't know which—from a kneeling position. He went down as the adrenaline-charged blows jackhammered at their heads alternately. Knife or gun boy had long since torn off down the alley. As the crate began to break apart, I saw a spray of blood under the alley light. Blood also ran from my brain. I screamed, "JET! *Stop!*" And then — blackness.

I slowly opened my eyes, and there were my two boys, one on either side of my hospital bed. Fred was on my right side holding my hand, and I reached out with my left and JET gently took it. I opened my mouth to speak, but Fred touched my lips with the fingertips of his free hand, halting my speech, which was fine considering the throbbing pain in my jaw. He softly explained, among other things, that I had a concussion and said all three culprits had been apprehended. He said two were easy to catch because they needed hospitalization—they were on a lower floor. My head turned toward JET as his sheepish smile turned into a big grin. I started to smile, but it hurt too much. "Are you all right, JET?" A childlike nod. "That was very brave, JET." A downward glance and blush. "Did you mess them up, kid?"

Direct eye contact and a devilish grin. "Yep!" he replied.

"That's my boy."

A WALK IN THE PARK

F red took care of the three of us—me, Kellogg, and himself. We began taking walks around the block and then to the park as I recuperated. Without me at the store, I believe Abel fully realized my value—but also JET's value, without my telepathic supervision and even Fred's presence. Za came to visit my apartment with flowers, wine, my favorite fat-free turtle candies, and fruit. What a sweetheart. I asked Fred why JET had not come to see me. Apparently JET was embarrassed, Fred told me, because he had seen my "underpants"! Fred was sworn to secrecy not to reveal this embarrassing mortal sin.

"Oh for Pete's sake, tell the kid I have no recollection past the blow to my head, and I want to see him," I exclaimed.

I really enjoyed the walks with Fred and Kellogg at Hamilton Forest Preserve. There was one stretch on our trail that had beautifully tall pine trees. We took to stopping there for a few moments; I would close my eyes and smell the pines. I remembered brief moments in time and took a mental snapshot for my sensory memories and mind's eye. I told Fred this, and we waxed whimsical about various experiences that had been, for each of us, brief moments in time that would become indelible memories. I told him I had many pictures of him— our first kiss, him on top of me, inside of me. I had known for some time, but now I was sure, I loved Fred ... and Kellogg. Kellogg knew. I couldn't figure out why I didn't tell Fred.

Maybe it took getting whopped across my temple or the subsequent crash to the concrete to come to this realization. I was told I had a concussion, but I felt as if I was having remarkable moments of clarity. Such a jumble of thoughts. This was the first time I ever felt as if I were getting older, as if I were tapping moments of my own history and experience. My feelings were strong for this pseudo-family triad I seemed to hold in my hand: Fred, JET, and Kellogg. So much had happened since I left Touhy. I had grown so much, experienced so many things, and met so many different people. I guessed I loved Tom when I married him—what my perception of love was at that time. This felt so different. I had left Touhy not wanting to become one of *those* people in love. *Were* those people in love? In a love I didn't understand, a love that hadn't hit me yet? An intangible, elusive love that I'd yet to experience truly?

We wondered if Kellogg could appreciate the smell of pine but figured he was more interested in the squirrels and chipmunks as he yanked against his harness toward a commotion in the bushes. Sometimes Fred would unbuckle the harness, and Kellogg would shoot like a bullet into the trees. Releasing a big sigh, I told Fred I would not be combing out the tangles and thistles in his fur when we got back to the apartment.

Fred skirted the issue, saying in his best Andy Rooney impression, "Did'ja ever wonder how they know a dog can smell a couple of parts per million of something?"

I queried, "Are you just making shit up?"

Once we were crossing an interior park road and came across a turtle the size of a silver dollar. Sure he would get turned into turtle hash by a car, I picked him up. The bottom of his shell had a beautiful and colorful design. There was a pond about an eighth mile off the path that I wanted to take him to. By the time we got there, the turtle was utterly pissed off, his head fully extended, jaws open, and his tiny claws paddling in an attempt to shred all three of us. I dropped him on the moss-covered water. Fred said he clearly didn't appreciate my kindness in saving his life. I told Fred sometimes it's not about getting a thank you—like someone you help and they don't appreciate it, but you do it anyway. Maybe it will occur to them someday, maybe not.

As we got back in the car each time, Fred would say Kellogg loved ice cream, so we would get some after our walk. Sarcastically, I suggested we were negating the health-imparting properties of our exercise regimen by eating ice cream. Fred cynically agreed completely but explained his theory of work and reward as it related to dog training, and it was imperative that Kellogg not be sent mixed signals. It was essential that he got a treat, his favorite treat, after performing well on the trails. Breaking from our *serious* dialogue, I couldn't help saying, "Now *I know* you're making shit up."

Fred, undeterred, insisted Kellogg required butter-brickle from Baskin-Robbins in a cup, which happened to be Fred's favorite also.

Humpty Dumpty
Had a Great Fall

J ET relished the additional responsibility given to him and
not in a bossy way. In addition to a general awareness of
maintenance, such as burned-out lightbulbs and slow-running
drains, he managed the busboys. If he did not personally set up
Table 5, he took pride in making sure it was set up properly.

At the end of an unusually mild winter, there was general
work being done on the exterior of the building. Contractors
were tuck-pointing, performing roof and signage repairs, and
when finished, washing windows.

Coming in one morning, JET was the first to notice that
the window washer's bosun swing had blown into T-5's window.
He called me over to look at it. It had shattered the exterior
Thermopane glass. Workers apparently cleaned up the sidewalk
beneath, or we would have noticed it coming into the building.
Safety glass, when smashed, breaks into a zillion pieces. The
outer pane shattered so precisely, it appeared surgically removed

from around the entire frame and was difficult to notice. The inner window was intact. Building management said they were aware of the damage, and the window-washing company was dealing with their insurance company for replacement.

I was starting my fourth year at the store and had begun some serious soul-searching. This had been quite a run and a lot of fun, yet I was getting burned out on Abel, his antics, and the whole La Ventana experience. I would be thirty-seven that year, and I'd never lost sight of my grand plan: I still wanted to make my mark on the world before I got too much older. I still had a good shape and energy to tackle a new project. I had talked indirectly with Fred about this, off and on, and I sensed his growing discontent as well. Not that he had aspirations to become a brain surgeon or an astronaut, but I knew we both longed for a change of scenery. The beauty of his work was portability. All he needed to set up shop was a laptop computer. I had two very important questions to ask myself. What did I want to do next, and did I want him to come along? If I did ask, there was a small presumption I was making. Would he want to accompany me? I needed to open a dialogue.

I was heading in early on a beautiful spring morning to prepare for Sunday brunch. The air had a new fabric smell rarely experienced in downtown Troy. I liked Sundays. They were peaceful, with no commuter traffic or diesel from buses and delivery trucks; even the fish trucks seemed to smell better. The early morning garbage trucks that usually leaked some putrid slop were absent today. It was seven in the morning, the sun was still coming up around our medium-high skyscrapers, and I had left Fred asleep after Saturday night's chicken cacciatore carryout, a little too much Chianti, and splendid lovemaking. Still spooked from the alley incident, even in the mornings, I would always exit the deck onto the street after parking Carlita, my Corolla.

I was smacked with what looked like a cop show movie set.

There was shattered glass strewn in a huge radius from the sidewalk to the middle of the street. As I scanned further, the street was cordoned off from both intersections, and rolls of yellow police tape surrounded the area like someone had TP'd on Halloween night. Uniformed cops, medical guys, the fire department, and cameramen from *Action 8 News* were milling about among squad cars and ambulances. I arced into the street to look up at our building, the Ivanhoe. It looked like the oversize Table Five window was gone, replaced by a huge gaping hole. The closer I got, the harder my heart began pounding. Shit! This was definitely us—I mean Ventana! Squeezing through the crowd to get closer, a cop held up his hand to block me. I informed him officiously I was the manager of La Ventana.

The chief investigator, a Columbo type named Detective Gwynn, playing it close to his ill-fitting suit vest, introduced himself and explained that the owner had apparently jumped with his girlfriend in some sort of tangled love tryst or impassioned act. Be it love or hate, this impassioned event had a motive yet to be determined.

I was in shock trying to take in this scene and construct in my mind what had happened. Abel would be the last guy to off himself over any woman, let alone a muscle-bound, in my opinion, drug-abusing dominatrix. And if the pink invader had been banging on heaven's door, it was still unclear if access had been allowed or denied.

My playing big shot manager paid off—sort of. Detective Gwynn asked me to confirm identification of the bodies. By this time I wasn't just shuddering; I was visibly shaking. Gwynn put a hand on my shoulder to offer some sort of support. We walked over to a huge lump adjacent to the curb, and Detective Gwynn lifted the corner of a dark vinyl drop cloth. Mangled limbs, twisted unnaturally, were steeped in a black cherry pool of thick blood on the concrete. Daleka lay on top of Abel in his ridiculous costume. They were handcuffed together! She was in tights, like a workout outfit, wearing fingerless black Lycra gloves. I can't imagine the everlasting shock of the first passersby to come across this horrific scene. Their feet were toward the building as Gywnn, after glancing over his shoulder, went to the curbside and lifted that corner. I grabbed at my mouth, barely containing a shriek.

"Yeah," I slowly murmured, almost inaudibly.

How surreal, how gruesome. My mind flashed to my dead uncle on a hospital gurney just after he had passed. Just like my uncle, this was the first time I'd ever seen Abel anything but alive—and usually bitching. His eyes were open, and there was a monster-like grimace on his face, his body structure crushed under Daleka's weight. Her face was mashed and distorted into the sidewalk over Abel's left shoulder. She clearly didn't come from the factory with wings, and her face showed it after an eighteen-story flight. I realized I had been holding my breath. I gasped for a millisecond and spun away, but I had looked long enough that I knew that image would remain with me for the rest of my life.

I flashed to a scene as a little girl on the farm, when a cow stumbled into the path of a log swinging from a crane boom to a woodpile. The weight of the log collided with the cow's head, illustrating the harsh reality of momentum and how delicate the bone structure of a skull is, even on a big animal. Turning away,

I saw fresh vomit on the sidewalk; someone with less visceral wherewithal than me had witnessed the bodies.

Looking up, I visualized what had happened. The kinksters were apparently frolicking on top of Table Five. I imagined the action must have been substance-fueled and as energy-packed as a photo finish at the Kentucky Derby. T-5 just couldn't take three hundred and fifty combined pounds of gymnastics plus a full table setting. Its legs must have bent toward what was left of the unrepaired single-pane plate-glass window, sending the lovebirds in flight. What a ride!

Gywnn released me to the restaurant, assuring me many questions would follow. I didn't know what was racing faster, my body or my mind, as the elevator doors opened on the eighteenth floor and I rushed to unlock the store, all the while calculating what I would do first. Clearly we wouldn't be opening for business. A couple hundred pounds of fresh food was there in various stages of preparation from last night and in anticipation of Sunday's brunch. It was eight o'clock, and the staff was starting to amble in zombielike.

Everyone was in some state of shock. I assigned Peter, a college student busboy, to make up signage saying "CLOSED UNTIL FURTHER NOTICE" in bold letters. I had already called Fred from my mobile phone by the time I got off on eighteen, and he called JET. I typically do well under pressure, but this was a little much even for me. I grabbed my notepad and began scribbling columns of priority items. With military efficiency, the staff cooperated with no discussion. Sergio captained the kitchen, contacting two fellow restaurateurs who sympathetically cooperated to take perishable product off our hands.

Suddenly something strange and eerie occurred to me. Dealing with Abel's remains would probably fall on me. At least the weight of Daleka's affairs wouldn't be falling on me, I silently smirked. My thought process, priority list, and attitude changed; I sensed that after the immediate dust settled, my whole life would change. That was an understatement. Sure, I could just walk away from this whole mess. Technically I was nothing but an employee, the hostess. This event would certainly force my hand into moving in a different direction. But there was no reason not to hang out a while to see what would happen. I had no idea what the disposition of the restaurant would be, if there would be irate creditors, outstanding loans, or even what the lease terms were.

I wondered how Fred would react, probably strange and unsure about the situation also. It was a relief knowing I would have his support through this madness, or would I? I was wondering what was running through his mind.

I mentioned this to Fred, and he said, "Me? I wonder what was running through Abel's mind!"

Abel's parents were both dead; he had a half-sister that I'd seen Christmas cards from but never paid attention to her last name. She wasn't from Abel's father and was married anyway. I shook my head, imagining, "Hello, directory assistance, I need a number for a Susan in the greater Duluth area." Fred and I continued the immediate business of canceling the brunch, rerouting the bakery delivery, and so on.

We stationed JET and Peter downstairs with a short and to-the-point report to disperse potential customers, hangers-on, and ghouls. The cops were inside now with their yellow tape marking off the trail of death from Abel's office to Table Five and La Ventana, the big window that was the restaurant's namesake. Fred had already ordered a board-up service and called the insurance company. Gywnn wanted to talk to the entire staff but of course spoke with me first and most. He had Abel's cell phone and, in front of me, wanted me to ID the contact list. Continuing with his Columbo act, he scratched his head and began exploring all possibilities with me. At this point he wasn't ruling out foul play.

The image of Ms. Za's shaking head and her comment about Daleka popped in my mind: "She walks in shadows."

The death trek looked more like a war zone than sexual fantasyland. There was no trail of garments like in the movies indicating T-5 was the pleasure destination. The violent tornado-like path included knocked-over chairs and a busboy cart, perhaps taken out by Daleka playing "swing the dummy around the restaurant." Abel's office was ransacked. Desk drawers were pulled and dumped; green business folders were strewn from the bottom file drawers; there were smashed wineglasses and bottles, pictures off the walls, furniture upended with a couple of cushions slit—total chaos. If Daleka was throwing this fit looking for something, it appeared she had not found her prize.

I wondered why Lieutenant Columbo had not mentioned the handcuffs in any part of his interview; my curiosity was certainly piqued. Maybe he presumed, perhaps due to my "management" statement on the street to gain access, that I would be offering a backstory on after-hours kinky play. I was still too shaken to overthink anything at this point. I would have my hands full cleaning up this figurative and literal mess.

I wasn't aware that AA had a formal will. I'd be contacting Larry Feinstein, his attorney, a gentlemanly older Jewish man, and we would have to collaborate on a plan. Larry had been around forever and knew everybody. I had met him a few times and liked him; he had a pleasant bedside manner. There wasn't anything he didn't seem able to handle, from a parking ticket to a murder trial, and all with prescient calm.

We met, and almost in a fatherly way, he radiated an "It'll be okay" calmness that I greatly appreciated. We both agreed, for whatever reason, that cremation had been mentioned more than once by Abel in a sober moment and mindful way. Funeral arrangements were made during the autopsy, and after somber commiseration over Abel, we threw a figurative match on the bastard.

The Aftermath

The lunch crowd was thinning out one afternoon not too long after we had put Abel to rest, and I thought I'd relax for a bit. In came Abel's accountant, Gloria, and attorney, Larry Feinstein; they suggested we go to the office. They proceeded to tell me they had documentation indicating I was in fact Abel's partner in the business! In light of Abel's death, I was now the sole owner of La Ventana! My ears were ringing as disbelief resonated through my brain. Next came the thought of a practical joke. It quickly occurred to me that Gloria was not the joking type and Larry, the lawyer, simply would not joke about a matter such as this.

Well, slap my ass and call me Aggie, Agatha, dumbfounded, or anything you like. I almost broke my nose fainting onto Abel's greasy desk in his—I mean, my—office at this news. I kept my mouth shut waiting for some explanation, mistake, or oversight. How could this possibly be? Why would Abel do this? Where *was* the paperwork, and what legalities were involved? What was the catch? Was this my dream realized? I had already taken the lead in operating La Ventana since the accident, but this was too much to comprehend. The entire staff seemed to have embraced me in my role of temporary boss. Judging by the staff's attitude and morale, they couldn't believe they were now going to be treated fairly. They were no longer subjected to Abel's condescending crap, his angry mood swings, and his basic irritating and rude personality. Who could blame them?

About ten days after I received this weird and wonderful news that I had transcended from hostess to manager to business owner, I was told I had visitors in Chez Neo to see me. Slap me again, but this time across the chops with a potential heart attack; there were two suits from the IRS wanting to see me. Thank heaven Fred was there and began to coach me before they came into the office. Besides his general street smarts, he had been involved in an FBI insider trading sting ... with the good guys. This meant he also had some IRS background and connections. Although this was good intel, it was not necessary to tell me to keep my mouth shut until I found out what the visit entailed. I would let them ask the questions or launch the first salvo. With a fixed stare, I sat tight-lipped, waiting for the bomb.

I had at that point seen the stack of ownership and partnership documents; most were legal gibberish to me. I could see Arrogant Abel had forged my name everywhere necessary in order to make me a legitimate partner. Abel had no shortage of signatures he could use to make it look authentic, with a different signature on each document. Smart. The next question would be, why? Abel wasn't the kind of guy to make me a benefactor out of benevolence; more likely, he wanted to spread the liability when he got busted for whatever rat's nest of shenanigans he had created within the books. Or worse yet, frame me as responsible for an embezzlement scheme he was perpetrating. Perhaps as a partner I could either be a tax benefit or his patsy for implication in tax fraud. Spoiler alert! Two sets of books in this type of business, and multiple registers as aforementioned, are standard operating procedure in the official worldwide bar and restaurant cheaters' manual. Hope I'm not divulging something the IRS isn't aware of.

We quickly called Larry and put him on speaker phone to brace for various outcomes of this meeting. If the house came crashing down on poor innocent me, we would expose my ignorance of co-ownership and forgery of documents. If nothing was found in the way of tax fraud or other offenses, I would smile, having not been aware of what *my partner* had done, and be on my merry way. The fact that the IRS was here at all indicated that something was amiss. If I *was* aware of my partnership, why hadn't I brought this to anyone's attention already? It was estimated the gamble was worth it, so we all sat, breath held and poker faces firmly in place. Neither Fred nor Larry had much to say when I commented the liability rested on me; the gamble was with my freedom.

The audit, surprisingly, uncovered omissions that I thought would fall on Gloria, the accountant, not me as a partner. It turned out the omissions did not have as much to do with Gloria as they did unreported income the IRS had uncovered. Was Gloria suspicious of Abel's antics? Sure, but any accountant can only work with the documents and information a client feeds her. The big question was the frequency and amounts of the transferred funds, both out and back, and whatever other financial sleight-of-hand maneuvering between the ledgers and checkbooks had occurred. That made me nervous—except the actual accounting after leaving my hands always balanced. Ultimately, fines, penalties, and additional taxes were calculated and identified as discrepancies due to Abel's bonuses and expense account for two tax years. They disallowed the items and claimed them as income. The tax owed was in the amount of $28,785.

With Gloria's assistance and my cooperation, a payment plan was arranged. It really had nothing to do with cooperation; I was the owner of La Ventana and therefore responsible for the debt. As far as Fred and I were concerned, good luck was an understatement, not having anything else questioned. Good luck did play a part, however; Fred later told me the IRS case manager was related to Larry by marriage. Proof of tax evasion was nebulous, and since the caseworker trusted Larry, a lot of case time was saved, making everyone happier.

Ultimately, as Fred later said, "Lucy, you could have been doing a whole lot more 'splainin'".

It seemed we were all ready to roll up our sleeves and get back to work. We would need a hostess, so Fred went looking for Jessica. She was no longer bartending where she had been, but Fred found her working at a restaurant toward the east end. She couldn't hit the door fast enough, giving about twenty minutes notice. When we rehired her on the spot, she was ecstatic. Not only was she going to make more money than she had previously at La Ventana, but I promised her she didn't have to sleep with anyone unless she was a willing participant. She informed me she was doing quite well in that department with a good guy who had money.

JET of course was in on the restructure and eagerly anticipated whatever promotion and title he presumed he would receive. JET, who had long ago undertaken whatever I threw him, got a chuckle when I suggested his new title would be *Mr.* JET. Fred and I knew any title was merely semantics. Regardless of titles, Jess was called hostess and handled the money. Jet became assistant manager but did not handle money. He received a raise, but the title alone thrilled him to no end.

And then there was Fred—what to do with old faithful Fred? He certainly was valuable to me, and the operation as well, and would be compensated with more than a few drinks. More importantly, he needed health insurance. We, Fred and I, decided to make him chief operating officer, with a low salary. He came and went as he pleased and used my office and computer for trading, nothing he was not already doing. The title was his idea, and he flattered me by saying he had plenty of fringe benefits, that was, me. I asked him to restructure the La Ventana organization. Under Fred's direction we kept La Ventana Inc., but Larry Feinstein drafted new incorporation papers in the name of Table Five. I became president and CEO, and the rest of the employees fell into place like well-fitting puzzle pieces. I was duly impressed, but not completely surprised, with Fred's business acumen as he prepared spreadsheets and an organizational chart with positions, wages, and benefits in a clear-cut order. I knew Abel's salary before his death and did not change it for myself. This actually meant a raise for me and more dollars going back into the business. Not only wasn't I stealing like Abel had, but Jess was starting at less than my salary and yet making more money than previously. Health insurance was offered through the corporation to part-time hourly employees who wanted to participate, with wages withheld to fund the benefit. We put Nonna Bella on as a part-time hourly chef, so JET was able to supplement a small policy she carried with our group plan. I felt pretty good about the whole thing.

Fred wore many hats. Jokingly I called him capital improvements manager also. Table Five's window was replaced with an extra-faceted pane on each end that we designed. It was a modified pentagon, with a windowsill jutting about fifteen inches out and over the sidewalk, after a variance was received from the city. Potted ferns on either side of the window framed the opening nicely. The design added strength, not that we anticipated another act of showmanship matching Abel and Daleka's. This new arrangement made Table Five even more of a focal point, with high-back maroon Naugahyde chairs with matching tablecloths. No one would be allowed to perform inappropriate acts below tables again, although there was still no specific way to police that behavior.

Business was better than ever, and Sergio was at the top of his game. The old crowd was still coming in, and new people also, with only minor talk of Abel. These elements, combined with an energetic staff and Abel's absence, created an excitement, as if it were truly a new place. Not wanting to induce too much change, we left the menu and pricing alone. We let Sergio prepare specials that Fred and I approved, as if we wouldn't? We didn't want Alba to get too involved in the kitchen, for obvious reasons, but she became good friends with Sergio, offered some tasty input, and stayed out of his way. She understood the high-strung Sergio and never tried to out-shine him by playing a 'chef card'.

THE HATCH OPENS

With Abel's lightly attended funeral service behind us, La Ventana was once again up and running. The reaction from regular customers was somewhat surprising. The auto message in my head was worn out from answering the question "My God, how terrible, what happened?" I began to wonder, were the questions out of respectful condolences or ghoulish curiosity? Apparently no one missed Arrogant Abel all that much. The next question was typically more to the point: "How's the veal picatta tonight?"

Midweek, while doing liquor inventory, JET came in with the cordless house telephone, the microphone covered by his hand. A guy named 'Hatch' was on the line asking about 'Sable'.

I cocked my head pensively, but before I could ask, JET shook his head. "I know. I was like 'pardon me,' but the guy repeated *Sable*, and then he like, cleared his throat, and said *Abel*."

I answered with my customary business greeting, and Hatch proceeded to tell me he was a friend of Abel and wanted to pay his respects. The FBI had called him from Abel's phone—apparently calling everyone from Abel's telephone address book—identified themselves, questioned him, and informed him Abel was dead.

Hatch explained, "Initially I thought it was a prank. After the call I researched the Troy obituaries and found it was true." Short of going into much detail, I told Hatch I was the new owner of La Ventana and briefly what had happened, minus the gore and costumes. Not much more than he had read. I didn't trust him anymore than anyone else at this point. My first thought was I wasn't buying anything he was selling. I figured maybe *he* was FBI or IRS and working me. The caller ID posted a number but not a name. He told me he was coming to Troy, again, to pay his respects, and get closure.

Fred remarked he thought this at least as odd as I did, cautioning, "Careful what you say, you might be setting yourself up to go 'down the hatch.' Besides, with Abel's burned remains, what respects would he have to pay?" We were collectively on guard, suspicious and distrusting of Hatch, and had yet to meet him.

Late in the afternoon three days later, Molly, the on-duty bartender, buzzed me to say there was a Mr. Hatch at the bar for me. I texted Fred, hoping he was near, and asked him to come to the office. I walked into the Chez having no preconception as to Hatch's appearance. A well-dressed, good-looking man about Abel's age stood to greet me. About average height, he had a nice smile and build, a little wider than Fred, and was wearing a sharp dress shirt and sport coat, graying at the temples through his chestnut hair. I could visualize him and Abel comparing notes on the ladies while knocking them dead with BS and good looks. I asked Molly to freshen his drink and told her we would go to the office. Molly pulled the soda gun from its holder and topped off Hatch's glass with 7-Up.

Apparently I had a curious look. He said, "I don't drink."

In the office we exchanged more pleasantries, and I told him Abel's office still felt strange to me. I recounted how I was hired and a few of my experiences there. Just as the conversation dribbled to a lull, Fred walked in—what a relief. During introductions Fred was curious as to Hatch's full name and asked in a subtle yet polite way. Hatch, also polite in a perfectly evasive way, told us that wasn't important, and he would explain as we chatted. We added slightly to Abel and Daleka's double-death accident but not much.

Hatch asked who was in possession of Abel's remains. Fred and I exchanged glances as Fred pointed to the top shelf of the bookcase in the corner. Abel was resting in a brushed nickel urn, conical in shape, with an ornate filigreed screw top, highlighted in copper. Hatch gave us a thoughtful look at first but apparently realized Abel didn't have anyone or anywhere else to reside. His eyes fell to the floor, and a faint smile came to his lips.

Hatch sat on the black leather couch, putting his arms behind his head, and leaned back. "I met Abel at the University of Colorado in a business class. We had one thing in common—actually two. We liked making money, and we liked to get high, not in any particular order. As young entrepreneurs we discovered quickly that simply buying weed to get high became expensive. We could buy larger amounts of pot and sell enough to smoke for free. We began dealing more than just enough for our own use and discovered it was *very* lucrative—and certainly more fun than going to school. We decided to sell more pot. A lot more. I was a business major; Sabel was in mass media and marketing. We complemented each other's skills.

"As our business grew, Sable got tight with another guy, a classmate who lived in southern California. We both went there for spring break and then the following summer. We found business in California to be really smokin', no pun intended."

I interrupted. "Why do you call Abel, Sable?"

Hatch smiled. "Like I said, Abel was in marketing and mass media. He had a way with words—a gift really. He could start a conversation with chicks, negotiate a deal, and sell just about anything to anybody. Cleveland, the kid from California, came up with the name Sable 'cuz sable was smooth, expensive fur. Abel was smooth, like sable. Sable-smooth Abel. Business really took off; I don't know how we managed to graduate. We took off for six weeks in Europe after graduation. Cleveland went also.

"That was probably the best time of my life—and I think for Sable too. We started in London, traveling to several countries, mostly hitchhiking. We stayed in hostels and met European girls who really dug Yanks—American guys. We had no connections, but we had some money and managed to get high and generally have a ball. We discovered a route we had heard of, called the 'hippie trail,' where young, carefree travelers would trek from England through Czechoslovakia, before it became the Czech Republic, all the way to Greece, Turkey, Iran, and Pakistan. California high rollers were sending Hare Krishnas, called Pilgrims or drug mules, to smuggle hash oil hidden in typewriter cases, if you can believe that, through international airports from Pakistan. The Krishnas actually believed they were doing it for their cause. The stuff was called 'honey oil.' A one-thousand-dollar liter bottle could be sold for eleven thousand dollars in the US—a tenfold profit. Initially we weren't doing that, but we learned the business and honed our skills.

"We came back to Colorado, picking up where we left off, dealing reefer. We started making *a lot* of money. We went back to California to widen our horizons and began jaunts to Mexico, getting into the hash oil market. We were doing so well I learned to fly; we already had a boat and then bought an airplane. It seemed we were always stepping up to a nicer plane and a series of speedboats that we used for transportation. I tricked out all our equipment with holes, or hatches, to carry pot or oil. I was pretty creative disguising holes in car panels, planes, and bulkheads on our boats, apartment floors, or closet walls, not unlike a squirrel hiding nuts. Except I never forgot where I hid the nuts. All these holes had a door or hatch. Each vehicle I owned had a secret door, always custom-made and cleverly hidden. Three guesses where I got the nickname Hatch.

"I was good at hiding weed and contraband or just making stuff disappear. After eight or nine years in this type of operation, the business was getting pretty big. No matter how well you organize and train your employees, somebody's going to talk too much and slip up. Somebody did, and the bales came tumbling down. But not before we buried over two million in cash in a mountain outside Aspen."

Just as I was thinking *this guy is making shit up*, I looked at Fred and sensed he was thinking the same. Fred figuratively threw his cards on the table; he wasn't playing anymore.

He calmly said, "Hatch, this is a very interesting story, and with all respect, I'm trying to figure why you are here and what you want."

In an almost sedate reply, Hatch looked directly into Fred's eyes with great resolve and said, "Sable could have just as easily been piloting our favorite thirty-eight-foot cruiser, but it was my turn for a run. I had left La Paz, Mexico, for Morro Bay, California. I was going to take two weeks, giving the appearance of a trust fund baby lolling his life away. I had forty liters of sticky Pakistani-Mexican honey oil on board. The Mexicans were distilling the THC from their own marijuana and mixing it with hash oil for a *real* kick-ass blend, not to mention an incredible boost to the profit margin. I was north of Morro, fifteen miles out from the coast, ready to backtrack and dock.

"The sun was shining, the twin Merc Marines were running great, and I'd just popped the top on a bottle of Heineken when a Coast Guard chopper gently descended so close to *Salus* I could read the guard's lips below the tinted face mask of his helmet. There was another guy sitting behind a .50 caliber machine gun poking out the side door. They indicated which direction I was to go. Not a whole lot of room for discussion. They followed me for a while, then peeled off when two Coast Guard cutters intercepted the boat. I did six and a half of a ten-year sentence in Adelanto State Prison. Sable never visited, called, or wrote."

Fred and I gave a confused look at each other.

"But Abel was there when I got out, and after almost a year of waiting and considerable planning, we went treasure hunting on Devil's Dimple, the locals' name for an area in the Sawatch mountain range in Aspen, to retrieve our cash. It hadn't been touched in eight years. A third of it belonged to Cleveland. But Cleveland was killed in a motorcycle accident with his girlfriend about four years into my sentence. Sable managed to get me that news indirectly.

"The cash had been heat sealed in heavy mil plastic and placed in waterproof military ammunition boxes. As well as we had stored the bills, our system was not impervious to moisture. Thankfully the government doesn't scrimp on the quality of paper and ink in our hard-earned dollars. The money stank so badly—all hundreds and fifties—Sable and I camped out for four days with pistols, food, and pot in a sunny spot in the wilderness of Big Bend Ranch State Park in Texas. We unpacked the cash and paper clipped it to kite string between trees, sponge washed it with Lysol, and let it air-dry. That got most of the mold odor out. Next we rented a hotel suite in the Dallas Hilton, bought some clothes irons, and spent an entire weekend ironing all the cash to bring it back to life. It took a while, but we laundered it again—this time through banks—and invested it. You can make a million dollars last a long time invested correctly." Fred nodded in acknowledgment. "We had some fun after I got out, but it wasn't like the old days. At some point we planned on reminiscing about this and other stories. That never happened ... this did.

"There is no liability telling you the story," Hatch continued. "I'm no longer in the business, no longer hands-on. Before Cleveland died, I knew he and Sable were doing something together, not reefer, maybe precious stones. We were going to talk about it, but with Cleveland dead, there didn't seem to be a rush, so we hadn't gotten around to it. I wasn't really interested anyway. They—Sable and Cleveland—weren't as hot as me. The statute is up on anything I've just told you; it's just fiction now. It doesn't matter."

After a pause I questioned, "So, Abel never got busted?"

Hatch got up and walked over to Abel, resting on the shelf. He turned around, now looking directly at me, and said, "No.

We never talked about me taking the hit either. Somehow it was one of the unspoken consequences, the price of doing business. Sable could have gotten cracked just as easily as me, but he wasn't at the wheel of *Salus*, so it didn't go down that way. *Salus* and all our vehicles were titled to dummy corporations. Sable was the most unique individual I have ever met. So why am I here and what do I want? Maybe there *is* honor among thieves."

I questioned, "Why the name *Salus*?"

Hatch looked at the floor, then at Fred, and then into my eyes as he said, "Salus is the goddess of well-being, or in other words, anti-pain. Abel named her Salus, maybe his euphemism for medicating his migraine." Hatch calmly, yet intently, kept looking at my face. "Did you ever have sex with him?"

My reaction was controlled shock and surprise. Fred sat poker-faced.

"No, did Abel tell you we had?"

"No," he said very matter-of-factly. "I didn't think so. He mentioned he may give you the restaurant before you told me or it happened. I just never thought he'd be leaving us this soon. He trusted very few people. It was kind of a double standard. As much as he enjoyed treating women nice, spending money, and helping them out sometimes, he was even a bit sanctimonious. His ulterior motive was more the chase; he didn't really respect and trust a woman that fell into bed with him easily."

I so wanted to blurt out, "It's not *kind* of a double standard—Abel would screw whoever he could and toss her out." But I didn't. Abel was dead, and it would serve no purpose. If Hatch got the damn urn and Abel out of here, I guessed that was okay.

"To give you La Ventana—he was showing you the tip of the iceberg. It is very flattering."

"Why *did* he give me the restaurant? What iceberg are we talking about?"

Hatch looked again at the floor and then out the window. "Abel was a very calculating guy. There are reasons for everything; actions cause reactions, and something happened to cause this reaction."

Hatch was skirting questions again. "Did you help him with his headaches?"

"I never realized they were migraines until close to the end. I thought he was buzzed on drugs or drank too much."

Hatch replied, "The headaches were always a problem, since he was a kid. Lots of things set them off. His parents didn't believe they were real when he was young; they thought he was faking to get out of school or some other duty or chore. His parents smoked cigarettes and played loud music in the car. They were assholes and wouldn't believe it was driving Sable insane. Lots of things would launch the headaches. It wasn't until late in high school that anyone seriously evaluated them. Even then they were misdiagnosed. In Colorado he worked with doctors trying to find out the cause. They understood they were migraines but couldn't figure out the cause—a tumor or something else? Smoking weed helped, but then it didn't, so he stopped smoking.

"I spoke with Abel, sometimes frequently; other times there were long lapses. We had drop phones and other ways to communicate. It wasn't prudent to be seen or electronically tied together. You do your time, but someone's always going to keep an eye on you; you're never free. Sable is free now, free from his headaches, free from his sex addiction, free from all his demons, free from the feds that always had an eye on him. They knew, through association; they just couldn't nail him.

We would meet at different places for weekends, sometimes in Europe, the islands, Canada, Norway. Yes, Lantana, you will need an extraordinarily large key to open the lock that was Sable. But if you do, it will probably be well worth the effort."

I asked, "I don't suppose you'd offer the location of the key or the lock?" His eyes were back on the floor until I asked, "Do you know why this happened to both of them—or why Abel and Daleka were handcuffed together?"

"I've got an idea," Hatch said, "but it's just my opinion, and everyone has one of those." Changing the subject again, Hatch asked, "Can I take Abel back to Colorado?"

Fred and I looked at one another, confusion on our faces.

Fred answered, "We technically have no right to him, nor can we find any next of kin. We've pondered what to do with him." After an almost uncomfortable pause, he continued, "Why do you want him? What would you do with him?"

Emotionless, Hatch said, "Take him home. Take him to his mountain. He can be free there."

Fred and I looked at each other. Fred flicked an eyebrow, as if to say it was up to me. I looked up at Abel's canister, then at Kellogg, sound asleep on the windowsill, as if our all-knowing dog would have the answer. My gaze slowly turned to Hatch, and I looked at his face and in his eyes. "You would scatter Abel on your mountain?"

Hatch waited a moment and said, "No, his mountain."

After another few moments, I said, "Yes, I think that would be nice."

THE OFFICE

When Kellogg wasn't with Fred, he would come to work with me now that Abel was gone, and stay in the office. I'm not one of those kooky dog owners that use baby-talk spoken an octave higher than normal or think dogs can reason, but the little dog was quite bright, and I had become very attached to him. Kellogg hung out quietly on the windowsill during sunny afternoons and was curious, sometimes to the point of irritation, about my desk. The office had long since been cleaned of Abel's belongings, including the black velvet Elvis paintings that I can only presume were an inside joke. There was one nicely framed print of a Buddha-like figure named Bodhisattva that I liked, so I left that hanging.

Fred would sit with Kellogg at the food-stained old wooden desk while he was trading and checking markets. Abel used to eat appetizers on the desk, and I had tried removing the spots to no avail. I ended up putting a desk pad over them. Fred liked our computer system because it was much faster than his laptop, plus he had a nice view of the skyline, even though it was out the back side of the building. Though Kellogg hung out on the windowsill, he also enjoyed sitting on the desk, picking stocks and making other important decisions with Fred.

I felt more secure when Fred was there. One afternoon I came in to steal a kiss from Fred and found him rubbing one of the novelty rhinestones left in the center drawer of Abel's desk. Fred was staring out the window while Kellogg sat on the sill. I joined them as Fred massaged a touchstone with one hand and petted Kellogg with the other. Suddenly a glint of sunlight flashed on one side of the stone. He glanced at me and back at the touchstone with a funny look.

He showed me where the finish had worn off one side, then he grabbed the two other stones from the center drawer, gave me a crooked smile and a kiss, and said, "Got an idea; see you a little later."

There were only a few people in the bar and I had some time before the dinner crowd started in, so I sat in the desk chair to put my feet up for five minutes and close my eyes. Kellogg, the little spring-loaded dog, bound from the floor to my lap. He lay there, making me warm and comfortable and ready to doze. Suddenly he hopped up on the desk sniffing around on the top. He began scratching and sniffing so intently his little cheeks were puffing in and out. There was something indescribably delicious about this desk, and Kellogg was going to find out what it was. It had been two months since Abel was gone and the grease spots were still on the desk, but I didn't think it smelled anymore. Then again, I couldn't smell one part per million like Kellogg!

I started pulling drawers out one at a time and putting them on top of the desk. Even though the FBI, IRS, and Troy police had gone over the office thoroughly, I decided to inspect it again. Removing the drawers and poring over the contents in great detail, I discussed with Kellogg possible unfound treasures and secret hiding places. I let him investigate each one. In the back of one drawer was a sumatriptan wrapper from Abel's migraine injections. I pulled the wide center drawer out, remembering all the crap we threw out. The police had taken, and not returned, Abel's beat-up Taurus .38, which probably ended up in some cop's sock as a backup gun or used as a plant for a dirty cop to bust someone. The gun was actually the only item noticeably gone. Not that I had inventoried the desk, but it just seemed like the medical wrapper, paper clips, coins, pens, notes, and so on were all intact. The bottom drawer on each side had been reloaded with files and paperwork after the cops' searches. They were too heavy to pull out, and I had already seen inside them.

Taking a break from the desk, I began looking at the two legal-size filing cabinets in the corner. Although investigators had taken Abel's computer and returned it, they had not removed the file cabinets. A copy machine was delivered for an investigator who spent the better part of a day looking at and copying files, removing and returning legal docs and tax returns that I had not inspected in detail.

I sat on the front side of the desk and began to peruse Abel's files one by one. This would be particularly interesting in light of my conversation with Hatch and the incredible backstory and insight I had gained into Abel's life. I zeroed in on what appeared to be three sets of medical files. I pulled out the farthest from the rear, which was simply labeled Colorado.

There were several folders, some going back twenty years, consisting largely of doctors in and around Boulder, beginning with the University of Colorado infirmary that treated Abel, for what were now being diagnosed as ataxia migraines, which caused problems with muscle control. This confirmed some of the conditions Hatch had mentioned and included an array of potential remedy drugs from that period, including brain scans. The underlying thread indicated that each specialist Abel had visited told him he should find someone more familiar with his particular condition.

The second file, labeled California, expanded on previous research and history, more treatments, more drugs, and more scans. It seemed odd that there was no paper trail, billing, or insurance claims for certain blocks of treatment. These procedures were being paid for in cash. Apparently doctors thought enough of Abel's case and condition and his cash that they were trying new procedures, with disclosures stamped throughout indicating treatments were untested and/or unregulated. I doubted this was being done out of genuine concern and had little to do with adherence to the Hippocratic Oath. Abel was becoming a pincushion and guinea pig, receiving treatments and experimental drugs administered for unknown charges. According to Hatch—"what the hell"— Abel had a cash cow from weed dealing to pay for treatments. The treatments were probably not FDA-approved, which often takes years.

The third file was labeled Clinics. Inside were individual folders labeled Diamond Headache Clinic, Chicago; Mayo Brothers, Rochester, Minnesota; University of Texas; and finally one that simply said, Norway. The Norway file had two clinics and a separate binder labeled Norwegian Neurological Sanatorium. This binder was thicker than the rest and appeared well worn, as if it had been reviewed often or had made several trips to the sanatorium.

There were lots of notes in the margins in two handwritings. One was obviously Abel's, and I compared the other to a note Hatch wrote that included the words "Sawatch Range," where he would be spreading Abel's ashes. The capital S in Sawatch appeared to be the same handwriting, as were other letters. Was Hatch more involved than he indicated in meeting doctors, reviewing medical notes, and helping Abel? There were X-rays of Abel's brain and reports on the effect of excessive sunlight and muscular tension. Notes and segments of reports were clipped and stapled to various pages. Searching on the computer, I found that these notes appeared to be in Norwegian, Danish, and Swedish, along with English. It was all gibberish to me, but I gleaned enough to know they were suggesting cutting open Abel's head. It would be interesting to speak with the Norway clinic out of curiosity. That would require an in-depth plan to get any information from them. Had I known this earlier, it would've been interesting to put Hatch on the spot regarding this. Now there was no way to contact him; the cell number he had called from was already defunct.

Several hours later, Fred returned to the restaurant with a Cheshire cat grin on his face so wide I jokingly asked if he'd just gotten laid. He had visited an old friend, Jerry the Jewish jeweler. No nickname was required. Fred explained he thought he now had a good idea as to what Abel and Daleka were into. Further, he thought he knew what Abel was probably hiding and what Daleka was trying to find.

Jerry had looked curiously at what had gotten Fred's attention in the first place, the worn rhinestone. Jerry explained upon first glance, two of the pieces looked like rhinestones, and one looked like cubic zirconium. The finish of either of these two faux diamonds should not peel or wear. Jerry whacked one with a hammer, expecting it to shatter. Nothing. Next he put it in a gem vise against a carbide grinding belt. The belt burned through the finish and continued to spin until it began to smoke. Interesting. With another machine, Jerry installed a carbide grinding stone and ground several sides of the suspicious zirconium cube, collecting the dust on a large piece of crisp white paper. He tested the stone with a Zec-Mate ultra-tester, an electronic gizmo that checks thermal conductivity of diamonds. It indicates, with a colored light bar, if the diamond is real or not and, if so, the relative quality and value of the stone.

Fred was disappointed at the reading, but Jerry told him, "Hang on; sometimes the Zec-Mate doesn't tell us the whole story." He went to a more powerful machine with a diamond grinding and polishing belt and, after a few moments, said, "Fred, these aren't five—and-dime rhinestones; they're rough-cut diamonds ready for processing!"

Fred questioned what this really meant and what the potential value was. Jerry, although excited, was more curious as to where these stones came from, what the coating on them was, and most importantly, why they were coated. Clearly someone went to some trouble to disguise these things as novelties. Likewise, cut and polished correctly, they could be quite valuable. Valuable enough, perhaps, that they must belong to someone, and someone was probably looking for them. In Jerry's estimation, these were likely smuggled diamonds. Smuggling diamonds in itself is typically low priority for law enforcement or the government, unless they are in large quantities or there's reason to believe they're funding terrorism or organized crime. The authorities' lax stance to stop diamond smuggling is typically due to the time, effort, and manpower it takes to make a case.

Jerry sent his runner to a nearby lab with the dust from the grinder for specificity and evaluation. The lab revealed the shaved dust was not typical rhinestone but coated in a mixture of zirconia (the correct word for the oft-used term zirconium) and moissanite silicon carbide, another diamond impostor, forming a composite sprayed on the stones and then polished, giving the appearance of shiny things that could be virtually any kind of costume stuff, for example, rock, glass, or quartz … but hopefully not real diamonds.

To the untrained eye, it's almost impossible to tell uncut diamonds, which in this case was just what Fred wanted to hear. The diamond grading system is based on color, clarity, cut, and weight, with cut potentially being the most important. The beauty of diamond smuggling, especially in raw condition, is that they are untraceable. Each time they are cut, they change. Laser imprinting or any type of serial number can be ground off, creating—viola—a new diamond.

Fred, and in turn I, received an entire diamond lesson from Jerry. Although DeBeers in South Africa is the most well-known for diamond sourcing, 80 percent of rough-cut diamonds actually come through Antwerp Belgium. Fred had been to Antwerp on a European vacation with his father once. I couldn't help but spout off what I knew from an art history class: Peter Paul Rubens, the sixteenth-century painter, practiced his apprenticeship there. I think Kellogg was more impressed than Fred.

Fred was still all about the value. Jerry's best guess, which was wide, was twenty to forty thousand dollars, depending upon how capably they were cut. Falling into the cart before the horse category, we didn't think it prudent to race out and try to sell them. On top of that, we knew nothing about selling questionable diamonds.

ENLIGHTENMENT

At the restaurant that night, I came out of the office and saw Detective Gywnn eating dinner with another guy. I'd had enough of Gywnn, so I exchanged a light greeting and walked into Chez to check on the bar. Fred ironically knew the man with Gywnn, another cop. His name was Mason—first, not last. Fred had gotten sloshed with him a few times; their conversation wasn't about cops and robbers but options trading. Fred initially did not think there was anything unusual about two cops eating dinner together. Suddenly he realized Mason was with the FBI, whereas Gwynn was a detective with Troy police. Having dinner together at La Ventana was probably more than a coincidence. We still didn't know if the Abel investigation was being classified as murder, murder gone wrong, murder/suicide, or an accident. Fred thought this a good time to find out—if not tonight, certainly the next time he could coordinate Mason and vodka cranberry cocktails together.

It was getting late, and the cops were still there chatting, the restaurant paperwork was done, and the receipts had been deposited. Fred suggested I feign sickness and go home, while he would lock up at closing time. Maybe after Gwynn had gone, Fred could catch Mason to strike up a conversation. Sounded like a plan to me, especially if he could incorporate a pail of vodka cranberry in the meeting.

Fred came home very late. Judging by his speech, it was obvious he'd had the better part of a bottle of Absolut and the conversation with Mason. There is a thin line between friendly conversation with an FBI agent discussing stock tips and a pending double-death case and possible diamond smuggling. You can't be too curious, you can't look like you're trying to get the guy hammered, and you have to be at least as smart as your opponent. I only wished I had been a fly on the wall to see Fred work. The conversation proved interesting and fruitful.

Mason told Fred, "Deaths like this require autopsies by law. The amount of adrenaline found in Abel's system was remarkable."

I questioned, "Wouldn't that be normal in the midst of the carnage due to the fight at the scene?"

"Ordinarily, but they took it further than general blood work. Abel was taking dexamethasone for his migraines. That stuff all but stops normal adrenaline production, the natural stuff that cranks you up in fight-or-flight mode."

Still waking up I said, "All the more reason Daleka tossed him around like a rag doll."

"You would think, but his system not only didn't have natural adrenaline or epinephrine, ordinarily excreted if you're fighting for your life, but there was some synthetic type of drug, unlike amphetamine, that the toxicology boys were still analyzing. Daleka however came back negative for that stuff but had a belly full of booze in her bloodstream, along with barbs—downers—so maybe they liked different buzzes or maybe they weren't getting high together. It raised a different and very interesting question: Abel should have been cranked up like Mighty Mouse and should have been able to bench-press a couple of Dalekas, so who was playing rag doll with whom? Also, they popped his top at the autopsy."

"Popped his top?"

"Yeah," Fred went on, "lifted his lid—sawed the top of his head off to take a look-see."

"Yuck!"

"It was difficult to tell, because Abel's skull was crushed so severely, but there was some sort of guck inside ..."

I interrupted, "Guck, is that a medical term?"

"A tumor or mass located toward a part of his brain that was putting pressure on a lobe that controls basic emotions: greed, anger, and maybe it had something to do with his migraines."

"What did they find in Daleka's head?"

"Mason didn't say specifically, but they called in an exorcist *and* a vampire killer."

Then it got good. Apparently the kinksters—now Fred was getting into the name game—were into piercings. "Like what and where?" I asked.

"Like the costume jewelry we saw Bora and Daleka wearing," Fred said while pointing to his crotch. "Abel and Daleka had nipple and genital piercings."

"How apropos."

"Mason said the trinkets were like huge stage jewelry."

"Oh, wow!" I said. "I just remembered the envelope the cops gave me with Abel's personals after they were done with the bodies. I didn't care to look inside."

Fred and I went directly to the office the following morning and into the closet. On the shelf, next to a spare electronic cash register, was a large, brown, Bubble-Wrap envelope with Abel's belongings the cops had given me after the autopsy. There was no next of kin, so the package was given to me, in case someone registered a claim at the restaurant. I hadn't given it any thought and likewise had no interest in examining his dance hall costume. I slit it open and dumped the contents on the desk. The bloodstained costume tumbled out, along with three pieces of jewelry that clunked on the desktop. Two were about the same size, and one was considerably larger, maybe for the pink invader.

Fred's eyes opened wide. "I imagine this stuff is more valuable than the novelty 'zirconium' we found in the desk." It was set in shiny tin-like stud settings like Bora's.

Fred burst out laughing. He had an idea we could make a ring for me from the huge stone. I fondled the stone and chuckled at the irony. That would be the closest Abel would ever have my hand to the pink invader.

THE SETUP

B ora hadn't been around much since the demise of Abel and Daleka but would come into Chez Neo occasionally on Friday nights. Fred learned that Bora—best described as Attila the Hun's granddaughter a few centuries removed—meant stranger in Czech. Sometimes one of her workout pals would come in with her; other times she would be alone. With an uncanny psychic ability, Fred would be there to chat it up. Occasionally she'd meet someone, a guy or girl, and leave with him or her. I would love to have been a fly on the wall with Bora the Stranger in the room *they* later occupied.

When she was with Fred, I would receive a report of the conversation. Bora genuinely missed Daleka, apparently in an emotional way. This continued to confuse us as to whether they were bi, straight, or gay and romantically involved. We really didn't think they were straight or hetero. Bora wasn't as interested about the reason behind the accident so much as hunting for answers of a different type, like where Abel and Daleka went besides the restaurant. She was unusually interested in Abel's office. I wrote this off to some sexual fantasy she jealously conjured of the kinky couple playing on the greasy desk. Fred thought, due to the ransacking of the space, that Bora was curious as to what they had been searching for and what had not been found that fateful night.

We now knew the oversize cartoon jewelry stuffed in her chubby earlobes, uncomfortably shoved over her stubby fingers, and hanging from her thick neck were real. With the backstory from Hatch about precious stones and the heads-up from Jerry the jeweler as to the value of the stuff he had inspected, we were fairly sure this was all tied to a diamond smuggling ring.

We were obviously done shrugging off this stuff as costume junk, although the observant cat burglar side of Fred always thought there was something peculiar about it. He couldn't believe how carefree and careless Bora was with the flimsy settings that held these multi-carat stones. One of her earrings almost fell out on the bar one night. Because we had never figured out the relationship between Daleka and Bora—friends, lovers, or just roommates—we didn't know for certain if she was aware of the value of her flamboyant jewelry.

Za witnessed these encounters between Bora and Fred. She surmised Bora was not quite as evil as Daleka but still dangerous enough to monitor. Bora knew Fred was "mine," so, although she probably thought she could wiggle worm her womanly attributes for his attention, Za and I believed her intention was gathering information, not romancing Fred.

I briefed Za on the questions Bora was asking—curious about my office and such. She had an idea as to how to extract Bora's motivation in a rather cunning way. Looking into her dirty martini as if it were a crystal ball, she told me she could possibly offer some assistance. I gave her a quizzical look. Since

Friday was typically Bora's day at Chez Neo, Za asked if I thought I could get Bora here this Friday, in three days. I was pretty sure Fred could. I was piqued by this, but it was also very important that it be handled carefully and discreetly, as there was assuredly no second chance with this caper.

Za said she knew of a man that was up to the job and very good at this type of work. Za said she would secure our interloper. She would offer this man $100, which he probably wouldn't take, but I should be prepared to pay him if necessary. I questioned why he would *not* take money for a job.

Za's lips flattened out as she arched one eyebrow, indicating I had just said something silly. Her answer was very simple: "He is a man, has an ego, and thrives on this type of job." That certainly had my wheels spinning as to what the job entailed. I had known Za for some time and trusted her. In the past we had run the gamut of discussions about Fred, Abel, and the overall La Ventana situation, although not the scenario of the diamond plot. I knew she was a sharp old bird and had been through some heavy events in her lifetime. I let her roll.

Fred enticed Bora to visit Chez Neo Friday night at seven for a drink, as if Fred perhaps had new information for her. The line was in the water. Za instructed me to happen to be bartender so I could pour Bora's merlot myself with a half shot of smooth premium vodka in each glass. Za—my slender double agent—would be switching that night to a nonalcoholic dirty water martini, still with the sidecar of seltzer. By design, Fred was sitting with Za when Bora arrived. Bora had seen Za plenty of times but had never made her acquaintance. Fred made introductions and asked Bora to join them briefly.

At precisely seven-thirty, Series 7 walked in with a thirty-something Black Adonis built like an NFL quarterback. Euro gals seemed to be more comfortable with biracial relationships than a lot of American white women, but it seemed every woman in the place was following him with her eyes. Za introduced Series 7 as Alexander and Black Adonis as Simon. In a short time it looked as if Bora was ready to play Simon says ... and it wouldn't be the PG version. Upon cue, JET poked his head in and excitedly summoned Fred for a preplanned emergency. Fred came back to explain he was sorry but would be detained. Bora did not seem to mind; two more vodka-spiked wines, and the Brothers had cast their spell. The four of them were off to what I hoped would be a heightened adventure.

Za texted me at midnight to tell me Bora and Simon had split off earlier and probably weren't headed to the pancake house for breakfast. She'd talk to me in the morning. Fred and I closed the store, tucked Kellogg under an arm, and went to his place to relax with a glass of wine and go to bed. We put ourselves to sleep talking about the silly stories we hoped to hear in the morning.

Fred suggested he would like to speak with Alexander, Series 7, about stocks, markets, and investing since he looked like he did quite well as a stockbroker. Cocking my head, I finally understood. Fred thought Alexander was nicknamed Series 7 because Series Seven is a stockbroker's license. I told Fred, yes, Alexander did quite well at something, but Series 7 denoted the 7 Series BMW he drove, not a broker's license.

"Oh," he replied.

We weren't sure what type of bedroom games Bora and Daleka had played or if they were lesbian or bi. We only presumed Simon was working with a full toolbox and was a master mechanic.

I met Ms. Za late Saturday morning at a coffee shop uptown. She did not disappoint. Daleka and Bora *were* lovers, yet the grieving process revolved as much around the loss of financial stability as pleasant or torrid sex or love in the relationship. Questioning Bora's sexual preference and presuming Simon had consummated at some level their quick friendship, I wondered what might have turned her around to be with a man. Was Bora not strictly into the fairer sex?

Za, again with the silly look, said simply, "Just because you're a lesbian doesn't mean you'd pass up a tall glass of chocolate milk like Simon." Point taken. However, Simon believed, by the terminology Bora used, her tastes leaned more toward lesbianism, though she claimed she was a Gillette blade, meaning she was bisexual. Quite masculine in her own right, she referred to Daleka as the bull dyke and she the molly dyke, and described in delightful detail Daleka's extensive collection of Johnson bars—gay speak for dildos.

In her inebriated and sexually euphoric state, Bora confessed she didn't know what was at the end of the financial rainbow but was sure there was a bigger pot than a few diamonds, more than the gaudy costume jewelry she wore. Bora explained she was haphazard and neglectful of the earrings and ring Daleka had given her until Daleka made her aware of their real composition and value. Initially in disbelief, she told Simon she decided, as a test, to cut glass with the multi-carat ring. The stone sliced a deep gouge in it, like an ice skate on fresh ice. She took the pieces to a jeweler unbeknownst to Daleka. Jokingly she asked what the approximate value of the "junk" would be if they were real stones. The jeweler scoffed and refused to waste his time until she demonstrated, maybe with the glass-cutting trick, that they were real. The jeweler informed Bora, judging by the size, that they were *ridiculously* valuable if cut properly. The jeweler suddenly appeared suspicious. Bora felt she was being detained; perhaps the jeweler was calling someone. Bora left in haste.

I suggested, and Za agreed, Daleka of the Dark kept Bora *in the dark* as to the entire scope of her dealings with Abel. This was anyone's guess, but ours was that Daleka didn't plan on spending the rest of her life—or her wealth—with Bora. Bora clearly picked up on that and was angry about it. So much for the grieving process.

This informational caper had turned out far better than expected from a single night session. Bora revealed much— some of which we already knew—but significantly that the diamonds were coming from Europe. She claimed she didn't know the source, and she admitted the rocks were smuggled but she knew nothing of the fencing arrangements or how much money was involved. Daleka had entered in the middle of this plot, replacing a murdered girl who had been dragged from the floor of the Hudson, and began to realize this scheme was large and lucrative.

Simon's report included much talk from Bora about home and the Parubice region. Za knew the girls came from the Czech Republic and supposed Bora was talking about home being the city of Pardubice. She spoke of a particular area and hotel and bar in Pardubice. I had been hastily taking notes, phonetically in my own shorthand, to share this conversation with Fred.

Bora spoke frankly to Simon and, in the heat of passion, or maybe just alcohol and greed, enlisted Simon to fish for information through Za, with compensation to follow. She even told Simon to bribe Za if he thought it would lead to the ultimate payday. This seemed not only risky on Bora's part but also revealed that she was desperate to work any means to an end. Bora knew less of the whole operation than we suspected. If Bora couldn't find the treasure, Daleka and Abel died hiding it from each other or trying to put something over on each other; there was definitely more treasure, but where was it?

Fred later wisecracked, "Oh, Daleka put something over on Abel, *over and on top* of Abel, all hundred and eighty pounds of her!"

THE PLAYPEN

There was a buzz surrounding the restaurant after the "incident" that created excitement for us all—Fred and me, the staff, even the new and old customers. For no apparent reason, other than Abel and his girlfriend drawing attention to La Ventana, we received a nice article from a restaurant critic with the *Troy Times* that was printed also in a larger restaurant magazine published in New York City. I was ecstatic that new customers and upscale folks I had never seen before were coming in.

In addition to new dinner customers, a single well-dressed businessman began coming into Chez Neo about twice a week. He would have two Captain Morgan and Cokes and make small talk with the bartenders. He remembered everyone by name, even chatting it up with JET, complimenting his fast work and curious about his name. JET told him, in his own words, that it was an acronym for his name. JET took to calling the guy "the secret man" because he would skate around the topic and not give his name. I never had the opportunity to engage the secret man without appearing suspicious, but considering the Hatch encounter and police still sniffing around the restaurant, neither JET nor I trusted him. Fred thought we were both paranoid and said he would talk to the secret man at some point. Later Fred overheard the bartender call him Maurice, or at least it sounded like that. Fred introduced himself with some small talk, and when, what sounded like Maurice or Morris finished his drink, said, "Nice meeting you," and left. So much for that.

Two couples started coming in, and they were gorgeous. We called them "The Models" as they looked like a page torn from *Cosmopolitan* or *GQ* magazine. If T-5 were empty, I seated them there just to show them off as flesh-filled mannequins. They ate healthy yet liked their martinis and expensive wine. They began bringing in equally handsome friends, becoming a larger group. I continued to place them at T-5 when available but told them to call for a reservation if they knew they were coming.

The most outspoken of the group was Sharon; she was beautiful and friendly and had a complexion so flawless it appeared airbrushed. She asked about renting banquet room A, the Playpen, for a party. We discussed particulars, and she decided to book it for a group of sixteen. This would be a buffet-style spread, with a selection of gourmet delicacies, some of which were special-ordered for preparation.

The night arrived, and I assigned JET to make sure they were in need of nothing. I'm not sure how Sharon handled the pricey event—whether she bankrolled the twenty-five-hundred-dollar foray herself, split it among discerning high rollers, or asked individuals to share in the cost of the posh get-together. It didn't much matter to me; I received 50 percent down, and she gave me the balance in cash upon arrival. A restaurateur's dream, paid in full and in cash—have fun, kids!

Among the delicacies were smoked lox, with mini bagels and cream cheese, fresh oysters, Peking duck, and beef tenderloin medallions, along with a half dozen imported aged cheeses, sourdough crackers, gourmet cocktail breads, and so on. Absolut and Tanqueray martinis were served by the pitcher, along with French and California wines of Sharon's choosing. A dozen bottles of high-end aperitifs, liqueurs, and cordials were placed on a bar table also. Mildly suspicious to me, Sharon asked that everything be set up by an assigned time as she would not be requiring wait staff unless she called—as much as saying, "Do not disturb."

A little over an hour into the event, I was managing the main room when JET came up to me with a wide-eyed, frozen-faced look. I cocked my head like the RCA dog, wondering and looking for a response. JET was well aware of the decadence that could occur in the Playpen. Looking in my eyes, he merely pointed his finger toward the Playpen. I knew there wasn't a problem with product—I'd made sure of that—nor was it boisterous. I quietly opened the door on the game room to see an action scene right out of a full-blown high-definition orgy. And there wasn't a cheesy Abel-like dance hall costume in sight. I had witnessed individual acts akin to this, but never this large and never with this many beautiful actors. Just as quietly, I closed the door and brought Fred back, if only for *me* to get another peek. This was cayenne hot. Someone should've had a camera. Then I noticed someone did. Short of stage lights and close-ups, this was better than an HD3D live-action epic.

There wasn't a whole lot that shocked me, but this was very close to pushing the over-the-top button. Fred scanned the room and quickly concluded that, moral issues aside, these were consenting adults in a private party. That was okay, until off in the corner, he noticed a huge mirror with a small mountain of cocaine, with long thin lines drawn out, surrounded by colorful straws. That was a definite liability.

I had kept JET's adolescent eyes outside the room during our observation, though I could not change what he had already witnessed. I came outside and told JET to hang the "Do Not Disturb" sign on the door, stay stationed *outside*, and summon me, and only me, if Sharon wanted anything. We didn't want any curious onlookers mistaking the Playpen for the restroom, and I did not want any of my staff subjected to any liability should this activity turn south. Jessica and I discussed if we should have gotten a cleanup deposit. We crossed our collective fingers and waited for it to be over.

As 1:00 a.m. approached—the end of the rental contract—Sharon made herself presentable, which clearly created a disappointed look on Fred's face, and asked how much it would be for two additional hours, in other words, until 3:00 a.m. Cocaine will do that to you. I told her three hundred dollars, one hundred of which would be refunded as a security and cleanup deposit. I was not as much worried about damage as I was bodily fluids, including vomit. Without a moment's hesitation, Sharon opened her purse and handed me three C-notes.

She leaned in and said, "I appreciate your understanding."

Ordinarily Fred and I would leave for the night, the restaurant would already be locked and building secure, the boys would do the regular cleanup, and JET would let everyone out. Considering the whole situation, we decided to stick around and close up ourselves. Besides, banquet room A, the Playpen, was not going to be used the next day. We knew the night would be late, but we were kind of high on getting the party bill in cash, let alone we had yet to hear the dollar estimate from Jerry the jeweler regarding Abel's genital gems from the evidence envelope. We guessed conservatively they must be worth at least twice as much as the trinkets from Abel's desk.

JET and Jess were happy to go home and agreed to open tomorrow. JET walked Jess to her car, and we retired to our own den of midnight tryst, my office. It didn't take long to think about all those gorgeous naked bodies, and we started playing around. Fred was getting a "tingle," as he would say, and I was horny too. I glanced over at the window in the office door out of habit. It had long since been replaced with real one-way glass. We started playacting like Sharon and her friends on the chair, by the file cabinet, and finally up on the desk, that awful desk. I threw a tablecloth over it from a stack in a cabinet.

Kellogg had long been a witness to our lovemaking sessions, and although initially it met with barking and concern, as if we were hurting each other, it had become a mundane and matter-of-fact behavior that humans apparently did. If it didn't draw blood, it was okay with him. In general he would sit in the window or lie on his bed, but no, not tonight—it was all about the desk. This time he was under it, and that would've been all right except Fred and I were on top of it. This became a distraction, as Fred was kicking at Kellogg under the desk. I suggested he finish one thing at a time, and apparently he thought so too. He closed his eyes, worked intently, and exploded inside me. I gave him a sexy eye squint and a big smile.

After dressing, Fred went to check on the party and bring back some snacks. I slipped some clothes on and crawled on the floor and under the desk, determined to find out what Kellogg found so interesting. I encouraged him, and he went back under the left side. I pulled out the bottom drawer on the right side, which locked on its track, preventing it from pulling all the way out. Kellogg shot across and beneath it. From the floor there was a panel covering the bottom of the desk, preventing access to the drawer from beneath.

Just then Fred came back with a plate of crab-stuffed mushrooms and bacon-wrapped asparagus tips untouched from the cokehead party. I asked him to pull the big drawer out. When it initially stuck on the locking mechanism, I could tell he was getting irritated; he gave it a hard yank. It freed, and he placed the drawer on top of the desk. Fred removed the hanging rack of files from inside the drawer and turned it upside down.

Kellogg jumped *into* the desk drawer opening and immediately began sniffing and licking inside at the panel, which apparently still smelled of Abel's greasy, salted fingertips. At last Kellogg had found *his* treasure. I bent down to see Kellogg on top of a piece of cardboard cut and fitted to the floor of the desk. I pulled Kellogg out, then the cardboard, and there it was—a manila envelope lying on the wooden floor. All three of us stood speechless. Kellogg broke the silence with one of his comedic vocalisms, "Rah-rwooo!" sounding like Scooby Doo howling at a ghost. Fred gently pulled at the secured corners of the envelope to free it.

The envelope was not sealed; the lip was tucked inside. Pulling the contents out revealed several documents, at least a dozen, maybe more. As Fred removed them, they looked like financial certificates embossed on heavy stock. Fred informed me that they were, in fact, bonds, and as he began reading them, I grabbed a pad to compile an inventory. There were bonds of various denominations from different countries—Czech korunas, Italian lire, German euros, Swiss francs, English pounds, and US and Canadian dollars. I jotted down and added the number of shares in each bond in their respective currency. Fred was busy looking up current values and exchange rates for the day and calculating the various foreign currencies versus the US dollar as I jotted the numbers down next to each bond name.

Kellogg caught our attention as he was still trying to inhale the desk. There was a piece of duct tape stuck on the back wall deep inside the desk. Fred peeled it off to find a stainless steel key. A safe-deposit key? On one side was stamped 823, and on the other was BSI. No other information. He handed it to me for inspection. I had learned about keys from Rich, the sandwich guy's, various properties. The key was high quality, and although it had what appeared to be a simple cut, there was multiple ribbing and stamping on the keyway, probably making it illegal, if not impossible, to duplicate without a shady locksmith. Yes, it was a safe-deposit key. Now, where was the box that it opened?

As Fred's fingers flew on the calculator, I realized there was one constant to all these physically different-size sheets and varying amounts: they were all in the name of La Ventana, a subsidiary of Satchland Corporation. They all belonged to me! There were several corporation names we couldn't even pronounce, let alone stumble around, this late on the computer trying to figure out what these things actually were. Fred, always conservative with his projections and rounding down for an initial rough estimate, totaled more than $1.48 million US dollars! If it had not been pushing 3:00 a.m. and we still had to lock up from The Models' party, we would've had sex again ... right then.

ANOTHER WALK

About a week later, Fred wanted to celebrate my birthday. Jessica was minding the store, and Fred collected Kellogg and me for a walk. We got to our park, but something was different today; we arrived on the far side, which had different paths that we rarely traveled. Fred grabbed a backpack from the Ford Taurus trunk instead of the usual plastic shopping bag as we headed out for our hike. We left the Hamilton Preserve main path and set off on a smaller path in a direction I was not familiar with. There were various ponds and streams and clearings with occasional tables throughout the park. What a good little planner my Fred is—he picked a particularly picturesque spot, with a small pond fed by a trickling stream. Out came a blue and white checkered thin plastic tablecloth, my favorite Mont du Claire red wine, a huge Papa's gyro to split, a short plastic water bowl and biscuit for Kellogg, and one raisin oatmeal cookie the size of your head from Nonna Bella. What a perfect day.

Crap! What *was* going on? I hoped Fred wasn't going to spoil this perfect day with a marriage proposal because the answer would be a disappointing and resounding *no*. Wait, maybe he wanted to have sex outside. I'd be too nervous for that, not to mention there would be too many bugs. Fred had poured the wine, handed me my plastic cup, and raised his for a toast. There was a brief hesitation as I held my breath. There was a proposal, the proposal of a lifetime, and it wasn't marriage or exhibitionist sex. Fred had been beaver busy behind the scenes plotting the adventure of a lifetime. He wasted no time with the details.

"Cheers! I think you should open a restaurant in Salerno."

My eyes were fixed on Fred as my mouth dropped open. Kellogg broke my trance by putting his paws on my leg.

"Excuse me," I asked, "you mean Italy?"

"Yes," Fred continued. "When you were setting up for lunch yesterday, I received my final confirmations on a few of the bonds I wasn't sure about. You're looking at closer to two million dollars. That has nothing to do with La Ventana's value or the hard number for the diamonds Jerry is still working on. There are a few more important diamond decisions to be made. Like who's going to cut them and where *you, he, or we* are going to unload them." Fred smiled.

I leaned my head to one side, slack-jawed, and started shaking my head slowly back and forth.

Fred began again, "You've dreamed about a European restaurant since you were slinging slop in Touhy from what you've told me. I know it's been a dream, but it doesn't have to be a pipe dream—not anymore. You've got the money to do it. I've given it quite a bit of thought and have a hypothetical plan. I'll run the scenario if you'd like to hear."

I stammered, "Ohh-kay?"

"Let's just start with some mechanics. Let's presume the dollar's fall in place with a realistic business plan. By the way, the BSI key that Kellogg found, I know what it fits, or at least where it goes. I scanned a copy and sent it to a friend in the trust department at Goldman Sachs in New York. It stands for Banque Suisse Internationale in Zurich, and *it is* for a safe-deposit box.

"Before you think I'm being presumptuous with your money, I do know this is your money and it's your life. I doubt this has truly sunk in yet, but you are very rich and you could really do this. Yeah, it would be a monumental life change, it's very bold, and it would be an immense amount of work. That cannot be overstated. If you want to do it, I'd be willing to assist and help with the project. And if you don't want to do it or don't want to do it with me, I'll land on my feet."

I knew Fred was thoughtful when it came to business planning, and I had a sense of how his mind worked. If he had a plan, I would be confident it was not haphazard. If we got along as well in business as we did in the bedroom, we would have a great chance at success. We actually did get along in business at the restaurant. He would offer a response if I had a question or make suggestions occasionally. Both were good. Our relationship spats were typically worked out quickly. We rolled with each other's better ideas, and this would be crucial if a project of this magnitude were to happen in the future. I know many problems over something silly come about when people become partners in business, and suddenly a small disagreement becomes a large one. But Fred was not my spouse, nor did he have any ownership in La Ventana or my newfound wealth. I still needed to hear Fred out.

Fred said, "If you think about it, you have a good team already on board. Sergio has talked about going back to Spain. Alba wants to go back to Italy, if for nothing else, to die there. She wants the best for JET and recognizes he's getting older and becoming his own man. He's already making his own decisions. Although she's proud, I'm sure Alba would embrace ideas for JET's direction.

"She likes to talk about her relatives and contacts in and around Salerno. We could give an international calling card to Grandma Alba, and if she had this seed planted, I'm sure she and the brunch bunch family members would burn up the transatlantic airwaves to establish connections. I've heard Alba rattle on about Guillermo, the family realtor, who I'm sure could check out availability of store locations and residential options too."

Alba had told me, over dinner, about the town where she lived—Senerchia, a twenty-minute ride or so from Salerno. Fred claimed it would be a nice area to check out.

Fred began again, "I know that sounds a little close to the family for *you* to live, but there are gorgeous towns and villages all around Salerno with forests and mountains, and Salerno is on the gulf. The realtor would be familiar with the whole area and probably knows restaurant people. Honey, quit shaking your head," he told me.

I held my hand up abruptly. "Fred! Stomp the brake! What the hell are you doing? You're blindsiding me with this whole thing! This sounds like a frickin' *Twilight Zone* episode, and it's a lot to take in. Yes, I mentioned Italy; I never said Salerno—I said Europe. I love Alba as much as everybody else, but if she needs to die in Italy, she knows how to get there."

120

Fred poured more wine and suggested listening to the rest of the story and then dropping it for the day ... or longer. He told me again he knew it was presumptuous on his part. I'll say! No one knew about the money, and right now we didn't know for sure if the money was free and clear, if the bonds were legitimate or stolen or possibly counterfeit—Abel was such a con man.

There was a long pause, such a long pause. This was very unusual for Fred. I was sitting on the picnic table, feet on the bench, Kellogg on my lap. We were both staring at Fred. He turned away from us, staring above the tree line at some puffy clouds. Then he stepped backward toward me, moving between my legs. Having put his wine down, he put his hands on my knees, then slid them to my thighs, leaning back into my body, his head slightly bent back looking over another tree line.

"You know I don't have any family, I'm self-sufficient, didn't need any money from you before this happened and don't need any now. Typical problems of couples are money or sex; we have no eight-hundred-pound gorilla in the room. I know I haven't told you, but I love you. I *love you*. Sex with you is incredible; I don't want for anything. I don't want for anything more ... or less. You know I thrive on "The Deal," putting the deal together, thinking the deal through, and love the deal when it comes together.

"I don't think I've ever let anyone into my life like I have you, and although you haven't come right out and told me your exact feelings, I know we would not have done the things we've done or continued to be together if you didn't really like me. You've made it abundantly clear you do not want to be married, and I'm cool with that. If we had found each other when we were younger, perhaps we would've had a kid, and being old-school,

I would've wanted to be married. And you know what? If that had happened when we were young, realistically we'd probably be divorced by now.

"I don't want kids, so I'm cool with our relationship, situation, and lifestyle as it is. I had no idea how you would respond to this whole scheme; I still don't. I know you are not indecisive, but having laid this groundwork made me think you would be receptive to it. It can be dialed in to your specs and implemented from any point forward. Anything can be changed, rearranged, altered, modified, or totally shit-canned. The same can be said about our relationship, situation, or lifestyle."

With that he turned around, putting his hands on my waist, and so deeply kissed me I thought I was going to pass out. He leaned back, still holding me with his eyes closed.

After another long pause, I whispered, "I love you too."

With his eyes still closed, the outer edges of his lips turned up into a gentle smile. He pushed in closer, leaning against me. Kellogg struggled to get out from between us before he got squished, letting out a big sigh and going into a prone position on my lap. We both laughed.

Fred took a long drink of his wine and sat next to me. I knew Sergio had talked about going back to Europe, Spain in particular. I had asked him where he would like to work in Spain. That conversation prompted him to show Fred and me a hand-drawn dream kitchen layout similar to La Ventana. It would be in Barcelona. It included a rough sketch of an entire restaurant. Depending upon square footage, he mentioned it would have a banquet room also.

We both knew Sergio's position. He felt he had already overstayed his own self-imposed tenure at La Ventana and in the States. He wanted to get back to Barcelona, his original home port. If we mentioned to Sergio a dream restaurant in Salerno, Italy, we were pretty sure he would be willing to help, invest six or so months in a venture, bringing his Americanized international flavor to a new stovetop, as long as he could travel back and forth to Spain to check out opportunities there. Barcelona is a quick flight from Salerno, so he could work even while training a new chef in Salerno.

Jessica's boyfriend, the one with money, was an investment banker/venture capitalist. He had been talking about getting into a restaurant or bar, and now that she was back at La Ventana, he was even more interested. Depending upon how solvent banker boyfriend was, he might be interested in a lease purchase of La Ventana. Of course the dissolution of La Ventana would be daunting unto itself as far as I was concerned. The good news was we perhaps had a built-in buyer with banker boyfriend; the bad news was this guy knew his way around the dance floor and was certain to be a tough negotiator. But Fred projected his usual confidence, and as long as he did, it made me feel better. We'd have to have an insurance policy if this whole venture fell on its face. And that policy would have to be a La Ventana buyback clause.

Thankfully Fred had not mentioned anything to anyone about this wild dream scheme. If JET got word of any of this, he would be beside himself with excitement. I presumed the Italian relatives would be excited at the prospect, especially after Alba would be informed.

It was easy to see I was overwhelmed, so Fred decided to divert my attention by making up some shit. He said he checked with United Airlines regarding a jump seat in the cockpit for

Kellogg, although he admitted Kellogg would be stubborn to learn Italian.

My wheels were spinning five hundred miles an hour with an anxious excitement. This really would be the chance of a lifetime, and with Fred's help and confidence building, I had the crazy thought maybe it was doable. Was my concern to do this without Fred or with Fred? I could be a tough businesswoman, but there would certainly be advantages having Fred helping in this man's world of business—and from what I understood, it was worse in Italy, with the Italian male ego.

Fred said, "I wish this windfall might not have happened just now. It's taken the wind out of my sails. How this must sound now that there's money involved and I say I love you."

I knew what he meant, but there was no way of knowing any of this was going to happen. We were both getting fed up with Abel and the gig before this happened, but now I owned La Ventana.

A good point. Why would I want to do this? Was there any reason not to stay put and simply operate La Ventana in my own style?

I had been staring into the lovely placid pond. After a long pause and sigh, I looked at my two boys, now staring at me intently. This *was* a proposal. "Oy vey," was all I could say, followed by, "What about the red tape, the sheer legality involved in such an endeavor?"

Fred explained calmly that it wouldn't be easy or without problems. This was simply an outline. This was not going to be a spur-of-the-moment decision, but I did have a great sum of money I considered a tool, a resource not to be squandered. I didn't even think of it as mine. I did love and trust Fred and wouldn't have been with him this long had I not. Maybe this event forced me to realize that. I hadn't consciously thought of love and trust or dependability and integrity as such. Sometimes I pinched myself because Fred seemed like that whole package I looked for in a guy—looks, smarts, generosity, and thoughtfulness.

But then again, you know what they say—"If things look too good to be true, well …" Did I really want to be this attached to Fred? Naturally I thought about the money, but I couldn't find fault nor extravagance in any of Fred's ideas or proposals. He wasn't suggesting taking a first-class Norwegian Cruise Line trip around the world with his and hers Ferrari waiting in a garage at a mansion when we got back. He wasn't suggesting putting anything in his name, nor did he mention compensation. He had been taken care of fairly in the past, and I knew he recognized his tremendous fringe benefit—me. I kept thinking we worked well together and already had some experience doing it. It seemed we shared the same business philosophy and would defer to others' expertise in questionable areas. By the same token, we never lived together, let alone in a foreign country, isolated from everything familiar. It wasn't like I, or we, played games behind Abel's back when he was alive or didn't take the responsibility of La Ventana seriously. Now it was mine … ours?

The thought of embarking on such a wild and colorful adventure had my head swimming with excitement and confusion. There were so many important matters to consider that I couldn't begin to prioritize them. Teetering on the edge of a ledge, I realized the master question was, "Do I want to do this?" The trickle down started from there. With Fred? Could I do this without Fred? Could I do it by myself? In reality, no. I would need plenty of help—probably three individuals to do what Fred was suggesting. Thoughtfully I cocked my head, batted my eyes in an exaggerated fashion with fingers folded under my chin, and said, "Tell me more."

We went back to my apartment to unpack the picnic supplies and ended up taking a nap. I was off that night, and we decided to hang out. I did some overdue cleaning and laundry. Fred decided he wanted French toast and bacon. He left, came back with groceries and laundry from his apartment, and made French toast as we continued to talk. We were fairly certain where the box was that the safe-deposit key opened. Of course the cops had been in Abel's apartment, but we were feeling larcenous and thought there might be a clue for us pertaining to our newly found treasure that they'd not realized. Just about the time we had our breaking and entering scheme worked out, I remembered there was a just-in-case key to Abel's apartment on the restaurant master key ring. Although our bellies were full and we were relaxed, we became too excited not to go there that night.

The darkness made us feel all the more stealth upon entering the place. It was neat, clean, and sparse, except for the bedroom that was decorated in "early bachelor" as you might expect. We half joked about bringing Kellogg and decided, considering how he pestered us in the office and it paid off, it wasn't really a joke. We brought him. Fred turned the apartment system fan on to clear the stale air. Searching the desk, dresser drawers, and small file cabinet, we found bits and pieces of telltale medical and restaurant information, but likewise, it was obvious the place had been picked over already.

There was a tall narrow bookcase in the corner, so we each picked a shelf and started grabbing books, flipping pages, and hanging them toward the floor to see if anything would drop out. This was nothing the police hadn't done, but you never know. There were books on traveling, but none on diamonds, precious stones, or anything relating to what we thought Abel might be into or that would give us any other insights. Interestingly there were books on Asian calligraphy, transcendental meditation, Taoism, Chinese philosophy, Hinduism, and somatic experiencing, a mind-over-body pain-reduction exercise. The back cover claimed "freedom from pain" and techniques to develop "mindfulness."

In the bedroom Fred squeezed pillows and peeled back the mattress cover, which was all it took to get his mind dirty spinning. "I think we should make it," Fred said seriously, his gentle way of suggesting sex.

"On Abel's bed?" I asked incredulously.

I couldn't believe he was suggesting this, or for a fleeting moment I was considering it.

Fred gave me the "what's-the-problem" shrug and nodded with his head to the corner, saying, "There's a desk—brought us good luck last time." That it did, and rather than tickling Fred's fantasy, I suggested he look under the desk to inspect the drawers instead. Kellogg thought Fred was playing and jumped on him while he was on his back, half under the desk.

He released a big "*Hah!*" I thought it was Kellogg startling him, but there, in wonderment, was a small brown envelope taped under the bottom right-hand drawer. Fred peeled it free and handed it to me. It was empty, but on one side read BSI/823, and on the other, there was a red shield with a white cross through the center, Switzerland's coat of arms. Across the bottom was "D. R." in Abel's handwriting. There wasn't much question that D. R. was Daleka, although we didn't know her last name.

Brushing himself off, Fred said it didn't matter that the envelope was empty since we had a key, but he couldn't help wonder who was in possession of the missing key. I passed on Fred's halfhearted advances to play around, promising him something at home.

When we got back to my apartment, it was way past midnight. Winding down, we got in bed and began talking softly and gently touching each other. We were never at a loss for conversation—what happened today, what would happen tomorrow, laughing about something, and talking ourselves to sleep. I rarely passed up a lovemaking session, but I was just as happy to see Fred dozing off. I was exhausted too.

I loved sleeping with Fred, and Kellogg typically didn't sleep on the bed when Fred was there. Somehow he sneaked up and we were too tired to argue with him, especially since sleeping was all we were going to do. Kellogg was happy to be included. Stretched out, vulnerable, and contented, he would lie on his back atop the covers between our calves, his four little legs pointing to the ceiling. Our quiet conversation would put him in a trance as we'd watch his chest rise and fall in a shallow rhythm, relaxing so completely he would lightly snore.

Even if I wasn't sure about uprooting my entire life for a restaurant in another country, some invisible force continued to pull me forward. The thought of having all the components within my reach to make this work was exhilarating.

The next day JET picked up on the fact that we were buzzing around in a different mode than our usual workaday schedules. We alluded to our decision to take a vacation to Europe. Fred and I decided we should take advantage of JET's enthusiasm and suggested he teach us some Italian. JET decided to take it a step further and speak only Italian at the restaurant. It became hilarious when the entire staff was trying to speak Italian. This was to the delight of some customers and the befuddlement of others.

BANKING

O nce again I was glad Fred was on my team; we had the ball, and it was Fred's serve. Deferring to his expertise as to what the hell to do with this kind of money was a relief to me. I didn't know what type of fancy footwork would be needed to make sure "we" could make it accessible without sending skyrockets to the IRS. Should we cash in the foreign bonds and buy US instruments? Would we use one bank to assemble all the funds? Should we spread it out in various countries? As Americans, with my Social Security number now attached to La Ventana, was it not all going to end up under one roof in one IRS computer anyway?

In a detailed format, Fred had neatly assembled an inventory of the bonds, factoring exchange rates, options on holding assets to maturity stateside or internationally, and ultimately facilitating various financial plans that included a complexity of other alternatives. This was where Fred shone. He was thinking diversity for growth and long-term security but also cashing some investments for capital expenditures and improvements.

This would also mean that our scratching days were over; if we wanted to go somewhere for a long weekend or even a real vacation, we wouldn't be traveling in a turd-brown Taurus, Toyota Corolla named Carlita, or Greyhound, nor would we be staying at Motel 6. Keep in mind this was a rhetorical "we," inasmuch as it was my money ball. And my liability.

We arranged an appointment with an investment banker at First Third Bank of Albany. This would be a second opinion relative to Fred's ideas. After the small talk and the how-can-*we*-help you propaganda, I received a smirk when I had questions about the bankers methodology for a diversified portfolio. He apparently interpreted this as if I doubted his expertise. As a waitress and hostess and having been in the service business all my adult life, let alone being a woman, this was one time I was not about to put up with any condescension especially since my assets were well into seven figures. I asked for the department head. Fred apparently felt my vibe and reasoned the doors were not getting worn out with business owners coming in each day with more than a million dollars in cash, not including the covert long-term value of the diamonds; we waited for the branch manager. Mr. Starched Shorts cleared his throat and assured us he could handle the job. After a round of twenty questions, the banker was still talking as I stood and said good-bye. Fred shrugged his shoulders at him with eyes skyward, and we walked out.

Another bank appointment, this time at the Intercontinental of New York, was met with an immediate hard sell that likewise annoyed me. Had the banker made a lame attempt at being courteous, I could've taken it. He all but asked for proof regarding the funds. Besides being rude, he was wearing a brown belt with black shoes. I had had it. "Mr. Dragatowich,

I don't know your net worth but I sense I could buy you, sell you, buy you back, and throw you away."

As we left Fred said, "That went well. Let me guess where you got that line—the sub sandwich guy?"

As we stepped onto the street, I said, "Yes."

This was becoming like a movie, where the hero has a check for one million dollars and no one believes it's real; he can't even give it away. I looked at Fred and said, "What do we need to do? Go to a Swiss bank with a leather attaché case and act like rich Americans?"

Fred stopped in his tracks, looked at me, and gently kissing my forehead, replied, "Baby, maybe you should manage the money."

Abel had a travel agent named Irene he had used in the past. I had worked with her for some of Abel's travel arrangements. She was brilliant. No sooner did Fred give her our itinerary than she was above and beyond expectations with flights, transportation, and lodging with an efficiency that seemed reserved for corporate executives and politicians.

Fred had showed me an outline of the places we would visit. Admittedly it was all quite exotic, as I had never been out of the country—nor even heard of some of the locales we would tour. Packing was a chore, in addition to making arrangements with Jessica, who would be running the operation in our absence. The list was tedious, seemingly endless, making sure she had all the contacts, suppliers, and emergency numbers. And of course we needed to make arrangements for our precious Kellogg.

TRIPPIN'

F ive days later we were sitting in first-class seats C and D on flight 704, bound for Rome and Senerchia via Zürich, Switzerland, and Prague in the Czech Republic. Feeling like a couple of big shots, we would show a Swiss bank how American high rollers operated. We had a few of the bonds inside a *Vanity Fair* magazine in my carry-on bag and copies of the rest. We'd both been coiffed and were saving our expensive new suits for our meeting day after tomorrow at Banque Suisse Internationale, yes, BSI, in downtown Zürich.

Fred had traveled extensively as a child with his father and several of his father's female companions. I'd never been to Europe but knew we wouldn't be staying at a Motel 6, if they had such places. We had plenty of time to talk, relax, and for me, fill in whatever small holes of Fred's life and upbringing I was still curious about. I knew Fred's father had ripped him off years ago, and not that that wouldn't be enough, but I was interested in other reasons they might be estranged. Although

Fred never came right out and said it, I got the impression his father was a con man.

His dad had married into a rich merchandising family, and his wife, Fred's mother, suffered some mental disorder when he was a little boy and had been institutionalized early in his childhood. She had since passed away. Fred's father was hands-off as far as nurturing a child, and about the only skill Fred was taught was business, the business of money and investing. Which is not a bad skill to learn, but there was still a little boy in there that should have had a chance to be one, a little boy that should've had a father.

There weren't a lot of stops we had not pulled out for this trip; we felt decadent with new clothes, first-class seats, and a four-star hotel. We didn't feel comfortable enough with "our" money yet, so we held off on a five-star. If you're wondering, this predicament felt like: you've got this money, but you don't; it's yours, but it's not; you're making plans with it, yet you can't. If this all sounds quite confusing—yes, it was.

Fred wasn't much of a suit-and-tie guy and felt a bit awkward with my apparel choice, but as opposed to Americans who buy their Rolls-Royce or Lamborghini with a checkbook while wearing jeans and a T-shirt, we weren't taking any chances calling on a megabank in a different culture and country. We would follow our script and play our parts.

Our flight was surreal, and in my mind, even the word "flight" had several connotations. We had taken flight from New York and La Ventana, taken flight into the unknown; that surreal flight was far more than first-class seats to Switzerland and Rome. It was a defining and frozen moment in time, like the pine trees in the park, a frozen snapshot at thirty-nine thousand feet above the Atlantic, causing me to realize my own utter insignificance with my dainty cheese tray and fine red wine. As we continued to sip our first-class alcohol, our conversational wheels kept rolling as if we were celebrating a sealed deal. But really we hadn't even scratched the surface; there was so much yet to be done—like everything.

Neither Jessica nor JET knew the details of our trip, except that we were taking a vacation with the excuse of a probable tax write-off for a restaurant fishing expedition. The three of them, including Sergio, would be minding the store while we were gone, with us hoping they would be keeping an eye on one another. We would be texting and, on a daily basis, checking numbers and so forth. I'm not sure what they thought of Fred. They knew he was not an owner in La Ventana but knew he was involved enough with me that they respected and obeyed if he gave them direction. We did have to level with Nonna Bella, sort of, meeting her nephew Guillermo over the phone and later explaining confidentially to him that we were interested in looking at restaurant spaces in Salerno, Italy.

Jessica delighted in the thought of operating La Ventana, even short-term, and depending upon how her relationship progressed, her banker boyfriend could visit the enterprise unencumbered by my presence. We hoped this would lead him to making a commitment and producing a down payment. I hoped Jess would keep a smile on the old boy's face with whatever feminine means necessary.

Unbeknownst to the staff, Larry Feinstein was preparing lease/purchase agreements, and Gloria, our accountant, was helping with projecting numbers, checking tax rates, and helping us with the development of a business plan based on La Ventana's numbers, juxtaposed to euros and an operation in Italy. This included selling a business and buying a business.

For once Larry and Gloria, independently, were missing their typical air of bravado and confidence. Apparently they needed some assistance due to the international nature of doing business in Salerno, Italy. The more we thought about possible options to this plan, the more it evolved and involved. The more it evolved, the deeper everyone's involvement became. There was still much soul-searching to do, so much to think through. Even if we did not relocate to Salerno, we would have a base plan for other European cities. To sound like some proverb, this much money was a responsibility, as well as a tool that brought with it a myriad of problems.

We had finished our drinks and snacks, and Fred was starting to doze. I could not waste any time second-guessing Fred's judgment in the direction I was headed with the money, let alone distrusting him. Distrust would be counterproductive. Why would I even think that way? Was the money already tripping the greed trigger in my brain? The door on our relationship had always been open; it had been light and free, yet with an unwritten rule of exclusivity. What we were doing now had great potential to change everything.

Fred knew I didn't want to be married, so it was never discussed. I liked to think we shared a comfort level in our relationship. It remained to be seen how lasting it would be. We would either ride out this adventure until there were three scoops of French vanilla ice cream in a bowl waiting for us on a cushy loveseat; or a "Road Closed" sign across the yellow brick road before we reached the emerald city. I was concerned about our living arrangements in either Salerno or Senerchia if and when this all happened. Hell, I was concerned about everything; we both enjoyed having our places and spaces.

Right now I was counting on Fred to stay on top of his game. I'd been impressed with his in-depth outlook and work in financial planning for future goals, not simply an Abel-like status quo approach. I was glad he gave me understandable explanations for the more complicated scenarios.

The heaviest problem I continued to ponder was the money; what was the right thing to do? Even the thought of it made my brain want to shut down or wander somewhere else. But I forced myself to focus and prioritize. I glanced at my watch and decided I had time before the next course of fat and booze to take a nap. "You're not in Kansas anymore, Dorothy," I chuckled to myself. I looked out the window and laughed out loud. "You're not in Nebraska either, Aggie," I thought, sitting in first class, as if I were holding a gold-lipped China teacup with my pinky up. I asked myself, "Do you hear the wind rushing past or the drone of the engines?" Either way, the drone had me asleep quickly.

I was standing in the lobby of the old Kline's department store in downtown Omaha, waiting for the manually operated elevator. There was no one in the store, but that in itself didn't seem odd to me. The elevator doors opened, and I stepped inside. The elevator operator was a thin, elderly man wearing a funny bellman's uniform, with a pillbox hat squarely on his bald head. His suit was navy and trimmed in gold. He flashed a toothless grin, stepping past me as the doors closed, leaving me alone inside. I waited a few moments and took hold of the control handle to see if the elevator would go up or down. The handle came off in my hand, and suddenly the car jerked in a downward motion.

I was being transported quickly down the elevator shaft, flanked by LED lights illuminating either side of the car, faster and faster. I was frightened at first. I was trying to convince myself this was a dream, but what if it were real? I concluded it did not matter. I would wake up or I would die; I might as well enjoy the ride.

The elevator car began to swoop, now traveling horizontally like a toboggan running through a tunnel. The lights burned brightly on either side of me; what had begun as a washed-out azure now changed in hue through the spectrum to a glossy navy blue. Racing through gentle and subtle curves so fast my peripheral vision was a blur, I closed my eyes. There was no tactile sense of speed on my skin or my hair or clothes. I began slowing down as it became brighter and warmer, as if the sun were on my face and upper body. I put my head back to enjoy the sun's warmth.

Suddenly my ride was bumpy, and I felt the rattling of a hard wooden seat beneath me. I opened my eyes to find I was holding worn leather reins in my hands. I was driving a single-horse buggy in the Old West. There was someone sitting next to me, but I couldn't tell who it was. Ahead were two lead horses with a rider on each; behind me, a team pulled a covered wagon. My brown hair was pulled back, and I was wearing a wide-brimmed straw hat. The road came to a wide free-flowing stream that we had to cross, but I could see there would be no difficulty, no danger. The guides decided to stop on our side of the stream, seeing a pair of huge oak trees offering generous shade. How strange—the horses were the same size and color, and it seemed to me as if they were whispering with each other; how I didn't know. I somehow knew we were stopping to stretch, refresh our canteens, and water the animals and ourselves. The riders turned out to be Fred and JET as they dismounted. They loosened the girth straps on their saddles and walked the horses along the stream a bit before they would be allowed to drink.

I hadn't noticed because he wasn't touching me, but Kellogg sat between the stranger and me on the bench. I still couldn't see who the stranger was, other than a person wearing a hooded robe. In slow motion I picked up Kellogg, holding him close to my chest, kissed him on the top of his head, and climbed down from the buggy, giving him a gentle toss to the ground from about a foot.

I walked to the back of the wagon and looked inside. My mom, Grandma Agatha, and Nonna Bella were there, but they were somehow interchangeable or melding from one to the other. Every time I glanced at Kellogg, he grew larger and was now the size of a cocker spaniel. I didn't know where we were or where we were going, but I was not frightened. I seemed to know many things intrinsically. We still had some distance to travel. I knew there was the threat of a storm and possibly the road farther ahead would be washed out and delay us.

My dad, my brother Chad, and Tom, my ex-husband, were there. Chad fancied himself a cowboy since he was a little boy, and he wore an ornate leather gun belt, with two Colt six-shooters. Deeper yet in the wagon sat Abel, in his dance hall costume looking eager to pick up a cowboy, a chicken wing in hand; Daleka, Bora, Za, Simon, Series 7 Alexander, Jessica, and her banker boyfriend wearing a suit made of hundred-dollar bills were also there. Kellogg was now the size of a German shepherd. Many of La Ventana's clientele were transforming into and out of one another. Lovey was with the ingrates, who sat in diapers. Robert the Repeater mumbled a nursery rhyme. It was total chaos.

Mrs. Amberley, my third-grade teacher at my Catholic grade school, St. Anthony's, was well out of her element here, just like in my school overflowing with nuns. She was an amazement to me then and now—why wasn't Mrs. Amberley a nun? As far as I was concerned, the St. Anthony's nuns were handpicked to be vicious; it seemed the meaner, the better. Sister Ivan, or Ivan the Terrible as we called her, was just as horrible and ugly as her name intimated. I remembered her in sixth grade, with that nasty wart on the side of her bulbous, bumpy, strawberry-like nose. That single black hair was more wiry, stiff, and menacing than ever, like it had gotten a special makeover at the hairdresser or a barbed-wire company. She had a bottle of sanctuary wine in her hand and a witch's hat, instead of a nun's habit, on her head.

I climbed up inside and began struggling toward the front of the wagon. It was cool and shadowy as I moved forward in the wagon. I saw my grandpa perched on top of a large wooden barrel with a painted label that read "JUDGE CORNMEAL." All these little faces were popping out from behind him and the barrel. It occurred to me that they were all Grandpa's "road companions," the prostitutes, timeless through the decades as they all looked thirtyish. As I got closer, their features softened; they were real people, gentle, helpless, innocent in their own way, with nowhere to go. Their faces and heads sat atop rat bodies the size of small terriers, like Kellogg, as they scurried around running amuck atop one another in the corner, wanting not to be trapped, but hopelessly so, trapped in their lives. Grandpa diverted his eyes from me. He had a silly embarrassed look on his face as he hopped off the cornmeal keg. As he got down, he turned toward the corner with the human rats. The label on the barrel had now changed, or maybe his legs had been covering a portion of it. The old-time script "JUDGE CORNMEAL" had become "DON'T JUDGE ME."

I climbed down from the wagon and went to the bank of the stream to get away from this menagerie. Kellogg, now over five feet tall and standing erect on his rear legs, walked up casually, with two folding chairs looped over his foreleg. He had a thin cigar pushed to one side of his snout, tucked inside his pink gum and black lip. The cigar had a wide red band on it that read "Suerdieck Caballero." He unfolded the chairs, giving me one and sitting down in the other as he looked into the flowing water. It seemed perfectly natural for me to ask, "You couldn't take that commotion either, eh, Kellogg?"

Kellogg replied, "No, it was disturbing and giving me a headache, but I'm here because you need my help."

"I do?" I asked.

"Yes, you've got a great burden and many concerns, so I'm here to help you sort them out. That, and I like you. Not any better than Fred, but you are the weaker female in our pack, and part of my job is to keep you safe, watch over and protect you. I still regret not being there to help JET in the alley." I smiled inwardly. I would have liked to have seen my little man, at over five feet, in action ripping at the crotch of one of the Chez playboys.

Kellogg looked wise as he continued. He suggested we discuss my various options and their outcomes and how to proceed with the money, helping me come to terms with it or reach a decision, if that was what I sought. To accomplish that, we could only have a conversation based upon assumptions.

"There's a possibility you'll never know who was separated from this great amount of wealth. And it's possible you don't want to know because this situation is very dangerous. Perhaps life-and-death dangerous. Let's assume it was not an individual. If the owner of the diamonds was a reputable dealer, would he not be reimbursed by insurance? And where did the money to buy the bonds come from? If there was an insurance settlement, would that remove the guilt from your mind?

"The loot, or what you have of it, isn't ready for retail; therefore it's not personal, nothing antique, collectible, or even finished stones. It's not even jewelry except Abel's, and that hasn't been cut to be marketable. In your mind this bizarre event has two sides. You face the moral dilemma of your integrity, honesty, and scruples. You're thinking you should return this stuff to its rightful owner. But the flip side is simply keeping it under the premise of discovering hidden treasure—finders keepers.

"Our presumption is Abel and Daleka were oriented to greed, which maybe became complicated with sex. This combination forced them to try flying eighteen stories, without lessons. Our nature, human and animal, is typically based upon greed. My nature is hoarding more food than I can eat, whereas humans enjoy amassing wealth, in this particular case, stealing diamonds is a means to an end. You're in this now, and it will forever change everything, no? You are the owner of ill-gotten gains that appear somehow legal, and the uncut diamonds are untraceable. Able and Daleka are dead—what could be more perfect? Only with a crystal ball could you know where the money came from, who it originally belonged to, and then what? More decisions."

Kellogg also pointed out something, although in the back of my mind, I had not considered. Bora had mentioned Daleka had many contacts, international contacts, contacts Abel did not have. Suddenly I wondered if this was part of a much larger scheme than we had imagined. In addition to my current angst, it crossed my mind that the amount of diamonds in our hands might seem large, but in fact, it might be small compared to an overall treasure. Maybe this involved something more, something of a greater magnitude—perhaps the smelliness of drugs, underhanded political lobbying, or even the sex trade. Was I getting paranoid or just thinking too much? Was I getting sucked into a cesspool of an underworld that revolved around thievery, graft, murder, and corruption? I was raised with a basic right-from-wrong foundation, and part of my moral Midwest upbringing was bearing heavily on my conscience.

Maybe Abel was a funnel for several suppliers. Kellogg went on, "Was he still dealing pot, or maybe something more than diamonds, while Hatch was incarcerated? Perhaps Abel had other contacts or connections to fence the goods and convert boodles of cash to bonds, and a legitimate place to park them. The kind of financial connections Daleka couldn't muster because she couldn't explain large deposits at a bank or brokerage house. Was she even a US citizen or merely on a long-term visa?

"Bora didn't really know what happened to Abel's last partner, Elisa; she just vanished. Did she get greedy and was therefore murdered? Bora mentioned there was a girl found heavily weighted in a deep part of the Hudson shortly after you were hired. Daleka and Bora arrived after that. Daleka perhaps had more experience, perhaps was sent here to follow up and finish the job Elisa had started. Had you spent more time with

Bora, under the guise of sympathy for Daleka, you might have learned more. Simon was enlisted and maybe mucked things up. Hindsight is 20/20, even for dogs.

"Elisa was probably just another insignificant Czech girl who thought she was a big shot, a real secret agent. Girls like her are good to use for work like this since they are rarely missed. Perhaps she did get greedy. Unimportant Czech girls are easier to get rid of because they are low priority in police caseloads. There are very few leads, and visitors on visas or newer citizens without attachments are harder to find; they become cold cases quickly. These European girls are no different than the 'tools' used in the concentration camps that Alba mentioned, no different than Grandpa's hookers; all are prisoners.

"Want something else to think about? Why were Daleka and Abel handcuffed together? The presumption is they were in performance mode for kinky sex. If it was wild sex that rolled them off Table Five, why did they both have their pants on when they hit the sidewalk? Columbo, hah! This *is* dangerous stuff, and you and Fred are in the middle of it."

"Are you suggesting they were murdered?" I asked, but received no reply. "How do you know these things? Who are you?"

I know these things because I am you, and your conscience, and your subconscious. I'm you trying to sort out *your version* of the truth, because you probably won't find the real truth. I am a manifestation of your perception of the truth. I'm the trusting dog within you. Think of it any way you like, but you must know the world runs on greed, and whatever goodness exists is shadowed by individual opportunity. If you battle this conflict—what to do, what's right and what is wrong—you'll find merely *your* perception of right and wrong. You are true to the way you were raised, and *you* were raised with a conscience.

"There are those that suffer living their lives how they think they are supposed to live, doing something they were told to do or *something they weren't supposed to do*. The extremist, the religious psychopath who chops off another's head in a belief he has punished the offender for his life of sin. The perpetrator relishes his own death, no matter how violently. He goes to his perception of heaven, owned and operated by his own personal God.

"Take me, for example. I just want to eat, fuck a dog, and sleep, not necessarily in that order."

"Don't look at me," I said, trying to make a joke.

"That's what I do," Kellogg replied. "It's my instinct, not a learned behavior from my parents; instinct and survival at its base level. Humans are the ones that are optioned out; most have their own agendas, their own stupid ideas of politics, diet, medicine, and religion. Cats and birds and dogs don't have to worry about that stuff—though birds aren't that bright."

Good grief—not only was my dog philosophical; he was a sarcastic critic.

Kellogg claimed he wasn't saying anything to further upset me but explained clearly he was glad he didn't have my problems; he and his kind would just die at the end of their life span, and personally, he'd made out pretty well. Canines were more adaptable than humans and, within reason, easier to train. He had to take the cards dealt, be it a three-by-five cage at the humane society, on the street like some feral island K9, or lucky as hell with Fred and me.

"Do you think turning over this wealth to anyone is going to make a drop of difference in the ocean of equalization for a good cause long-term?"

"You're trying to trick me, Kellogg; you are dissuading me to rationalize something I'm not sure of. And I must be insane already, having a conversation with a five-and-a-half-foot dog sitting in a lawn chair chewing a cigar."

"Even if you knew who the money belonged to, most assuredly procured by illegal means, what would you do? Give it to the 'authorities'?" he emphasized with contempt. "Now that you've seen the pathetic rats behind the cornmeal barrel, wouldn't it be wonderful to give some money to them? You saw them as rats and then realized they were gentle humans with problems of their own. Wouldn't it help that tiny faction of the world, Aggie?"

I glared at him for using that name, my name.

Kellogg glared back. "Give me a break; what are you going to do—swat me on the rear? I'll bite you. What do you think the authorities will do with the wealth? Spread it about the needy, or among themselves for sex, a Lincoln, and drugs? Hell, I don't know; maybe it will go somewhere worthwhile. If you keep it and get away with it, you can designate to have it used for your means of good ... if that's what you choose.

"Or go back to Touhy, get comfortable in your Daisy Dukes, but I won't be there. I know you didn't steal that money. Isn't that why you left Touhy? Not to steal money but to discover yourself; not to grow old in Touhy. Don't get me wrong; there's nothing wrong with Touhy—you simply wanted a different life for yourself. And you found it in spades, Aggie. It doesn't mean you can't do something good with the money, including taking care of yourself, your family, the Tratorios, even the rats in the wagon and the humane society, where I came from.

"You could make smaller, real, and meaningful changes, not like a movie star or celebrity dropping gazillions on one major cause, another penny tossed in a wishing pond. This is a great opportunity, with great responsibility."

The cacophony of voices and commotion rising still made us move farther from the wagon, to the edge of the shade.

Kellogg said, "What do you think the hens in Touhy are gossiping about today? Do you suppose they're saying, 'Wonder how Juanda is doing on LaSalle Street with her ad exec job. How 'bout Samantha, a big shot in the garment industry in New York? Aggie Lantana sure had balls to start a restaurant in Italy.' And meek Margie claiming she's not "missin' not a thing, right there in Touhy." Is that where you want to be?" The dog continued, "It does take balls to persevere, and I would find it reassuring that you have Fred's right between his legs next to you.

"By the way, let's not forget that without me agitating around your desk, you wouldn't be on this jet in this dream. That was *my* instinct working. Because I'm domesticated, I'm trained to abide by your rules. I no longer climb to your tabletop and eat your cereal; I only pee where I'm supposed to. To an extent, we are all alike. My behavior and subsequent guilt, as evidenced by my tail between my legs, are driven by repetition and avoiding a swat on my butt. I perform how I know you want me to behave. I openly show love; I am incapable of hate like a human. I can even be trained to attack but not kill. Your species is mandated by repetition and training in much the same way *if you let it.* You have the choice to form your own opinions about what is right and wrong. You can break the chain if you are brave enough.

"You had the fortitude to leave Touhy, not strictly for financial success but to follow your dreams and your heart, even if that was not consciously your motivating factor when you left. So let's wrap this thing up, Aggie."

Ooh, this dog just burns my ass, I thought.

Kellogg rose, folding his chair and gently leaning it against the back of mine. Ironically, he patted me on the head and briefly stroked my hair with the side of his paw, then turned and began walking toward the water with one last glance at me, his Suerdieck Caballero still comfortably tucked between his lip and incisors.

My mouth opened and I tried to speak, but nothing came out. I wanted more; I wanted Kellogg's security and protection, but he kept walking. He looked so calm and serene, so natural as he stepped into the stream; his head disappeared beneath the water with a quick swirl above it.

I stood up looking around; our chairs were gone, as were the horses and buggy. Everything was gone except the covered wagon. It was as if I were on a soundstage, except there was an endless horizon in all directions surrounded by nothingness. I walked to the back of the wagon; my grandfather was now the only person inside. This time he looked straight at me. He telegraphed a rainbow of emotions through his eyes and expression. I leaned forward, narrowing my eyes as I tried to understand. He slowly closed his eyes while making a sweeping gesture with one hand that looked almost like a blessing. The sides of his mouth curled into a subtle, unfettered smile. He had the same knowing smile that was attached to his face for eternity when I last saw him as he lay in the casket at his funeral. I stared at him, thinking I would be unable to forgive him. I slowly pivoted on my heels, knowing I would be leaving soon. Instead of doing an about-face, I completed a 360° turn. The wagon and Grandpa were gone, and suddenly, effortlessly, my soul felt cleansed, as if I were a little girl coming out of confession for the first time. I had forgiven Grandpa.

I woke up in the wide seat of the first-class cabin feeling like I had been in a coma. Fred was looking at me. I looked around and back at him as he asked me if I was okay.

"Yes, I was dreaming."

He said, "That must've been a pretty heavy dream."

"Yes, I was thinking how perceptive Kellogg is. Do you think he likes cigars?"

Fred just smiled, rolling his eyes in a circle.

I looked at my phone to see what time zone we were in. There was a text. My eyes got wide, and I began slowly shaking my head side to side while looking at Fred.

He looked at me, cocking his head in question, and I said, "My grandmother is dead."

BANKING, PART DEUX

I called my family, from a quiet place, as soon as we debarked the plane. I talked with them regularly after I left Touhy—not enough as far as they were concerned—so they knew of my European trip. Gram had been such a big part of my life. I felt terrible and helpless that I couldn't be there and could only send my love and thoughts.

The following morning in downtown Zurich, we walked into the Banque Suisse Internationale, acting as visiting diplomats for our appointment and were treated as such. Greeted immediately by a clerk, we were offered Swiss coffee and an array of small decorative biscuits that looked like lacquered props for a bakery ad in *Restaurant* magazine. A Mr. Brunati welcomed us into his executive office on the third floor; the office looked as if it were right out of a James Bond movie. The walls appeared to be burled walnut, with three-by-five-foot painted portraits of stuffy bank presidents from the past. We were seated in plush oxblood leather chairs. When Fred pulled my chair out, I almost curtsied.

I introduced Fred as the COO for Table Five Inc., our latest corporation under the La Ventana Inc. umbrella. Not completely true, but they weren't going to check, and I reasoned it gave us more credibility. Fred, although not a La Ventana officer, had power of attorney, along with Larry the lawyer, and therefore check-signing capability if something should happen to me. Larry and Fred were aware I had a transfer-on-death document that enabled the greatest percentage of assets to go to my family in Touhy, Nebraska, presuming these assets were really mine if I died.

We showed Mr. Brunati the group of bonds we'd brought, along with proof of the others. I'd also brought copies of Abel's notarized death certificate and documents indicating my ownership of La Ventana. Brunati politely reminded us he had only agreed to our meeting because of Abel's La Ventana account. He seemed a bit more at ease now that he fully understood the situation of my ownership, although he was aware of Abel's death. We briefly explained our interest in depositing and borrowing against the bonds as collateral and generating income as needed for our Italian venture by selling shares of existing bonds. As I filled out new paperwork eliminating Abel and installing myself on the account, Brunati began valuing the bonds at today's rates.

I explained the T-5 corporate papers would include transfers and disposition of the business in case of my death. In other words, I was the only one on the account, just as Abel had been in the past. At this time Mr. Brunati gave us a quizzical look as he summoned a minion to his office. The assistant then disappeared with copies of the La Ventana ownership documents, corporate paperwork, bonds, and my birth certificate and passport, presumably to take to the legal department. We knew he was curious, if not suspicious, that I was Abel's partner. Abel had no partner when he started doing business here. At least that's what we thought. Brunati did not yet know how much money we had to deposit. Acting a bit pretentious, I informed him that this was, in fact, only a portion of the assets we planned on bringing in.

Fred mentioned the safe-deposit box.

Brunati asked to see the key. "Are Mr. Rice and Ms. Rudiski aware you are opening the box today?"

I was stunned—*who are Rice and Rudiski?*

Fred jumped on this with surprising confidence.

"Yes, Mr. Rice is aware; tragically Ms. Rudiski perished in the same accident with Abel Connelly."

Crap! I could barely come up with Abel's last name on the fly, and Fred was hitting a home run making shit up because Brunati didn't as much as flinch. There was nothing remarkable about his inspection of the key as he picked up his intercom and called for a glorified teller named Griffin.

Fred, Griffin the teller, and I took a long walk and then a lift down six floors from the third-floor office.

In the elevator I squeezed Fred's hand and whispered, "How?" Apparently he knew I was asking how he had arrived at the names.

He exhaled through his mouth, drew a large breath into his nostrils, and said, "I was guessing Daleka's last name was Rudiski. We saw "D. R." on the little key envelope marked 823 in Abel's apartment. I didn't come four thousand miles to get hung up on one question from a snotty banker. Mr. Rice was strictly a guess, but I'm thinking that might be Hatch's last name."

Then I thought about Daleka's first name. Who told me Daleka meant "darkness" in Czech? And now Rudiski! I isolated "rude" out of Rudiski, combining the first and last name and coming up with; "Rude Darkness" or the "Rude Dark One" or simply "Dark Rudeness." How creepy.

Griffin, in his tweed three-piece wool suit, heard us whispering, curious about such a deep elevator shaft in the building. He told us the shaft had been excavated to access a vault, created when war was imminent in Europe. Then, it had been cemented over to protect masterpieces of art, gold, and other valuables from the Nazis.

Through a series of chain-link gates, accessible by magnetic security badge, iron doors, and electronic keypads, we walked down a hall with numbered doors on either side. Griffin selected a door and, with a single master key, entered an oblong room approximately twelve feet wide by forty feet long, with floor-to-ceiling small lockable stainless steel doors. There was a ladder with thin rungs that rode on a track close to the ceiling to access the top boxes. A small metal table supported by angle iron next to the door had four metal catalog drawers above it.

Griffin pulled a drawer and began flipping through index cards until he found the pink three-by-five he was looking for and placed it on the mini-desk. I removed a pen from its holder as Fred looked over my shoulder. "Abel Connelly dba La Ventana USA" was on the top line. On the next line, with several spaces in between, were the names William Webster Rice III and Daleka Rudiski. The only signature on the card was Abel's; the last entry was a year ago June. I signed beneath it, "Agatha M. Lantana dba La Ventana USA." Fred patted me on the side of my butt.

After a very officious, "Very good, ma'am," Griffin led us to box 823, which he pulled out and presented to us as if it were a bottle of fine wine. We carried the black metal box to a small anteroom. I gasped and Fred sighed as I lifted the lid of the elongated box. The contents were sparse—only a rubber-banded bundle of cash and a single sheet of heavy stock stationery folded in thirds, with what appeared to be Japanese character writing on it. Fred carefully refolded the paper for my purse and gave me about half the cash to count. Together we counted six thousand in euros, about seven thousand dollars US. I put my stack in my purse, and Fred stuffed the other bundle in his slacks. We returned box 823 to Griffin and trekked back to Brunati's office.

Brunati returned shortly with a white-haired, impeccably dressed executive, who he introduced as Mr. Everett Ebersohl, director of Foreign Investments. Mr. Ebersohl walked straight to me, hand out, introduced himself again, and in so many words said he had some disappointing news.

"Excuse me?" I said in a dumbfounded way.

Mr. Ebersohl explained that corporate investment accounts started at twenty-five million USD minimum. Abel's account no longer held the minimum amount, and BSI was actually waiting for a promissory note from Abel that had never come. BSI was in one respect happy that we were there to update the status on the account. For Abel to have had an account at BSI meant he had held, and disbursed, dispensed, or otherwise disposed of over twenty-five million dollars or was laundering a boatload of money for other "investors."

On shaky ground, we were nervous to ask anything about the La Ventana account for fear it might be margined, in which case they would be asking me to satisfy the debt. Thankfully that was not the case; there was about one hundred euros left in the account.

Since we couldn't do business with BSI on a corporate level, there was no reason to open a regular account in Switzerland. We closed the Ventana account and relinquished the safe-deposit box key. We continued making small talk with Mr. Brunati as he shredded in front of us copies of the documents I had just generated. It came as no surprise, since we now had no relationship with BSI, that he wouldn't give us any history regarding Abel's twenty-five million in assets or what had happened to it. He informed us there were fees involved in closing the account and a charge for the two missing safe-deposit keys. Thankfully the BSI account closing cost and keys were only 122 euros. I happily signed over the money in the account and paid the balance out of my pocket, with Abel's cash.

We walked out of the bank famished and looked for an expensive restaurant in which Abel could buy dinner for us.

Fred knew by holding my sweaty hand that I was nervous, so in an effort to calm me down, he said, "Everything will be fine."

I muttered, "Yeah, everything will be ... fine."

My first stop in Europe had proved to be a great learning experience. We found that havens for the uber rich, like Banque Suisse Internationale, along with other Swiss megabanks didn't do business with paupers and penniless ilk such as myself, worth less than twenty-five million. In one respect we were disappointed there was not additional treasure in the box, but maybe it was a blessing in disguise. Finding more assets than the six thousand in cash might have opened a Pandora's box if someone was looking for money along with diamonds and bonds. Now that the BSI account was closed, we didn't have to worry about unknown parties related to BSI that might haunt or hunt us down had Abel ripped them off—maybe even the secret man, who was still hanging out at La Ventana. At least we were being reimbursed for the fancy clothes and first-class airfare with Abel's cash from the safe-deposit box.

We would arrange a bank interview in Italy, presuming they would accept our chump change, and present the same plan proposed in Switzerland: selling off bonds for income and restaurant build-out money. We still had the estimated value of two million US dollars.

I giggled to myself, wishing I could get more advice from my five-and-a-half-foot dream dog. What would Kellogg do? We still didn't know what the cost basis was for the bonds from Abel's desk and therefore how much in capital gains tax I would encounter. Regardless of potential tax consequences to Abel, I was hoping *my* cost basis was zero due to Abel's death date.

Last Train to Czechville

W e took a train from Prague to Pardubice, Czech Republic. It was fall, and the landscape was beautiful and exploding with color. Fred had done his own detective work, having assembled details from the *setup* with Za. Bora had been very informative about persons and places in her liaison with Simon, but I still wondered what the hell we were doing here. Fred had given me bits and pieces of the Bora and Daleka connection to this place and clearly thought it was worthwhile to visit, although in his own words, it would be a treasure hunt. He believed this was the hub of Abel's diamond dealing.

It was early afternoon when we checked into the nice but modest Hotel Dante. After freshening up, we went to the hotel bar for a cold one and to initiate reconnaissance. The rest of the day was intended to relax and get acclimated to our surroundings, having a full day tomorrow and going back to Prague the following morning.

The wooden bar was very long and old, with a lot of character, and had been repaired many times, making it look like a patchwork quilt. We were immediately entertained by the bartender, who, being accustomed to tourists over the years, told us the only English he knew was bathroom, taxi, beer, and telephone. Mikael, a lanky man about thirty, initially told us he had never heard of Bora and Daleka, which was interesting since Bora, never in her life imagining we'd be at Dante's Bar, had told Simon about this place, and she certainly knew Mikael.

Fred surprised me by producing one of the rough-cut diamonds from his pocket and placing it on the bar. Nonplussed, Mikael began playing with it like a little soccer ball, batting it around with his thin index fingers, and then he spun it like a top. I didn't know Fred had brought it, probably so I wouldn't be nervous about it or his intentions. Mikael was no stranger to playing poker, judging by his emotionless face.

"What is this?" he asked as he nodded at the stone.

He still wasn't sure about us, and who could blame him? He now "guessed" he did know the girls.

"Oh, yes, Bora—thought you said something else. Bora called to inform us Daleka had passed."

Fred told Mikael that Daleka and a man named Abel had given him the little token, saying that it had originally come from home, in other words, here.

Mikael continued fingering the stone. He said he was only a bartender, not a jeweler.

Fred jumped on that. "I didn't know it was a jewel. I thought it a talisman or what we call a touchstone."

Mikael pushed out his lower lip, raised his eyebrows, and scoffed in an international facial expression indicating he didn't know or, more likely, "Oh crap, I just stuck my foot in my mouth."

Of course we were lying, he was lying, we were all lying, and we all knew it. We maintained we were Daleka's friends and had gotten the token as a gift from her; we were on holiday in Europe and curious as to stories we had heard from the girls. It seemed common knowledge they had been "close friends" around here also. We continued our edgy, tight-lipped conversation a while longer and left. We didn't think we could learn anymore, and none of us wanted to get tripped up further in our tall tales.

As we strolled along the downtown street window-shopping, Fred suspected a casually dressed man, fiftyish, was following us. After another block of stop and go, cat and mouse, we were sure. Fred told me to go into a store with a sign for wigs and earrings. If the guy followed me into the store, Fred would double back. If the guy stuck with Fred ... it didn't matter; he followed me into the store.

Fred was in the store and on us very quickly; I had never seen him posture like this. He was definitely in this guy's space.

"Can I help you?" Fred asked. He was now face-to-face with this man; the man's jet-black hair looked as if it were dyed, and his complexion was rough, perhaps from bad acne as a teen.

"My name is Boris Lazarof, and I understand you were a friend of Abel?"

Fred replied, "Wouldn't it have been easier to ask directly instead of frightening us?"

I'd seen Fred work, but again, not like this; I liked it.

"I'm sorry. My intention was not to frighten, but, you see, this is a rather sensitive matter. Could we go to my office to discuss it?"

Crap. Now what?

"What is this about, and how far is your office?" asked Fred.

"It regards Abel's business associate here in Pardubice. It is not far, but too far to walk," Boris replied.

Boris was too slick not to have prepared answers for anything Fred might ask or suggest. We agreed to go, but we would follow him in a taxi. We climbed in the back of a cab, telling the cabbie to follow Boris's car, and we gave him the street address. The driver spoke English much better than we spoke Slovak; his name was Anton, and he claimed he did not recognize Boris. We asked where we were going; old downtown was the answer, and the office building was old also, but reputable. We got out, and Fred asked Anton to come back in thirty minutes and call the police if we weren't out on the sidewalk in forty-five; he agreed. Fred paid the fare, telling Anton he would tip him when we came back out.

Boris took us to an office on the sixth floor, which was orderly, somewhat dusty, and looked as if it was not used often. It was likely a drop spot used for its address and probably clandestine meetings such as ours. Within its dingy walls were a file cabinet, three chairs, and an old wooden desk and chair, with a weird-looking handset on a multiline tan office phone from the seventies. Boris started by commenting what a terrible thing had happened to Daleka and Abel. *Good; we're not wasting any time retelling Abel's failed flight plan.*

We asked if he had made Abel's acquaintance. Yes, he had first met Abel about twenty-five years ago. Abel was just out of college and traveling through Europe with two friends from the States. They were wearing backpacks, staying in hostels, and hiking the "hippie trail." Apparently the same "hippie trail of honey" Hatch had referred to. Boris claimed he met Abel in Prague.

"We became fast friends. It was a very fun time; someone would say a wild time. Plevel was cheap and plentiful; we drank beer and grappa made in the hills."

Our faces indicated we did not understand his terminology—at least, plevel.

"Plevel is marjanka, or marijuana in English, and grappa is a very potent ... you say, maybe, moonshine. Every day was a holiday, and we made ourselves good and sick with it," he said with a laugh. "We met girls and also had much fun. That was the first time Abel traveled alone out of his country, and he was ... sowing wild oats?" he said, flipping his eyebrows up quickly. "I met a girl on that trip and continued with her. I married her; I'm still married to her." Boris was becoming friendly, but Fred wasn't about to let his guard down. Boris finished reminiscing, "Our friendship continued, and Abel met my boss several years later; they were both in the restaurant business."

Supposedly Abel became friends with Boris's boss, who was Abel's partner in a restaurant investment. He was out of town and had asked Boris to meet us. This was an immediate red flag, a snake pit of deceit. We didn't tell anyone we were here. Boris obviously received an immediate call from Mikael due to our conversation in the bar. Fred didn't want to cause friction with Boris, and yet we knew we were on to something and this outlandish scenario required further explanation.

"So, how is it, Boris, that you found us in Pardubice so quickly?" Fred queried.

"Of course Mikael called me, innocently enough, knowing Daleka and having made Abel's acquaintance. He was more concerned I would like to extend my sympathies regarding Abel, not knowing Daleka as well."

Now he was really making shit up.

Boris continued to spin. "I called my boss, knowing that this would be important to him." Abel and his boss had met in this office several times. He told us it had been almost a year since Abel's last trip over here and played it close when we asked if Abel and the boss invested in any other businesses. He said he thought so but quickly dropped that also. Boris did not mention the boss's name, nor did we ask.

As the conversation ensued, I presumed Fred did not press on the boss's name because Boris could and would've made up anything he wanted.

Fred later told me maybe we really didn't want to know the boss's name. If the boss was *"The Boss"* of the illicit organization we suspected Abel had worked for, it would be more needless information that would put us in more peril.

Boris continued a respectable job of making shit up, and we were doing what I considered a commendable job of fabrication also. Boris's nameless boss claimed he was in the middle of a deal with Abel and wanted to know about Abel's business files and any curious personal effects that had been left behind. I drew an immediate blank trying to answer that.

Stunned for a moment, I think Fred realized we all knew why we were here, but it was difficult for anyone to break the ice, pun intended. He pulled the stone from his pocket to show Boris. I understood his logic: instead of playing more cat and mouse, toss out the Abel and Daleka gift story as told to Mikael. Fred told him there were actually two stones like this, and he had given one to a busboy. He continued that, due to the nature of the deaths, our government had taken Abel's files to audit; they also took anything else they wanted or found of interest. The police had had first access to Abel's office in addition to the bodies. They returned Abel's personal items, including the two stones. Fred did not mention the third stone. He claimed La Ventana's operation was in a shambles, as was the business paperwork.

At that point I spoke up. I told Boris that Abel was, to me, a very private person, and although I worked for him, he never spoke of relatives except that his parents had passed away. Abel had given me a key to his apartment for emergency use; I did visit the apartment after his death. Again, the authorities had already been there, and I did not find anything of interest or value. We simply didn't know anything about Daleka, but she and Abel were very close in their friendship.

We were fairly certain Boris knew what had happened and that *close* was an understatement; they were deathly close, handcuffed together! Boris diverted his eyes from us with that information and shook his head negatively. Bora was never mentioned in this conversation, so we did not bring her up. Fred segued back to explain there were just too many players and too many officials climbing about after the incident and fingering everything. We did our best to convey that this was all there was—two rough-cuts and a big mess back in New York.

We discussed later that even torturing and killing us for information we didn't have would be of no use, and someone would have to dispose of our bodies. Apparently, and thankfully, Boris thought the same. The IRS comment was the only thing that wrinkled Boris's stony face. Surprisingly, he informed us that Fred's diamond in the rough was valuable and that we should exchange a gift or somehow get the other one back from the busboy. He then asked where we were headed when we left Pardubice. I deferred to Fred to answer.

There seemed to be no liability, so Fred told the truth, pretty much. He explained we were on a multicity touring pass through Europe and could visit as many cities as we wanted in our ten days. This was a crafty marketing tool for United Airlines in that tourists initially thought they could visit a lot of cities. Considering it took half a day to travel anywhere, how many cities could you possibly visit in ten days? Fred continued that our itinerary included Rome, but we had flexibility among Barcelona, Brussels, or Paris, so we were open to suggestions. Boris told us that if we were going to Belgium and were interested in diamonds, we should pass on Brussels and instead visit the diamond district, aka the diamond quarter in Antwerp.

If we went to Antwerp, Boris suggested we visit a tavern called Stamineeke at Vlasmarkt 23. There we could talk with the owner Geoff, whom Boris had seen a few weeks prior. He half-jokingly suggested we ask to speak with Elba Hax. Apparently Elba was a legendary diamond thief from the 1700s and in some circles a password for black-market inquiries. Although Boris said we should seek out Goeff, we weren't sure if that was his opportunity to have our throats slit outside of his own neighborhood.

I asked if I could use the restroom. Boris said it was on a different floor and needed a key, but he would take me. I looked at Fred, who nodded his approval while pulling his long-distance calling card out. He asked Boris if he could use the phone to call the restaurant in the States—the connection was much better from a landline—and he would meet us on the street. Boris scanned the room as if to do a visual of any junk Fred might put in his pocket. We were remiss in not asking if he had known Elisa, the suspiciously missing Czech girl Bora had mentioned and Daleka had presumably replaced. That might have been a risky question that would likely have gone unanswered, but it would have been interesting to see his reaction.

Anton, our cabbie, was waiting when we came out at the thirty-five minute mark, and we returned to the backseat after our good-byes to Boris. After a bit more small talk, we realized what an interesting character Anton was and great fun too. Fred seemed anxious to condense our visit in Pardubice and bump up our departure for Antwerp to the morning, skipping a full day here. He asked Anton if he was available for hire for the rest of the day; he was.

Anton had been a cabbie his entire adult life, as was his father, and both were lifelong residents. We enjoyed having a local driver who we felt was on our side. His tip would certainly reflect that.

Since our pockets were bulging with Abel's cash from the bank box, it became a joke when it came time to pay any bill; each of us would say, "Here, I'll get this one." Then it changed to "Abel's got this one!"

In a gesture of good faith, Fred gave Anton the equivalent of about one hundred dollars to show us "his" Pardubice. This thrilled Anton to no end.

Anton asked if we were in trouble. We nervously laughed and said no, but we weren't sure what to expect during our last appointment with Boris. Half in jest, we suggested we might have trouble at our next stop, though.

Anton explained his first thought was we might be outlaw people, but then no, not if we might have needed help from the Czech Policie. "Are you American policeman?"

"No, no," Fred said. "We thought we might have trouble with that man, and we wanted to be prepared."

Anton nodded in acknowledgment and seemed to further embrace acting as our official Czech guardian. Pardubice, despite being the capital of the Pardubice region, was not the hottest tourism spot. Most people had never heard of it. Anton gave us an interesting ride around his city of ninety thousand. It was a manufacturing hub that included one of the largest plastic explosives factories in Europe; we were very close to it. I suggested Anton did not have to stop there for a closer look. He told us his son worked there. He also told us we were close to the city's edge and he wanted to show us some of the beautiful Czech countryside. We were out of the city quickly and stopped at a scenic overlook. As he reached for the glove box, Anton suggested we get out.

I grabbed Fred's knee, and he tensed up also.

Anton apparently sensed our trepidation, held up his hand, and said, "No, is all right."

We exited from each rear door of the cab, watching Anton intently. He removed what appeared to be a miniature-size egg carton for six eggs. Placing it on the car trunk, he opened the box to what appeared to be grayish ping-pong balls nestled in foam rubber inside the container.

He said, "My son makes these at the explosives plant. They are not a toy but for defense. The gun law here is very strict. You can have a gun in your home but not in your car or on your person; you get in very much trouble. Driving the taxi can be dangerous in some parts of the city. I have been robbed twice; it was very frightening. Let me show you how this works."

He took one from the case and, scanning the empty lot, threw it very hard at a large rock on the edge of the parking area. It exploded with a pistol-like report, very loud. Since we didn't know what to expect, it scared the hell out of Fred and me. More impressive was the damage it created; much like an M-80, the concussion and rapid expansion created a small divot in the hard ground in front of the rock.

Anton removed two more and, handing them to Fred, said, "Here. I want you to have these balls."

Stepping forward to intercept the explosives, I quipped, "Fred already has balls; I'd like these."

Anton, almost blushing, shook his head and reluctantly handed them to me, saying he thought they were too dangerous for a woman.

Carefully holding one in my left hand, I spun around, tossing the other in the air, snatching it quickly, and whipping it with deadly accuracy into a thick-gauge metal fruit can, still half full, on the ground. The piercing crack upon impact was the same as Anton's as the can exploded into shreds, fruit and sugary syrup disintegrating into the air.

Anton's eyes got wide as he smiled, and his eyebrows went up. "Wow! How you do that?"

I told Anton I played baseball with boys growing up in America.

Apparently Anton Junior made these devices and got them "very cheaply." He also traded them for many different goods, including other weapons. Senior proceeded to pull a black rod, about ten inches long, from his trunk and gave it to Fred. It was a heavy steel telescoping baton; Anton explained, "Like the policie use." Anton refused any money for the devices; we presumed he knew his generosity would be reflected in our tipping.

We asked Anton for a fine restaurant close to Hotel Dante where we could walk back to our room after dinner. Like a proud ambassador, he told us of the best Bohemian eatery in the city. It might be within walking distance, but he did not want us on the street after a big meal and in the dark. It was too early for dinner, so he proposed he would pick us up at eight o'clock, and we could text him ten minutes before we were ready to go "home." Anton suggested we could look up the menu on our smartphone and make sure it was acceptable. Fred finally put the name of the restaurant in his phone after three attempts to understand the uber-long name, seemingly all in consonants.

Back at the hotel, we decided to lie down for a while. As I was hanging up my blouse in a sun-weathered freestanding wooden closet, it suddenly occurred to me. I spun around and said, "Crap! Too bad we couldn't tear into that old desk in Boris's office."

Fred calmly turned his back to me while unbuttoning his shirt and said, "Why do you think I let you go to the bathroom alone with Boris?"

My mouth fell open when I saw the business-size manila envelope tucked inside his waistband against his back. He pulled it out, tossed it on the wobbly room desk, and sat on the bed, motioning me to come over. I sat down next to him.

"Checking out the desk came to me about halfway through our conversation, honey. You couldn't have done better! The best I could come up with was circling the block to see if we could slide the latch back in that old door with a credit card. I'm not exactly an expert in that field, and I got an awful feeling in my stomach imagining being busted for B and E in Pardubice, Czech Republic. Your bladder was brilliant! I had to move quickly. I was scared; I didn't know how far away the bathroom was and if 'B-Boy Boris' would unlock it and double back to check on me. I went straight to the bottom right-hand drawer and felt underneath. There was nothing covering up the envelope, like under Abel's desk. But it was taped pretty well.

"That's part of the reason I want to go to Antwerp early tomorrow. Number one, it was in my mind we were coming here for something, and we found it. Number two, if they notice it's gone, I don't want to be around to get shot. And number three, I'm hoping, if it's been almost a year since Abel was here, they don't know that envelope even exists. So the acid test is if whatever is in that envelope is in La Ventana's name or it's more cash; then the trip was really worth it. And since 'Bebopper Boris' danced around Abel and the other businesses he may have been in, even if there's nothing but dirty pictures in it, there may be another clue to who knows what."

I got up, grabbed the envelope, pulled a nail file from my purse, and sat down again. Smiling, I handed the file and envelope to Fred. He sliced it open to find several crisp stock certificates, stuck together, so there were more than it appeared. They were all made out in La Ventana's name and dated almost two years ago. There were nine certificates; Fred had to spell the companies out while I wrote them down as they were all European. Again seemingly all wall-to-wall consonants, this batch were stocks.

Fred began to look up the stock values on his phone. The first two companies were bankrupt, but upon the third, Fred exclaimed, "Bingo!" Seven of the nine were operating companies. But something to do with how the European markets settled, Fred couldn't access the values until Monday. Folded within one of the certificates was what appeared to be a Polish cashier's check made out to La Ventana in the amount of eight thousand euros, or about nine thousand dollars. None of these papers included Satchland Inc., like the bonds from Abel's desk. He must have stashed these in case of emergency while visiting Pardubice. That probably meant he also had a bank account in the area, but that would be impossible to locate. At any rate, we would still blow out of Dodge first thing in the morning, but it seemed unlikely anyone knew of this stash made out to La Ventana.

Our conversation turned to Bora as we realized we'd be dealing with her on a much different level when we got home. She hadn't known we were traveling to Europe, let alone Pardubice and Hotel Dante, but we were sure Mikael and/or Boris would be calling her, telling of our visit and the diamond. She would know for certain we were much more familiar with everything than we had let on.

Through our many conversations with Bora individually, Fred and I needed to corroborate our stories. Surely we would be revisiting Daleka and diamonds. Daleka wasn't off-limits in our conversations, but there was a bit of apprehension when her name came up. It was clear Bora was still upset about Daleka's death, and I actually felt sorry for her. From my perspective, she loved Daleka, in addition to counting on her for care, financially and emotionally. Because of her death and the incredibly weird circumstances surrounding it, neither Fred nor I brought up their relationship or other issues we thought might spook her from giving further information. Besides, their relationship didn't matter relative to what was important to us.

We sensed from Boris that Daleka was probably another expendable messenger, like Elisa had been, for Abel, not a partner. Their sexcapades likely began after their business relationship. Yet we were confused why Daleka was on the Swiss bank box roster. Perhaps this was the inception of greed and infighting if Abel started withholding diamond information from Daleka. Or was Abel merely using Daleka for fringe benefits, letting her think she was a bona fide partner in the big score and telling her she had access to the Swiss box?

This also necessitated being delicate with questions to Bora about the time frame when the girls came to the States and why. In one respect, some things didn't matter anymore. Considering our "little" money secret, it was time to start distancing ourselves from Bora. Our priority would be to find out who the other players were and try to figure who killed Abel's last "partner" and how much danger we were potentially in to evade the same fate.

We both knew a few drinks induced animated conversation from Bora. You just didn't know when she might say something significant. Even if a diamond-related story didn't dribble from her mouth, her European stories were quite interesting. She spoke of how varied her culture was from ours, but having it told by the voice of one who had lived and breathed under communist rule was surreal. When she explained what was known as the "Velvet Divorce," when communism was nonviolently ousted in 1993, her Czech-accented dialogue sounded much like a television documentary.

The communist government was not like a basin of dirty bath water being tossed out after 160 years of communist rule replenished with fresh and new. It was anything but an honest and new democratic regime, as it was purported to be, for the new Czech Republic. Bora likened the political change to racial issues in the United States starting when slavery was abolished.

Czechoslovakia was a civilized country, basically continuing to be run by the same people. But just as Americans are ingrained with the old ways, they resist change; they don't necessarily believe in the old ways but cannot embrace the new. The life of some Czechs was still cheap or valueless, just as sick, hungry, and homeless people still languish in the States.

She told the story of an elderly man near where she lived who died of a heart attack. "No one would take responsibility to bury him, and he had no money. Your government is not like that," she said.

I thought, *Sweetie, you've been watching too much American TV.*

Bora went on, stating that communism and democracy are both driven by power, greed, and corruption. It sounded like Kellogg talking to me in the dream. She was very young but soon learned the new democratic system had been quickly corrupted. There were civil unrest and gross inequities between classes. It sounded like America to me. Another cocktail, and her comments would become more entertaining and humorous, as her accent and tongue became thick.

We would have time to discuss our game plan. Right now we would make love, take a nap, and begin packing for Antwerp after dinner. I put the stock certificates with the bonds, and we got into bed.

Diamantwijk

Antwerp greeted us with a chilly drizzle in late afternoon. Ordinarily we would have taken public transportation, but with bulging pockets, courtesy of Abel, we were strictly cabbing it for the duration of our trip. Besides, we would be taking a hit on converting the euros back to dollars when we returned to the United States, which was a good excuse to live it up. Fred was accustomed to the tiny European hotel rooms, and I was getting used to them. Our room at Hotel Leopold was a bit nicer than Pardubice but just as small. What passes for a queen bed in Europe is half again larger than a twin in the United States. It's all but impossible for two to use the bathroom simultaneously unless your mate is in the shower. After a quick cleanup, it was down to the hotel lounge for a pint of Duvel, a delicious Belgian brew.

We sat at a small café table for two overlooking the quaint downtown street. It was getting dark as we plotted our next course of action. Our surroundings were so attractive we had no regrets coming to Antwerp, regardless of whether we received any information concerning the diamonds. We didn't know how to approach Geoff, if we found him, and even if we did, to what end? Who would open up to two American strangers stumbling into a bar and asking suspicious questions about diamonds? The last thing we wanted was to get in any trouble here; our money had been "made," so to speak. Not only did we have the bonds and diamonds at home, but a nice chunk of cash from the safe deposit box in Zürich. If the envelope from under Boris's desk drawer had been discovered missing, our arrival here would hardly be incognito.

Parroting some of the facts Jerry the jeweler had told us, but in greater detail, Fred read from the Antwerp tour book. Eighty-four percent of rough-cut diamonds pass through Antwerp, about twelve billion dollars per year.

After a lovely dinner in a nearby restaurant, we retired early to our room. We could accomplish what we needed to in one day, so we booked a nine-thirty flight to Rome tomorrow evening.

Instead of an early-morning concierge pitch for a motor coach, spelled B-U-S, we planned our own tour route and ordered an English-speaking driver to get a taste of the city and then go on to Diamantwijk, the diamond district in the city center. We dismissed our driver after a few hours. Although pleasant, he was hardly as much fun as Anton.

Diamantwijk was about one square mile, housing almost four hundred shops with three thousand five hundred diamond brokers. As we wandered about and perused various shops, we found ourselves on the Vlasmarkt Street Boris had mentioned, before purposely looking for it. We walked past the tavern Stamineeke twice, scoping the area and planning an escape route, though that was silly. There was one door in and the same door out, with solid storefronts for the entire block. Time to do this.

Once inside we sat at the bar, not too far from the door, and confidently ordered two pints of Duvel, as if that would make us sound like locals. It was already three o'clock, and due to our 9:30 p.m. departure, we wouldn't be having our usual late European dinner. We decided to split one of the enormous sandwiches listed on the chalkboard menu, choosing sliced sausage with a strong Bavarian white cheese on crusty wheat bread with suicidal horseradish. A burly, bushy, blond-haired man in his midforties, wearing a bright red apron that rose to the top of his chest, appeared through a swinging door from behind the bar, as if he were performing all duties, including throwing sandwiches together.

When he returned with our order and put the plate down in front of us with extra napkins, Fred casually said, "Thank you, Geoff." That got his attention.

Giving us a puzzled yet suspicious look, he asked if he knew us. Fred smiled and said no, but mentioned that Boris had suggested we visit, have a drink, say hello, and ask if Elba Hax had been in lately. Before Geoff could say anything, Fred was pulling the rough-cut from his pocket and placed it on the bar.

Geoff's arched one eyebrow as he calmly said, "No, I haven't seen Elba. What did you want to do with that?" he said as he nodded toward the stone.

Fred apparently had already rehearsed this in his mind. We still had Geoff's attention, and he appeared unfazed. Fred continued, saying he'd like to buy more of "these," preferably larger, but we were obviously new to the area, not familiar with pricing, the market, and so on. I thought this could be taken one of two ways. We could be high rollers, cash-heavy and ready to buy, or we were greenhorns and had no idea what we were talking about. At least Fred was cutting to the chase before Geoff could diffuse any questions or tell us he was too busy to engage in lengthy conversation.

Geoff glanced over his shoulder at other customers but also needed a moment to digest and ponder his next move on the game board. He walked away briskly. I gave Fred a nervous smile as we simultaneously put our hands on each other's legs. We watched as Geoff spun around from two customers at a tall table against an unfinished common brick wall and disappeared into the kitchen. Racing out again, he grabbed an oversize pitcher, put it under a draft spigot, pulled the handle, and flew back in the kitchen, all the while with a cordless phone tucked between his ear and shoulder.

He delivered the pitcher of beer and a meat, cheese, and fruit plate to the tall-table customers and, looking austere, came back behind the bar to face us.

Fred, again wasting no time, asked, "Did you talk to Boris?"

With no hesitation Geoff replied, "Yes, but I won't be able to help you. Clearly there are plenty of stores to buy diamonds within walking distance. Will you have anything else?"

Fred said, "No, thank you," as he pushed a few bills toward Geoff. We each finished our last bites of sandwich, Fred finished his beer, and mine, and Geoff laid change in front of Fred's plate. He thanked us and invited us back. As we stood, turned, and began to walk away, he said, "Oh … Elba Hax hasn't been here in a couple hundred years."

We walked up the block, and now it was time for us to be looking over our collective shoulder.

I began, "What did you expect Geoff to do—expose his operation to a couple of greenhorns? Explain that a couple of expendable pawns like Abel and Daleka saved *them* the murderous trouble by rolling out of a window on the eighteenth floor while attempting the ultimate orgasm? Maybe we should have asked him if we could get Abel's pension package auto-deposited in one of our accounts."

"No, wiseass," Fred replied. "Why do you think Boris would mention or direct us to Geoff in the first place? If anything backfired on Boris from our visit, he could say Geoff saw us firsthand; Geoff could form his own opinion and concur that we didn't look like international cops, we didn't know anything and were just moneygrubbing greedy bastards like everyone else. All we had to bargain with was a lousy little uncut and were trying to act like big shots. We were farcical, acting as if we might know as much as Abel about this caper and try to benefit from it. All it cost them was *our* time and *our* money. So now we or *you* don't have to be looking over *your* shoulder for the rest of *your* life—just another five hours until we're out of Antwerp."

"Oh," I sheepishly said after a moment of silence, feeling more like a jackass than a wiseass.

I asked Fred why he insisted on keeping all our valuables with us at all times. He told me a story about a trip to Germany when he was young, with his dad and one of his girlfriends. Her jewelry was stolen from a hotel room on the trip. For us, the valuables meant the uncut rock, cash, and certificates, the last batch of which we did not yet know the value. Most of the places we stayed did not have house safes, and Hotel Leopold was no different.

We came across an antique dealer with Oriental art in the storefront window. We decided to go in as Fred pulled out the paper with the Japanese characters printed on it. The owner was Asian, sixtyish, and wore a colorful Oriental smock; he had a gray Fu Manchu about six inches long. The store was full of Buddha-like statues and related prints and engravings.

He had a thick Asian accent, but once again, his English was better than our Chinese, Japanese, or Dutch. He was very curious and interested in our document, and although perhaps not completely fluent in this particular dialect, he was knowledgeable in general as to what he was looking at. For starters, they were not Japanese characters; they were a Chinese or Tibetan dialect of Sanskrit.

He proceeded to tell us that Chinese characters are logograms and number in the tens of thousands. Functional literacy alone requires a knowledge of three to four thousand characters. The more involved the characters, the more knowledge it requires to translate and decipher them. His interest was clearly piqued, as he knew many of the characters but not all; he pulled from a shelf a huge book identifying many of the diagrams.

He believed, in general, this was a confession of sorts or redemption and had to do with transcendental meditation and somatic experiencing between the mind and body. The practitioner was trying to enter a silent state of bliss and tranquility, ultimate mindfulness, and freedom from all worldly attachments.

"Pain?" I questioned.

"Perhaps," said the man. Some of the characters were very involved, expressing feelings and emotions. "The finer the nuances are, the more studied and proficient the scholar interpreting the writing must be," he continued. "A misinterpretation or mistranslation of a particular character, or combination of characters, could alter the entire meaning of the message." He pointed to a single character that meant Buddha and only Buddha. That was in contrast to many sounds and symbols in the Chinese language that have as many as twenty meanings. He suggested the approximately two hundred characters on the page were significant for someone to have gone to the trouble of capturing such obscure detail.

Looking at Fred, I said, "That's what the books were for in Abel's apartment—research and information."

"There is an expert in Chinese art history at the Art Institute of Chicago I dealt with several years ago," said the owner. "I don't know if he's still there, but if anyone could give an accurate translation of this message, it would be him." He spun through an old-timey Rolodex on his desk, jotted down a name and number, and handed it to us.

He refused a ten euro note Fred tried to hand him. Fred placed it on the counter anyway and said, "We have an American friend named Abel, and he insists you take this."

We left the store, turned a corner, and walked down a side street, lost in the moment. We were flipping from topic to topic—getting to the airport, what the Chinese characters might mean, what Rome would hold for us—and suddenly, there were two unsavory individuals a hundred yards away coming toward us on the sidewalk.

There was no time to develop a plan, but I wasn't sure we needed one yet. Fred instinctively grabbed my hand and pulled me toward him as he stepped off the curb, crossing the street at an angle. The two, in a mirror image, stepped off and crossed also to intersect us. One was black, and one was white; the latter wore a bulky athletic jacket, his jeans as dirty as his blondish hair and unshaven face. Both were unkempt and to me looked drunk or stoned, or was it an act? The black guy, in a full-length crumpled London Fog topcoat, was just as rough and formidable-looking. A coat like that could hide everything from a shotgun to a midget beneath it with a shotgun.

Involuntarily I exclaimed, "Shit."

Knowing Fred, he had already seen what I was just inputting. Storefronts on either side of the street didn't look open, but there was a small parking lot on the side we were heading toward and a church. More disconcerting, there was no one around—no one. I could scream and no one would hear, and then what? No people were around the cars in the parking lot. The church was a poor bet; no one on the street meant no one in the church. Going inside would probably be worse. We'd be cornered. I felt the pressure from Fred's hand, not only pulling me closer but pulling back, slowing us down as our adversaries continued to beeline toward us on the sidewalk. They were spreading apart slightly as they advanced.

Fred spoke in a calm, mechanical voice that forced me to focus on his orders. "You ready?"

"What?"

"The ball. You got the ball?"

"Yes ... oh God," I mumbled.

Fred let my hand go. "You have the ball? Breathe. Pay attention. You have the ball?"

"What? Dammit. Yeah." Topcoat would be my man, on my side. My ears began ringing, buzzing; this was happening, and there was no one around.

Fred quickly said, "Throw it in front of his feet. Throw it hard. Hear me? Right in front of him. Very hard."

I didn't reply; they were on us. I was so frightened I was afraid I was going to crush the ball in my windbreaker pocket. I pulled my hand out. Peripherally I noticed Fred had spread away from me. My guy was picking up speed; he was going to hit me—knock me down. I flashed red-hot, an internal rage. The buzzing increased in my head. It was like my alley incident with the Chez Playboys, but JET couldn't help—he was four thousand miles away. This guy was all three of the playboys in one. I was incredibly pissed. Staccato images flashed. Abel and Daleka's anguished faces on the sidewalk. Boris, Geoff, paranoia, the coyotes. I *was* paranoia.

I couldn't see anything except this figure and the sidewalk in front of him. Fred was gone; everything was gone. The ball left my fingertips like a bullet. The flash, the gunshot-like report, all in slow motion; his dingy white tennis shoe fragmented in shreds, bright red blood exploded smattering the concrete sidewalk!

My head snapped to see Fred's right shoulder dip down and forward, his right arm swinging up from his waistband in one fluid movement. The baton deployed as his arm swept across and backhanded the right kneecap of his opponent, who screeched and crumbled to the sidewalk.

Another millisecond, and the black guy on the ground was screaming in what I can only presume were Dutch curse words. I did not look at his foot; I didn't want to—I couldn't.

Fred was above Athletic Jacket and screaming, "You fuck! What d'you want? Got it now? You happy? Was it Geoff? Did Geoff send you?"

Athletic Jacket was screaming back, "You crazy! I no know. Just want money!"

I stepped toward the black guy. He was in shock, wailing and rocking on his rear while clutching his foot. He saw me, dropped his foot, and began cowering and flailing and waving me away. Wailing louder, he flapped the topcoat, indicating nothing was inside. He screamed for me to get away. The blood was now overrunning and ruining the starburst design the detonation had created. *I'm creating street art? I am insane. My head is on fire.*

Fred shook me back to reality. "What happened to *in front* of his foot?"

I was in a robot-like trance and yelled, "I *was* aiming in front. Should we help them?"

Fred grabbed me, pulling me by my bicep. "They weren't after us; they're muggers!" He started pulling me away. "Cops in Antwerp won't like Yanks assaulting citizens with handheld bombs."

The entire event had taken less than twenty seconds. What was happening to us? What were we becoming? What had we already become?

Fred still had a firm grip on my arm as he pulled me along and around the first corner. "Walk quickly; don't run." Fred hailed a cab and instructed the driver to deliver us to the Leopold, but about a block away, once he knew where we were, he told the cabbie to let us out. We went into another brewery, the Bierhuis Kulminator, and sat at a small square table covered with an aqua-colored tablecloth. I ordered a shot of slivovitz and a 7-Up. Fred had a half pint of Duvel. I must've been trembling. Fred leaned forward, pulling me by the collar, up from my chair. He spread my lips with his mouth and kissed me, calming me with his warm breath.

"Never a dull moment with you. Abel's got this one."

AH-ROMA

We had to connect through Rome to get to Salerno and had an extra day due to leaving Pardubice early. We decided to take a whirlwind tour of the city the following morning. Again, with the good luck we had with our cabbie Anton in Pardubice, we hired a driver through the concierge at the Palace Hotel, where we stayed.

As Rich, my sub sandwich shop boss, would say, "It's only a quarter more to go first class," and we had lots of quarters courtesy of Abel.

We planned on reimbursing ourselves at some point with the bond money but as yet hadn't, so it was nice to have Abel's cash. I still felt guilty about spending money I didn't feel was mine. We weren't rock-star spending, but being so cash-heavy, we didn't want for anything.

I had called New York before our flight to get any updates before meeting the Tratorio family. Kellogg couldn't have been in better hands than Nonna Bella. We had done a few trial run sleepovers to make sure everyone was comfortable with the arrangement. Nonna loved fawning over the little dog, allowing him to sleep in bed with her. Kellogg ate up the affection, and I'm sure that was not all he was eating up. I could only ask Nonna not to feed him creamed pasta or cannoli, and the only threat I could contrive if she fed him rich food was she'd be cleaning up from both ends of the little dog. JET assured us everything was fine with Kellogg and at the restaurant, but the secret man was becoming a regular at Chez Neo, which was unsettling to hear.

Between Nonna's family and their extended contacts in Salerno, including the family realtor, who was already checking out store locations and residential options, we didn't feel as blind considering the monumental life-changing decisions we were facing. There would still be a million details daunting to both of us. The realtor, Guillermo Perico, had already found a few restaurant vacancies. One in particular still had equipment held for back rent. It was not unusual for used equipment to be discounted thirty to fifty cents on the dollar, or in this case the euro. Guillermo was a member of the Salerno Chamber of Commerce, a valuable resource for banking, visas, citizenship, and even medical approvals. I was afraid my precious Kellogg would be quarantined but was relieved to find out he needed only current US vaccinations and a canine virus shot once in Italy. One thing I would splurge on: Kellogg would have his own seat for the transcontinental flight. I didn't care if I looked like a crazy cat lady—only with a little dog.

All the famous places in Rome reminded me of watching the old movie *Roman Holiday* with my gram. My poor gram; I felt so bad missing her funeral. We passed on the Vatican as it would have taken an entire day to visit, a good portion of that waiting in line to get in. We figured we'd be back here one day, with or without a restaurant operation.

Salerno

Stepping off the Jetway at Salerno, we expected only Guillermo Perico, the realtor cousin, to greet us. I had been repeating his name in my mind for days; I kept thinking I would call him Signor Paprika instead of Signor Perico. To our surprise, an entourage greeted us as if we were celebrities or returning war heroes. Our first challenge was convincing the group we were staying at the Hotel Annalena in downtown Salerno, not at one of the nine houses offered to us. With all my rehearsal and having talked to Guillermo, or William, on the phone, the first words out of my mouth were, "Good morning, Signor Paprika!" Thankfully he laughed, but I'm sure he didn't think I was clever—just another stupid American.

We relaxed, if you could call it that, for the rest of the day, deciding to tour our prospective locations in Salerno and Senerchia the next day. The Tratorio clan would make sure we would have food and drink until our sides split.

In Salerno there was no shortage of good-looking women that surely didn't escape Fred's lascivious eye. I almost thought I saw him scoping out a female dog, with international romance for Kellogg in mind. Wait, what's this—little old me was receiving lustful attention from good-looking Italiano men? A tinge of jealousy from Fred? That was good for everyone— well, just me, I suppose. I was glad Fred recognized I was still a commodity.

We were invited to a relative's home in Pontecagnano, about twenty minutes from the airport. If there were ten people meeting us at the airport, there were another ten at the house. Of course the throngs of Tratorio family members were most interested in hearing about Alba and JET—I mean Joseph— and cousins and so forth back in Albany. We couldn't blame them, but we were tired from traveling and more interested in speaking with Guillermo about restaurant and residential properties than visiting with relatives. We realized this was a great excuse for a party, but the red table wine was beginning to make our tongues thick. Thankfully everyone else had a head start on drinking, and we managed to leave with Guillermo with a good two hours of sunlight still left in the sky. He wasn't drunk, so he suggested we drive around.

Guillermo turned out to be a great guy, speaking English well enough that we had no problem communicating. He was very well versed in his business and had some connections with restaurateurs. He suggested we go about five miles in the opposite direction of Salerno to look at a condo, an apartment, and a small house for rent in neighboring Bellizzi. If this all worked out, we planned on renting for at least a year to get organized and up and running before we would buy a house. We drove by them all, thinking the condo appeared to be the best deal for us due to lack of maintenance and it was newer than the apartment building.

Fred looked at the odometer leaving Bellizzi for Salerno. Approximately twenty kilometers or about twelve miles, not a bad commute to the restaurants, about two miles farther than my current drive to La Ventana. We drove by three restaurant locations and the one with used equipment that was on Via Nizza, in a nicer section of the business district of downtown

Salerno. A cursory look showed it as most promising. Guillermo would have keys and/or appointments to get into spaces tomorrow. We got out of the car and peered in the window.

I am better versed in restaurant equipment than Fred, but we would certainly be negotiating a deal together. The stuff didn't look bad and wasn't beat up. We thanked Guillermo for the sneak peek, and he delivered us to Hotel Annalena, where we were happy to arrive, checking into a quiet room to relax.

Hotel Annalena was built on a picturesque parcel of land that overlooked the city of Salerno. After freshening up and relaxing in the room, we became reenergized after our tour of the area and decided to go to the lobby, where computers were set up in comfortable anterooms with views out large windows. Fred wanted to catch up with communication, and this seemed a better idea than trying to punch condensed texts into a cell phone. I grabbed some bottled waters and nuts from the bar and came back to our private chat room and our own little party.

First was a text sent to JET, giving him our email address. He was instructed to e-mail back from the office computer after receiving an address Fred had just created. We requested daily dollar numbers for La Ventana and Chez Neo, and then of great importance, updates on Nonna Bella and Kellogg. Next would be Jess, presuming she was at work, for any info she might have after our JET conversation. We would have already heard from Larry the lawyer had there been anything earthshaking on the home front, so Fred wrote him only to update him on our progress and that we had successfully made it this far. Last would be a note to Jerry the jeweler.

Predictably JET was back to us quickly. He gave us the information requested, starting with the numbers in our prearranged code. They were average for the days of the week he was telling us about, which meant good. Good for us and Jess, who would feel much closer to the operation running it herself. She would undoubtedly be sharing those good numbers with banker boyfriend. And we all knew how bankers felt about good numbers, especially when they belonged to them.

JET reported Bora had gotten out of hand again and had been asked to leave and the secret man was still hanging around. We didn't go into much detail regarding him because we didn't want JET acting suspicious. JET wrote that the secret man finally mentioned his name to him and spelled it "Morris," as opposed to "Maurice," as Fred had envisioned. Fred and I continued running scenarios as to who the secret man might be and his motivation. We had not ruled out that he knew about the diamonds or the bonds or both. He could just as easily be an undercover FBI agent or, the strangest scenario, a legitimate businessman on a temp job in New York, as he claimed.

Nonna was fine, and JET jokingly announced that we might have a hard time getting Kellogg back, as he was quite accustomed to sleeping on the pillow next to Nonna's head. It appeared to him, at least, that Kellogg had put on weight. *Wonderful—not only an ugly little dog, but a fat ugly little dog.*

In came the note from Jess. She reiterated the sales numbers and mentioned the Bora incident. It had nothing to do with Za but was another minor confrontation with Nonna. Bora had begun a rant about Americans, and although Jessica wanted two busboys to escort her out, JET had insisted he could handle it himself, which he did. I wasn't thrilled with that since I knew Bora carried pepper spray in her purse. Fred said JET knew that also and would be much faster than Bora, especially if she were drunk.

Ding! The e-mail chime sounded as Jerry's mail arrived. He said he was at the "Donut Shop," the name they called the off-track betting parlor with Wi-Fi in Rensselaer, just across the Dunn Memorial Bridge from La Ventana. The boys loved conversing in their own unique language. With two newly minted and disposable Gmail accounts, their conversation would go up in coded vapor anyway. Fred could decipher Jerry's gibberish and said Abel's jewelry diamonds were odd weights but of great value if he found the right someone to cut and perhaps market them, unless we were planning on doing the marketing. The overall shapes were such that Jerry was uncomfortable cutting them. He explained they would cut nicely, and with cutting comes small pieces called melee, or chips, for a larger ring, fill-ins on a brooch, earrings, and so on.

"Maybe we should keep them as genital decorations?" Fred typed in as part of his wisecracking reply. I asked Fred if he just couldn't help acting like a thirteen-year-old boy.

Jerry wrote back, *"I'm redesigning them for Lantana to model."*

I nudged Fred out of the way and typed, *"As long as you make a **stud** for your wife, Katie—she could probably use one. L."* That was the end of the Jerry communiqué for the evening.

Jerry had admitted he didn't have the skill to cut the rocks and wasn't going to risk slipping with a tool, effectively ruining the value in an instant. We knew the gem cutter's job was extremely difficult. They have a specialized knowledge of stones, tools, and techniques to maximize weight and shape. He thought they would be worth at least seventy-five thousand dollars by the time they were cut properly, all beautifully untraceable. Jerry was hopeful, as were we, to employ one middleman who could both cut and unload the jewels.

Fred and I spent a restless night discussing the commitment. It would be my signature on the documents—my money. As final as that sounded, in the big picture it also depended on what kind of deal we could negotiate on the space. I was having a hard time with any downside to this. Not to be negative but just being realistic, I had the wherewithal financially to absorb failure, and this *was* the chance of a lifetime.

The next morning Fred and I were enjoying our continental breakfast, alfresco in the Annalena Café, when Guillermo came to collect us. We had called Guillermo last evening and instructed him that he would only need keys for the first two properties to inspect. We were most interested in the space at 15 Via Nizza and understood we would be meeting the property owner, the titleholder on the equipment, and the ex-restaurateur himself.

Guillermo instructed us to stay calm no matter where the conversation went. He explained that hot-tempered Italian businesspeople crank up the volume at a moment's notice but also have watched too many American movies. They think if American businessmen don't like the deal, there is a brief emotional outburst, and then they shoot each other. Fred said that might not be too far from the truth.

We arrived at the Via Nizza property shortly before ten. The landlord was walking the perimeter inside the store, mostly staying away from the other two, who already appeared to be in an altercation. Guillermo greeted all and made introductions as we feigned no Italian at all, with the possible advantage of eavesdropping on a perfectly audible Italian conversation. We had inventory sheets for the contents, and Guillermo knew that although some items were noted "not for sale," this was a bargaining tool since the equipment owner wanted to get out from under his equipment and the restaurateur wanted to reduce his debt.

The discussion became a game of haggling, and after an hour, it was decided we would simply pay the balance owed on the equipment—all of it. Suddenly we realized we were halfway through cutting the deal. The place had been vacant for some time, so it was easy to tell the landlord, also the owner, would be quite pleased to have it rented. Another half hour, and I was signing a one-year lease, with an option for two more.

We played the same game most home buyers in the United States do. We gave him a deposit, and the lease was contingent on selling La Ventana. So we felt we had arranged a great deal overall. We depleted more of Abel's cash for a deposit on the equipment, with the promise to wire the balance.

Selling a restaurant is much more difficult than selling a house, in Italy also, but we told our new landlord we did have a prospect in mind. Bottom line, we secured the place for the equivalent of a few hundred dollars, and Guillermo suggested he could do something with the equipment if we walked away from the entire deal. Everyone left happy, in particular me.

STATESIDE

The entire trip was beyond overwhelming, but the flight back seemed almost to be the best part of it. Besides our first-class accommodations, we were heading home. We had half a legal pad of notes dedicated to our new cast of characters, with the secret man at the top of the list, another for the diamonds, one for moving, the sale of La Ventana including the business, inventory, and so on.

Fred and I weren't celebrating nor being self-congratulatory, but the realization that we were going through with this was sinking in. It was surreal, I thought. *When did my mind cross over from no, to maybe, to going through with it?* We had been through so much, and yet had we even scratched the surface? It seems you will never be sure of some decisions, so you just have to forge ahead. In the back of my mind, I knew I could still bail, but that seemed less an option now.

We couldn't help our conversation returning to the secret man, even though there was no evidence supporting our suspicions. After considerable contemplation, genius Fred said he was either a good guy or a bad guy. Brilliant. Fred gave me the classic deadpan droop-eye look. "If he's a bad guy, one of us mice is going to end up with our tail in a trap. If he's a good guy, it's still bad. He's probably with the IRS or the feds." Just what I wanted to hear. There were times, and this was one of them, that I thought we were in over our heads with this charade.

We returned to the restaurant business grind, and so did the secret man. He would visit Chez Neo at varying times but always within a window between five-thirty and seven-thirty. He'd drink two Captain Morgan and Cokes with extra lime, stay for an hour, and leave. I asked the bartenders what he had been talking about; they said it was mostly chitchat, the weather, and how busy he'd been that day, in a nebulous and nondescriptive way. The conversations about Abel and Daleka's terrible demise were a thing of the past. Other than cordial greetings, I could never get enough conversation without it looking like an interrogation. He was smooth. Fred decided to engage him once again. Since JET had informed Fred the secret man's name was "Morris," he asked, "First or last?"

"Short for my name," said Morris and began his sports and weather gossip.

Smooth, Fred had to admit, smooth and suspicious.

Morris claimed he was an independent contractor working for a company in California; he mumbled the name quickly and didn't want to dwell on it. He did utility analyzation work for local governments. He was doing some work for Troy and a few other suburbs outside of New York City. In Troy he was evaluating and analyzing city electrical usage.

I questioned, more like pestered, further, and Fred snapped back, "Look, he pays cash. What am I going to do? Card him for his age?"

My Cheatin' Heart

As they say, something's gotta give. Fred and I had so much going on, it seemed sometimes one or both of us were going to explode. If something could try a relationship, this was it. Our daily conversations included the move to Salerno, which was still ultimately my decision.

The money weighed heavily on my mind; my money and La Ventana belonged to me. But it was not what you think. It wasn't me being greedy or wanting to hoard the money; I still had to make the ultimate decision. Fred, rightfully so, did not want to sway or force me into the decision, which I appreciated. If this fell apart, there would be no one to blame, or reward, but myself. Fred did the best he could by saying he would support me regardless of my decision.

Banker boyfriend was in receipt of the documents from Larry the lawyer. I needed to finalize the lease/purchase of La Ventana with the banker before the deal, or maybe even Jessica, became stale to him. The clock was also ticking on the space and equipment in Salerno. I still had doubts that the whole project was too soon considering all that had happened. It had been many months since Abel and Daleka died, and although not directly involved, I still felt an unresolved cloud hanging over my head. The situation was unnerving with the FBI, IRS, and Troy police, let alone potential criminal dogs who might be lurking or sniffing around corners. We were still concerned there was a Mr. Big somewhere coming for the money and diamonds. I reasoned my indecision was just that. Would I ever be ready for the deep end of the pool without just diving in?

Fred and I began calling the new restaurant Tavola Cinque, Table Five. This gave it a personality and a life of its own, something tangible to look forward to. It had already become abundantly clear that I could not do this alone. I needed Fred. I didn't think or believe this to be a bad thing. I did love him. If anything, I hoped the pressure of all this wouldn't destroy our relationship. Sometimes when the daily issues got too heavy, he would instruct Jess and JET to handle the rest of the business day right through closing up. He'd tell me to meet him at one of the apartments, and he'd walk in with a Papa's Tapas gyro and a bottle of Roditys, with a fantastic lovemaking session and nap to follow.

JET came into the office one hectic morning while I was finishing up with Larry the lawyer, who was leaving. Larry had just explained that responses and correspondence had stopped from the banker regarding final contracts for the La Ventana sale.

"Ms. Lantana," JET started, "I got to tell you something what happened while you were gone."

I corrected, "I have got to tell you something that happened, JET."

"Yeah, that's what I meant. I heard Mr. Larry talk about Ms. Jessica's boyfriend, the one who's buying the La Ventana?"

"Yes, JET, Mr. Larry is a little worried about it, and so am I."

"Well, that's what I mean. When you and Mr. Fred were gone, Ms. Jessica was kissing another man." A sudden silence. "There was no one around; they were in the Chez Neo alone, and they didn't know I was there, or like, I could see them. Then Ms. Jessica was arguing on her phone with somebody; I think that Ms. Jessica's boyfriend maybe found out; maybe he's mad about it."

"What did he look like JET, the man Ms. Jess kissed?"

JET said, "Hmmm, I don't know."

"Well, was he good-looking ... like Mr. Fred?"

JET crossed his arms and looked at the floor deep in thought. "Hmmm ..."

"Was he good-looking like you, JET?"

JET looked up quickly, his eyes large. "Maybe good-looking like me, yes."

I laughed and nodded. "I see. You *are* very good-looking, JET."

JET blushed and looked back at the floor.

I mulled this new development over with Fred, after telling him that JET certainly didn't have anything on him in the looks department. We weren't exactly sure how to handle this, but we were obviously beyond upset if Jessica's promiscuity squelched our deal. It raised trust issues, which are significant with anyone in business, let alone the general manager dealing with an operation doing the volume of La Ventana, three registers and two credit card machines. Abel would fire someone on the spot for irresponsibility of this magnitude. We decided to confront Jessica with it directly.

We called Jessica into the office, and then we simply explained that the banker seemed to be reneging on the restaurant deal and wanted to know what she knew about it.

She proceeded to tell us, "I am so sorry, Lantana, I didn't know how to tell you. I had no idea if it would still go through or not. It all happened so quickly when you guys were in Europe."

This was not what Fred and I wanted to hear. Fred was staying calm, me not so much. In an angry tone of ultimate disgust, I exclaimed, "Jess! Do you have any idea how important this deal was to everyone, including you? I have no idea what I'm going to do now. How am I going to salvage this? I just can't believe ..."

Jessica interrupted, "God, Lantana! How was I supposed to know he was still married? He told me his divorce was final. He lied about everything, all while he was fucking me! I didn't know it was his wife; she was here for lunch with her friend! I thought she was just a customer calling me over to her table either to compliment or complain. I was totally blindsided. She started making a scene, calling *me* a slut! I had to walk away before she disrupted the entire dining room."

Fred and I simultaneously said, "Shit."

PLEASANT CONVERSATION

After Za set up Bora and Simon, they didn't come into Chez Neo for some time. But then they did, and they appeared to play the part of an item, they didn't need Za or Series 7 for company. Bora never came in by herself to visit Fred, which was okay with us, and she never wore the diamond jewelry. We weren't sure why she had stopped her questioning, having earlier as much as invited Fred or Simon to be a partner in an operation she had little notion of. We knew she was grasping at straws; she had no clue what she was truly hunting for. She didn't know any more about the sum total of the loot than anyone else, and we were sure the Czechs had contacted her. If there had been a secret, it was out, and we all knew it was diamonds. So that begged the question: "How many and where were they stashed?"

One late afternoon Bora and Simon came into Chez Neo. Fred was at the bar as I walked in, said hello to the lovebirds, and went behind the bar to assist him. Simon caught Fred's attention and called him over. Leaning back, Simon held his hand over his mouth and whispered something to Fred. Simon stood up with Fred and both walked around the corner toward the office. Fred gave me a backward glance and a shrug. I finished updating the time stamp on one register and sat with Bora, who was sipping a wine and dabbing at her nose as she appeared to be crying. I quickly pulled out my international biracial bisexual matchmaker guidebook and hat and asked what was going on, as it was clear Simon was the center of the discord. She asked if I could break away for a few minutes to get some fresh air. Okay.

JET had used Carlita, and it was parked at the curb, so we decided to go for a short drive. We turned a corner off the main street as Bora went into her purse to replace her handkerchief with ... a nickel-plated over-under .22 caliber derringer which she pointed at my midsection. She suggested we go to my apartment. I had little choice but to comply. As opposed to the alley incident, I had a few moments to analyze my situation. On the plus side of the column, I had slacks and flats on for kicking, I was on my home turf, and I had the Beretta in my purse. The negative side carried the fact that she had this little toy euro-gun that could still put a hole in me, and if that didn't work, she was capable of snapping me in half like a dry wishbone. I wondered if bossy Czech women ever tangled with a Nebraska farm girl PMS'ing.

A hundred things ran through my mind, not the least of which was that this was a concerted and scripted effort between Bora and Simon. It was clear to me that Simon had coyly removed Fred from the Chez. Was he conducting his own interrogation, or just giving Bora the opportunity to strong-arm me?

Bora had not buckled her seat belt. If I could distract her, maybe to get something from her purse, her phone, only for a second, I fantasized back-fisting her bulbous nose into an explosion of blood, slamming on the brakes, grabbing the back of her head, and slamming her face into the dash, relieving her of the little gun.

"You know, Fred carries a little derringer also."

"Simon will take it away from him," she said flatly. "Simon is talking to Fred in your office." I visualized Simon closing the door and spinning the deadbolt behind himself. Fred could be a bit of a scrapper, given his wrestling experience, but he surely remembered the conversation of Simon's military background. Regardless, Fred was more likely to use his brain and negotiate his way out, if there was a way out.

I clunked a bit in the hallway before unlocking my apartment. As anticipated, the Nose, Mrs. Hannity, opened her door to do what she did best—snoop. Bora's attention was momentarily diverted as the dog on springs launched, hitting Bora in the face. The Beretta, safety off, had been palmed in my hand while getting my keys as I spun around. Bora, now startled and off-balance, jerked both hands up as I knocked the hand with the little pistol back with my purse. With no time to respond and Mrs. Hannity to my left, I reflexively fired, catching Bora dead center through her left hand. In single-frame slow motion, I heard and watched the .32 slug penetrate and spray blood out the back side of Bora's hand as the bullet hit and stuck in the wall. With no time to deal with the Nose, I yanked Bora in by her top while tripping her hard to the floor and slamming the door, giving the Nose a sort of wave-off.

I think Bora was in shock; she didn't have much fight left in her. The gun had come out of her hand, and I kicked it across the room, continuing to hold the Beretta on her.

"Good boy, Kellogg!" I congratulated as he nervously peed on the floor. Throwing a roll of paper towels at Bora, I was so angry I considered making her mop up after Kellogg. She began wrapping the towel around her dripping hand.

I growled, *"What?"*

"I vant the die-mahnds!" she screamed.

"There aren't any!" I screamed back.

"You shot me!"

"Fuck you! You were going to shoot me."

"I'm bleeding to death."

"Wrap the towel on your hand. What is Simon doing with Fred?"

Bora expounded, "Simon and I know Abel and Daleka were partners."

This wasn't the time to explain that Daleka was no more than another minion, like Elisa, in the plot, and she, Bora, was even lower on the totem pole.

"Simon is getting information; we will compare your stories. Simon and I are the partners now; we are replacing Abel and Daleka."

Again, I wasn't going to waste my time explaining she and Simon were partners in vapor.

I proceeded to talk plainly, saying we were all in the dark regarding any cache of diamonds. She was aware of the ones in my desk and knew about Abel's jewelry, presuming she had had a private showing of Daleka's genital jewels. She said she had a couple of raw diamonds in addition to the jewelry we had seen her wearing, but more importantly, she admitted that Daleka and Abel were running some sort of operation.

Daleka had told her it was too dangerous for her to know any more about it. That she would ultimately be in on the whole thing and share in the big payoff. *Yeah, right,* I thought as I rolled my eyes.

Simon would be along any time "after" he found the diamonds in the office. Of course that cranked my antenna up; so these rats were in the hole together. Crap! Where and how was Fred?

Just then I heard the fumbling of keys in my door. Before Bora could give any warning, I jumped to the back side of the door as it swung open. Simon pushed Fred into the room, slamming the door behind himself. I popped out, jabbing the Beretta's barrel squarely behind Simon's left ear. Perhaps the trail of blood leading to Bora on the floor and the crimson-soaked paper towel around her hand put Simon in a cautionary mood.

Fred didn't seem any worse for wear. I told him to get the peashooter from the corner, where I had kicked it out of the way. Fred looked at Goliath on the floor, gave me a flat-lipped smile, and picked up the little gun. He explained he had let Simon rummage through the office, telling him all we had was the *two* rough cuts and the genital gems.

Fred mentioned this was a little early in the day for gunfire in the apartment building and we had better wrap up before the Nose had her SWAT gear on and the cops arrived. We collectively agreed they had some rocks and so did we; if there were more, we weren't aware of them. Of course they didn't know about the fortune in paper assets. Whatever Abel and

Daleka might have stashed or already fenced had disappeared the way of the eighteenth-floor window when the birds flew.

So Daleka screwed Bora on the loot or didn't figure on dying so soon, and Bora and Simon had a pittance of what likely existed. To continue an investigation to find more diamonds would only be dangerous, incriminating, and ... where would they start?

We pled ignorance and suggested that we all be happy with what we had. Before Bora could process too much information, I also informed her that when the cops arrived, her gunshot wound was due to breaking and entering into my apartment. I was on my property when I used my weapon; her weapon was illegally concealed and likely unregistered, and somehow I doubted she had a federal gun card. If she didn't like that scenario, we could instead work on a kidnapping charge. I wouldn't say we all parted shaking hands, but they left. Bora glared at Fred's face and then down to his hand, which still held the little gun. He looked at me, and I nodded, at which point Fred flipped the barrel release, popping two .22 long rifle cartridges on the kitchen counter, and then handed the pistol to Simon, quipping a double entendre: he didn't want blood on his hands anyway.

Fred sat in a chair and stared at the floor. We still had some 'splainin' to do to the Nose, but Fred decided to handle it; he'd flash that winning smile and make up some shit. I opened a bottle of my Mont du Claire *and* brought out the Jimedor tequila. Most importantly, I sliced a thick chunk of extrasharp cheddar, his favorite, for my hero, Kellogg.

Fred explained that, although suspicious of Simon, he was blindsided by his ultimate tack to get into the office. Fred's guard was down under the impression there was loyalty between Simon and Za, but there was none.

I told my story and said there was no need for apologies inasmuch as Bora suckered me also. But Kellogg got the drop on her when he overshot his jumping trick, typically into my arms, and hit Little Attila in the face.

"Overshot?" Fred said incredulously. "Are you talking about my finely tuned and calibrated killing machine Kellogg? That was protective instinct," Fred stated confidently.

I replied, "If that was instinct, blowing a few toes off that poor mugger in Antwerp was a perfect shot too!"

Looking down at Kellogg, I said, "You know what? You *did* get the drop on Little Attila. Thank you, but let's call it teamwork. I think you're lucky you had backup today."

I gave him another nugget of cheddar while spreading paper towels over his wet spot on the floor.

SIMON AND
THE SECRET MAN

Za was still coming into meet Series 7, Alexander, and occasionally AMG Mercedes. Walking into Chez from the office, I was shocked to see Za and Series 7 sitting with Simon. Za was by definition angry that she had trusted Simon. I think it made her feel as if she were getting old or losing her edge, let alone having been betrayed. Exhibiting no telltale body language, she sat ultra-cool and emotionless with the two, me knowing she'd slice Simon's testicles off if she had the chance.

Next the secret man came into the bar while the other three sat at Za's café table. Simon abruptly stood up, unnecessarily refreshing his own drink, and started a conversation with the secret man. This became more interesting when Simon sat on a stool next to the secret man and they began to chat and drink. Before the bartender overheard anything of substance, they both stood, laid money on the bar, and walked out together.

About an hour later, JET came flying into the office while Fred and I were reviewing lunch receipts. Spitting like a machine gun, he said there had just been a shooting in the parking garage. Fred told him to calm down and tell us what he had seen and heard. JET said there were cops all over, and a crowd was being held back to the sidewalk. From what JET could see in the darkened garage, though floodlights were set up, the two front doors were open on what JET thought was a late-model Dodge Charger, the window shattered on the passenger side, with plenty of blood on the tan interior of the door. Bodies had already been bagged and were being rolled out when JET overheard people in the crowd talking about a white guy and a black guy in the car. JET closed the door as he left the office. Fred and I stared at each other in silence.

It came as no surprise that Troy's Detective Gwynn showed up the following morning with a barrage of questions regarding both men, as he knew they were in Chez Neo the night before. It seemed he was making a point of not giving up much about the identities of either man. We couldn't press anything without appearing overly suspicious.

There would be no reason for us to withhold information—information he either knew or would find out anyway—so we told him about our two customers, a man who called himself Morris and Simon who knew Za. We knew Za would keep a cool head and presumed she'd be questioned by Gwynn, but naturally we gave her a heads-up beforehand. We played as dumb as we could but were hit by lightning when Gwynn suggested they would be reopening Abel's case. Fred and I were certainly not mentioning my ownership of La Ventana, let alone the massive amount of assets that mysteriously now belonged to me. This would all be coming out if they didn't already know.

A few days later, Fred saw FBI agent Mason on the street late in the day and seized the opportunity for conversation. He invited him up for a cocktail. I didn't know if this would be good or bad—probably both. We could use some fresh intel, but a very large can of worms was already open and we didn't need any more of a mess on the floor. I was not in the chat, but Mason did not mince any words, nor did Fred in his descriptive repeat of the crime scene.

Whatever transpired the car, the heated exchange that became an intimate gunfight, was supposedly unknown. The homicide detectives concluded Simon had drawn his .38 special first, firing three rounds into the secret man, whose name Mason did not give. Fred coyly mentioned he knew him as Morris and he was a relatively new customer, giving Mason his history. Mason remained silent on the name. Apparently the secret man was more than a municipality utility consultant unless carrying a small-frame .45 is de rigueur for that occupation. He was also quick enough to pump two .45 caliber slugs into Simon before he lost consciousness. The thick and slow .45 bullet, by design, created maximum damage entering Simon's chest and then generated larger holes exiting, making an utter mess of the Dodge, let alone Simon. Having shot quite a bit at the farm, I said, "I'll bet their ears are still ringing from those things going off inside a closed car."

Fred rolled his eyes and said, "Yeah, I'm sure they were worried about their ears."

Fred danced delicately with his line of answers to Mason's questions. It was common knowledge the two had been in the restaurant before the shootout. He hoped he could open the door for more intel. Mason offered that the FBI had been watching Abel and Daleka for some time before their deaths, knowing they were into something illegal. At least this was the story Fred was told. He didn't mention diamonds per se but alluded to a grand scale of illegal activity. Common sense indicated this was a big enough deal that the FBI was involved. The secret man was apparently wearing a device, but Mason claimed the conversation was being recorded, not transmitted, so he had no cavalry for backup. There was no way Mason would tell Fred what was on the tape.

This was becoming more complicated by the minute. If the FBI had been tracking Abel and Daleka's suspicious behavior, things should've been redirected away from La Ventana now that they were dead. Now, with a (second) double murder, they would be reopening the Abel/Daleka case with a new investigation centering on foul play, double murder, murder suicide, kinky love angles, smuggling, and most important to me, probably tax evasion. With murder there's a motive; where there's a motive, there's usually money. Where there's money and crime, the IRS would be holding hands with the FBI to see if there was a business involved as a front for the crime. Fred, sensing my nervousness, pointed out my money was technically legal, and so far no one—that we knew—was aware of the stones. Perhaps, but even with Abel dead, discovery of the money would be made at some point, and where *did* such a large sum come from?

So, why was I nervous? Maybe because I'd been listening to stories from a man-size dog. Fred continued to tell me there was nothing to be nervous about. And when I believed that, little red monkeys would poke from Carlita's tailpipe, smoking cigars and whistling Dixie. Perhaps Kellogg's theory of the lovebirds being thrown through the big window was not far-fetched, dog pun intended. I had told Fred about the dream but didn't include specific intimate conversation with Kellogg. I didn't want him to think I had totally lost my mind.

Shattered

A few days later, Fred and I sat in the office mulling over these latest developments. There was something going on with Fred, and had been for a few days. His mood was pensive, there was an uneasiness about him. After a considerable silence, a weak smile turned somber, and he spoke.

"I've got a confession to make. I didn't expect this whole thing to explode like a bloated carcass in the desert sun, not yet at least. There's no way to hide this, and my involvement anymore, Lantana. Morris, Cliff Morris, *was* a secret man, an undercover FBI agent … and so am I. We were working with U. S. Customs. Our pal Simon fucked up our little corner of a three-year global sting of which diamond smuggling was just a part. That's only the tip of the iceberg, there's another team heading up a separate investigation that involves things including drugs and the sex trade.

"That halfwit Gywnn doesn't have a clue as to the entire scope of this—just the Abel/Daleka case. Cliff Morris was my friend. A friend with a wife and two kids in the suburbs. With his training and understanding of all the players, including knowing about Simon and his Special Forces skills, I'm surprised he didn't recognize the slim-framed hammerless in an armpit holster Simon was carrying."

I burst out laughing to Fred's bewilderment, wondering what the hell was going on. What the hell was he talking about? I was first dumbfounded, next exasperated, and then angry. This couldn't possibly be happening, I wanted to scream, but no, I decided to retaliate; "I never trusted you from the onset; you must have known that, or should have. Not that real gentlemen don't still exist, but you were too good to be true, and several times you were too much of an actor. Sometimes your acting fell short. I questioned your comments and behavior that seemed suspicious—your disappearing to do trades, the contacts you had so readily available. I suppose you figured bedding me down was your 'seal the deal' moment, you figured everything was 'butter and roses and puppy toes.' Do most women you play, buy into that? Don't get me wrong; you don't do too badly—with what you have to work with. Guess you can't learn everything from pictures in your spy manual."

Yet Fred didn't miss a beat—was he acting? "You just don't get it, and you can't conceive how large this is. The whole thing was a setup. Mason and I were collaborating on the case. We set Abel up. We found him in southern California operating a restaurant along with running his own book. He didn't know who we were; he was anxious to get out of there, before he was shot by some low-level thug he'd ripped off. We offered him an opportunity. He thought I was a kingpin in some other crime organization. *I'm* the one who put Abel in this restaurant he thought *he* owned. The government owns La Ventana.

"You were the perfect patsy for stumbling into this theatrical production. It might've been anyone, but it was you, and you were perfect with your greasy spoon experience and bookkeeping savvy. You were probably supposed to die by accident, at least on paper, which would have been our opportunity to expose the ring. Your murder would have been better. Murdered by a mugger perhaps, hey, maybe even blame the Chez playboys, but Abel would have pulled the strings behind the scenes. Abel realized he screwed up simply murdering Elisa and dumping her in the Hudson. He could've used her as the patsy, but doing it his way, he had no body to produce. If you were found dead the scam would be authenticated and Abel could testify that you were an embezzler, with the money you stole returned to him! He would claim you were the one who forged the partnership documents; you collected the bonds and hid them in the desk.

"But; Daleka turned out to be a double bad guy, playing both ends, and instead of just taking her cut, she got greedy and wanted more. She would have been our key to busting international crooks up the ladder. She was getting the diamonds to Abel, who was peddling them to our fence, a government agent. You know him as Jerry the jeweler. In receiving the diamonds, Jerry's job was simply to string Abel along until we had solid evidence for a bust. Abel's intention was to implicate you. We planned to complete the bust before you were killed of course, maybe creating the illusion of your death. Likewise, all the bonds *are* real, but you can't keep them; they belong to Uncle Sam, like the restaurant.

"We didn't know Daleka, or Abel for that matter, was going to die; no one really knows why that went down the way it did. Must have been the icing on Abel's cake when she began titillating him with her S&M act. How cool was that? Abel thought he was making millions while getting his crank yanked."

Talk about a sucker punch. I hadn't felt like this since my husband, Tom, deceived me and made a lame attempt to cover up that he'd been cheating. It didn't take him long to realize I was too smart or he was too dumb. I was devastated by that—and now this. I held back my parallel emotions of exploding in anger or crying, remembering Dad telling me, "Big girls don't cry."

Closing my eyes, I leaned back in my chair. Unlike the ringing in my ears during the alley incident or when I was blowing off half of London Fog's foot in Antwerp, a serene calm washed over me. My nostrils flared as I inhaled deeply, filling my lungs, then slowly exhaled through an ooh shape I made with my mouth. I reached in my purse and slowly pulled out the Beretta. The double-clicking sound as I chambered a round was utterly deafening in the quiet office.

I opened my eyes to see the frightened expression on Fred's face as he scooted up and sat erect on the sofa. *"Okay! I'm making shit up!"* he yelped.

I glared at him intently. "Really? Pretty funny, huh? Why would you, or the FBI, pluck Abel out of California 10 years ago? And Kellogg found the bonds, or is he an FBI dog?"

After a long pause, Fred opened his mouth and shut it again. He quietly stood, walked around the desk slowly, and gently took the Beretta from my hand. In one fluid movement, he ejected the live round onto the desk and released the clip, then set the pistol down. Putting his hands under my elbows, he raised me from my chair and, with that smile, wrapped one arm around me and his other hand behind my neck.

Putting his face next to my ear, he softly said, "I'm sorry, poor attempt at dark humor, I guess I can't take this anymore either." Then in an attempt to make me laugh with a Fredism, he whispered, "What's up with butter and roses and puppy toes?"

I sucked in a big breath, exhaled loudly, and all but yelled in his ear, "Asshole! So what *do* you think happened?"

Rubbing his ear, he sat down and pulled me onto his lap. He said been thinking about this, off and on, for days. He apologized again; I had a hard time imagining he could even come up with a story like this, but his theory was largely the same as the story he had just told except he was, thankfully, not an FBI agent. Maybe Abel had put my name on the business because he *was* expecting me to die, or perhaps his plan was to cash the bonds, faking his own death and disappearing to another country with a different identity. He could afford to leave me with the restaurant. Hatch said there were reasons, or scenarios, why Abel gave me the restaurant. Maybe this was one of them.

Even if he had disappeared and I figured out his deception, why would I force any issue? If La Ventana were in debt or had a tax problem, I would still be happy to have the restaurant, being the savvy greasy spoon girl I am. I could dig it out, turn it around, and make it a success. *Wait till Fred feels my size eight in his balls after the greasy spoon comment.* Whatever Abel's plans, they did not include me.

Fred started, "obviously he didn't select you personally, because you just walked in, but it couldn't have worked out better for him. You were absolutely perfect for the job for the reasons I mentioned. Larry Feinstein mentioned that Abel spoke of plans to retire to another country by himself. Once Daleka became more than a business partner, he probably toyed with the idea of including her. Yet I can't imagine that happening with Bora in the picture, can you?

"Larry said he had given Abel a couple of boilerplate restaurant sales contracts he was to mull over and plug in options for the sale. The contracts were anything but standard. In a convoluted way, they included transferring funds, making it difficult to find out where the proceeds would actually end up. Getting back to you, my little flower, besides having all the skills he needed for the job, the frosting on his cake was having a gift-wrapped beautiful doll like you show up on his doorstep as if custom-ordered. I think Abel was more a sociopath than even you imagined. Screwing you would've been the ultimate prize. I don't think he knew where to draw the line between pleasures of the flesh and keeping his eye on the prize. But that was okay; there were plenty of hood ornaments and foxy females in wine sales."

Okay, maybe Fred redeemed himself for the greasy spoon girl comment.

Just when everything should have been simmering down, it was back to a rolling boil. Fred hadn't learned anything from Mason relative to the identity of the secret man. If Morris was an FBI agent, Mason wasn't letting on, which would make perfect sense. A dead FBI agent involved in a shootout, that he had lost, would be a delicate matter and handled unlike a civilian murder. Besides a poor showing for the agency, the investigation would be confidential. It would be handled as quietly as bunny paws on cool concrete.

If the Abel and Daleka death case were reopened, we were worried the IRS would scrutinize La Ventana and Abel's history with fresh interest. Fred had had conversations with accountant Gloria regarding "hypothetical scenarios" about other assets in La Ventana's name that were discovered after Abel's death. Gloria was no idiot; Fred could tell her wheels were spinning at high rpm. Likewise, Gloria was smart enough to know her job was to answer questions that were asked—and not ask questions she would later regret knowing the answers to.

She explained there was no record of purchases of stock or bonds and therefore no paper trail until they were sold. What would we say when we sold these investments? Where did they come from? From Abel. How was it that he had a million-plus dollars in bonds? I don't know, and he's dead. What was the cost basis of the stock? I would need to convince the powers that be that I was not aware of the bonds; they were purchased before I was aware I was a partner, and the cost basis would be Abel's date of death. It still reeked of suspicion, but there was nothing to do except wonder when and who would be asking any of those questions.

Gloria informed us it was common to find assets from dead relatives. For now we would continue making plans for a new restaurant, continue to act relaxed, in our high state of anxiety, and reassess what to do with La Ventana now that we had no built-in buyer.

Bounced and
Canceled Czech

After Simon's death, for reasons unknown, Bora still came into Chez Neo, although seldom. Sometimes alone but usually with one of the original entourage. We didn't care if they were gay or straight, but either way there was no open affection between them and Bora. Bora was still grieving Daleka, but it appeared time was healing that wound.

Bora had gotten mouthy with Za on more than one occasion, but Za, ever cool, just looked at her silently, infuriating her all the more. The same was true with Nonna Bella Alba Tratorio. Except she seemed always up for an altercation, perhaps a fistfight with Bora, because a simple catfight would be below Nonna's standards. This verbal volley was usually ethnically oriented, boasting childish one-upmanship. Sometimes their paths would cross when Nonna Bella came to visit with Sergio in the kitchen. Sergio enjoyed conversation with Alba and trading cooking tips.

I happened into Chez one evening when Alba, on her way out, decided to chat with Za. Bora came in, obviously inebriated, and the calm conversation escalated to anger rapidly. Za became vocal this time, and had this not been frightening, it could have been a comedy sketch on the Tower of Babel. The three of them cursing in Romanian, Italian, and some obscure dialect of drunken Slovak almost had me laughing, except I didn't want anyone getting hurt or glasses getting smashed. I caught JET's eye to defuse the older gals as I swept Bora by the arm out of the bar. I hooked my arm through her bag so there would be no access to the peashooter inside. JET escorted Nonna out in a different direction, and Za simply finished her martini and left.

Za would have been the only one to relate the straight story regarding the instigation of the matter, but I dropped it as of no consequence in the long run.

A few days later Nonna Bella dropped something off for JET and popped into the kitchen to say hello to Sergio. Bora was in Chez. She mumbled something under her breath that piqued Alba's attention. Alba squinted a killer look at Bora as she flushed red, muttering what I was sure were Italian curse words through her clenched teeth. I quickly defused this confrontation and whisked Nonna out of Chez Neo. Fred later told me whatever was going on, it was becoming a feud between the two hot-blooded women. At that point we told Bora she was no longer welcome at Chez Neo.

On a Wednesday afternoon, I was at my desk looking over some freshly printed flyers showcasing our new promotion, "Italian Night," in an effort to pump up weak Wednesday evenings. We enlisted Nonna Bella's help, with Sergio's approval, to assemble some Italian dinners with Chianti served in half and full carafes and an Italian breadbasket, with olive oil and fresh-ground Parmesan served at the tables. The labor-intensive lasagna was made from scratch in restaurant trays. Nonna was in her glory directing the preparation and assembly from her recipe with helpers. The regular menu had been pared down, but a few items were available.

JET was scooping Kellogg's litter box into a garbage bag when suddenly we felt a faint vibration through the floor of the office, which butted up to the kitchen. There was a commotion and thumping, culminating with what sounded like a muffled gunshot. We both jerked to our feet and bolted toward the door. Racing into the kitchen, we saw Alba facing the back stairs that led down to the alley. She stood statue-like, one hand covering her mouth, the other on her chest. In a slow, mechanical movement, her torso rotated toward us; she was ashen-faced, eyes wide as if she had just seen a ghost.

The three of us stood silent for a moment. Almost in a whisper, I asked, "Where's Sergio?"

Alba shook her head from side to side.

Deliberately I walked toward the corner, peering down the unlit staircase. I could see a crumpled figure at the bottom landing. Flicking the light switch, I saw it was Bora. I spun to JET and told him to call 911 for medical and police; I told him to tell them someone was badly hurt, perhaps worse, and to come to the La Ventana sign at the alley door, which would be open—not to come through the restaurant.

Suddenly Fred and Sergio appeared in the kitchen, having received abbreviated information from JET as he ran by them on his way to the office. As Fred looked at me, I mouthed "BORA" and pointed down the stairway. Without a word, he went downstairs. I asked him to prop the door open with a wooden wedge and wait. He gave me a hand signal and directions to take Nonna Bella away from the kitchen. I took her to the office with Sergio, sat her on the couch, and instructed Sergio and JET to sit with her until the police arrived. When I'd held Nonna's hand, it was cold and damp. I looked her over quickly; when I was behind her, I had pushed her hair up and away from her neck, inspecting for damage or blood. There was none.

On the way back to the kitchen, I autodialed Larry the lawyer from my cell phone. Thankfully he answered and said he was not far away and would come directly over. When I looked down the stairs, Fred was crouching over Bora. He looked up and shook his head. I could see blood on the floor, and Bora's body was twisted in an unnatural position. Her head was more than ninety degrees past her shoulder. No one needed to be an expert in anatomy to conclude her neck had snapped.

Fred asked, "Is anyone with you?"

"No, we heard thumping and a bang, maybe a gunshot," I told Fred, still on one knee.

He held his hand in the air, thumb up and index finger out like a pistol and said, "Yes, there was a gunshot. Come down if you care or dare; this is one canceled Czech."

The rather narrow thirteen-step concrete staircase was painted battleship–gray, with a red steel handrail along one side—a rough ride if taken in one step. A few steps away, I stopped. Fred pointed to her right hand and, with his pen, pulled back her thumb, exposing Bora's little nickel derringer clutched in her thick hand. It would be interesting to hear Alba's rendition of what led up to this incident, but Bora was still clutching the pistol after it went off, putting a hole in her left leg above the knee, presumably during the tumble.

Blood was soaking through her pale rose-colored slacks. Ouch. I subdued a snicker through pursed lips since she still had an elastic bandage on her left palm from my .32 slug passing through it.

Fred and I hurried back to the office. JET was sitting on the couch with his arm around his grandmother's shoulders. I was a little surprised when Fred told JET to go back to the door at the alley and stay with the body until the authorities arrived. I guess Fred thought JET was ready to see fresh, violent death before it was dolled up and laid in a casket. I closed my eyes momentarily with a mini-thought. *My little boy is all grown up*; some pseudo-mother. *Is this the new me? Having JET guard a mangled corpse with a bullet hole in her leg? Just another day at my restaurant?*

Fred told JET, "When the police come, be polite, but you know nothing of what happened."

JET got up, acknowledging without a word, and closed the door behind him.

We asked Alba if she was all right; she nodded. "Can you tell us what happened?" I asked. We knew she had seen her own share of death, but we wondered how involved she was in this incident.

Alba began, "I-a had my back to the stair. I working on antipasto tray, and I hear Bora—she behind me; I just know it is her. I no turn around right away, but I look up an' see that Sergio is gone from kitchen. Then I turn around. Her eyes are sharp like-a knives; she staring at me, omicidio in her eyes," she said, gesturing to her face—"omicidio." She paused as if she were done speaking.

Fred asked, "What did Bora say? Did she want something?"

Alba was clearly very upset and speaking quickly. "Omicidio on her face. She want me to go with her, out the back. I don't move, and she show me her gun. She start backing toward the stair, ordering me, come with her. I no know what to do. I am scared; now is a-madness in her eyes. We got to stairs, and she turn for moment to look down. Maybe foot was maybe-a stuck, maybe she a-slip, lose balance a little. I think maybe push her, not hard, but she already off-balance, and she fall down stair. Just like that!"

"Okay," Fred said, rubbing his fingers on his forehead and looking down at the floor.

JET came back in the office, telling us a small crowd of police and medical people were gathered in the kitchen and wanted to speak to the owner or manager.

Fred looked at me and said, "Let's both go." He put his hand on JET's shoulder and told him to take his grandmother to the back corner of Chez Neo and sit with her until Mr. Larry arrived.

I whispered to JET on the way, "What does omicidio mean?"

JET opened his mouth but paused and then said, "Murder."

Fred stopped me in the hall on the way back to the kitchen. He briefed me a bit on the direction he thought we should take with the police with our latest catastrophe. Basically we agreed our plan was "We know nothing."

As we walked he said, "I looked through Bora's billfold. Her last name is Lazarof. Ring a bell?"

I shook my head negatively.

He continued, "There was a family photo in the billfold; we met her father in Pardubice."

I was still drawing a blank.

Fred said, "Boris, Boris Lazarof."

RETURN OF THE URN

A few weeks had passed since Bora's death. Fred and I were in the office discussing details and new options on Italy, the disposition of La Ventana, and satirically what could possibly happen next. The intercom rang, with bartender Molly informing me that Mr. Hatch was back and had something for me. I asked her to have JET escort him back to the office.

As was JET's way, he knocked twice and let Hatch in. I thanked JET as he pulled the door closed behind himself.

Hatch paused with his back to the door for a moment looking around the office and then came over to my desk carrying a cardboard box. He was wearing khaki slacks and a yellow knit top, with a small green alligator on the left breast. It looked as if the box was heavy as Hatch set it down on the desk, though he appeared relaxed and carefree. With a smile he mentioned there certainly seemed to be a lot of excitement around the restaurant lately. Fred and I offered a superficial smile in return as Hatch unfolded the box top, reached in, and let the box fall to the floor. Abel's urn was in his hands, which he replaced on the desk.

Steadying the urn with one hand, he twisted off the top with his other. Removing the lid, he dipped inside, pulling out a Charter Arms .44 caliber Bulldog revolver. I recognized it because my ex-husband, Tom, had the same model, purchased from my brother Chad. "That's going to be awfully loud in here, Hatch," I commented.

With no hesitation, Hatch replied, "With any luck, it won't be making any noise." He filled his other hand with a Taser from the urn.

"I'm really sorry Cleveland and Abel won't be here to share their cut of diamonds and bonds, but I'm afraid you won't be able to enjoy them either. Actually you knew Cleveland as Morris. Or was it Morse or Maurice?" he said with a smirk. "Cleveland got quite a kick out of chatting with you, Fred. He said the name differently just to play with you."

Fred and I offered blank looks to little effect— what was there to say?

Hatch decided to confide, "I kind of fibbed. Cleveland didn't die in a motorcycle accident years ago. The three of us—Cleveland, Sable, and I—were still working together, but like I said, I was too hot after doing time. Sable and Cleveland had gotten out of the weed business as soon as I was busted. Somehow Cleveland bartered a warehouse of weed for a sack of diamonds after the bust. Abel got his feet wet in that business, and it spun off with some European contacts he nurtured. Once they developed the connections, it was a no-brainer compared to weed. Rocks are easier to steal, hide, and move, and you deal with a much better class of people. Sure, they're still cutthroat scoundrels that would sell their own mother for a dollar, but at least they're not potheads. Unlike weed, diamonds don't stink, and there's a lot more cash involved for moving a lot less volume. I stayed out of the business in the United States, but I started running some of the game in Poland, Norway, and Belgium.

"Just as my salespeople got me busted by talking too much, Cleveland got enough information from your staff that you were out of the country—you know, loose lips sink ships and all that. After Sable was gone, we knew you had found the rocks and probably the paper. Why else would you be restaurant shopping in Italy? What a bizarre turn—we weren't sure what happened to Sable; the cuffs were supposed to release, and only 'Daleka the Slovak sumo wrestler' was intended for the high-dive act. Next, poor Cleveland got away with playing possum for so many years just to get bumped off by Simon so close to the end. It's created so much more work for me."

Fred interjected, "So, Daleka was slated for *murder* out the window? That had to be a lot of preplanning to swing big Daleka around."

"Oh, Fred, *murder*? You make it sound so evil when you use that word. Daleka was a greedy gold-digging worker bee bitch who became a liability some time ago." Sighing, he said, "Sable and his kinky shit. I told him to be careful—she could kick the shit outta both of us—but he assured me he would be cranked up on something, and she would be downed out and lethargic. He said he would take care of it. Him and his sex toys. The cuffs were supposed to unclip; they either didn't, or she got the drop on him—we'll never know.

"It was getting personal for Sable; he had found out something very disturbing about Daleka. He was going to tell me all about it after the dust had settled." Hatch kept going, "I told Sable both those Czech girls were bad news. Sable maintained it didn't matter who you were dealing with, you were going to get screwed in any business if you weren't careful. The difference is, in this business there's very little negotiating, and you can't sue your associates—you're playing with your life.

"And then there was Simon and Bora. They would have slit each other's throats for an extra dollar if they had the chance. Bora was too dumb and greedy for her own good. And trying to kidnap the old woman, Alba Tratorio! That was an act of desperation and stupidity. No managerial ability compared to Daleka. She did herself in with no help from us.

"Simon was just as greedy and was actually trying to negotiate with Cleveland! Trying to negotiate with a bargaining chip he didn't have. Cleveland and I weren't sure what we were going to do with him, and to tell the truth, I have no idea how the son of a bitch got the drop on Cleveland—just not like him." I smiled at the thought of Hatch telling the truth. "Cleveland was recording their conversation in the car, but I'll never get to hear what went down."

Just then two knocks sounded on the door and the handle spun. Mind flash—JET in jeopardy. I knew Fred was probably ready to spring, and if Hatch turned around and I could offset his balance knocking the urn into him. The door didn't open; Hatch had locked it behind himself when he came in.

Hatch didn't even turn around. "Tell 'em you're busy; you're talking business on the phone."

"I'm busy right now, JET. I'm talking to Sergio in Rome."

"I want the diamonds and the paper . . . and the key," Hatch demanded.

I started, "We don't . . ." but Fred interrupted me. Not knowing what I was going to say, he decided to jump in. Having closed the Banque Suisse Internationale account in Zürich, we returned our key, and in fact they charged us for the two missing keys we had never found.

Fred said, "We don't have a key, but we have ..." Fred started opening the center desk drawer.

Hatch barked, "Careful!"

Fred continued slowly opening the drawer with his right hand, while he held the left out to his side. With two fingers he pulled out the small manila envelope with BSI 823 and Daleka's initials on it and handed it toward Hatch. "I think this was Daleka's, but there was no key inside."

Hatch told Fred to toss it on the desk and move back. He put the envelope in his pocket. "Daleka had a key all right," he snickered, "but it wouldn't have opened anything but a gym locker in Boulder. Abel showed Daleka a signature card to prove she was on the account," he added, continuing to chuckle.

"The rest is in the fireproof," I said, pointing to the steel locked file cabinet in one corner of the office. "Everybody's looking for diamonds, but all I have are a few pieces of jewelry."

"And the paper?" Hatch asked.

"Yeah, in the fireproof."

I didn't want to look at Fred. I didn't want to see his expression. I could've said something else, anything, but I didn't want anybody else getting hurt. Fred knew I now regularly carried the Beretta, but he didn't know exactly where it was or if I'd have a chance to use it. Hatch told me to unlock the cabinet, put the bonds and jewels on top, and step back. I complied.

Hatch grabbed them and, looking at me, ordered, "Let's go. Fred, you're going to stay here and be quiet while Lantana walks me out of here. She'll call you after I'm down the road. Look at me." Hatch's expression was pure evil. "I can't impress this strongly enough. Don't be stupid or play hero. I'll fuck her up; I don't give a shit. I honestly have nothing to lose. Let's go."

He stuffed the jewelry in his slacks, then looked at the bonds to verify them, folded the envelope in thirds, and put them in his back pocket. He secured the Taser in his waistband beneath his shirt and took me by the arm, with the .44 Magnum hanging low by his side in the other hand. He told Fred, already sitting in the desk chair, to roll toward the window facing out and relax. I was to lead out, turning immediately into the kitchen and down the back stairs.

I unlocked the door, opening it slowly. In the hall I caught the shadow of a figure with my peripheral vision. Intuitively I dropped deadweight to the floor, pulling out of Hatch's grip. Someone or something wildly slammed the door open. I was going to roll away from the threshold but didn't have time. I heard the deafening blast from Hatch's short-barreled revolver and saw the muzzle flash. From the floor I saw a body yanked from its feet, slamming against the wall across from the doorway. Before the person hit the floor, a burst of shots tore over my head so quickly it must have been a fully automatic weapon. In slow motion Hatch's body jerked sequentially, like a strobe light, backward as a spray of warm blood hit my face and red splattered in my eyes as if whipped from a paintbrush. Hatch's body thumped to the floor, and someone rushed in, kicking the Charter Arms from his hand. It was Mason!

Hatch was within an arm's length of me. Unlike each of the Czech girls' faces, which appeared contorted in emotional anguish and pain, Hatch's expression was grotesquely serene. The bullets must have passed through him; bright blood contrasting against the yellow shirt began to pool beneath him. Mind flash—Fred was hit by the pass-through bullets.

I was stone-cold petrified, immobile on the floor—in shock I suppose. I wasn't even shaking, but I was suddenly gasping for breath; I had forgotten to breathe. JET rushed in, falling to the floor almost on top of me. Frantically, almost crying, he said, "You all right, L'tana, L'tana ... L'tana?"

"Yes, JET! Yes!"

Fred rushed from the chair, sliding down to me.

I looked to the hall. The man who was down was being helped slowly up by another agent in full combat gear. He was wearing a vest, but was short of breath and holding his chest, muttering quietly; I think he was swearing.

Detective Gwynn, aka Columbo, was on the scene also. I was picked up and escorted with Fred out of the office and into Chez Neo. "Your boy JET should get a bonus for today's job," he said.

I was coming back to reality, although the ringing in my ears had yet to subside. I looked around for Jessica and JET. "What about the customers? What's going on? We've got to ..."

Gwynn interrupted. "I'm afraid the restaurant is closed; this is a very serious crime scene at the moment."

Fred was shaken also as Jess stepped up to the plate. "You guys take it easy. We've got it handled; the customers are being handled. We're going to say we've had a power outage in the kitchen and we won't be open tonight."

I looked at JET for his explanation.

"I heard that guy lock the door when I left; I never liked him anyway. You know, you *can* see people through that mirror window during the daytime when the sun comes from the outside window. I already thought something was wrong before you said you were on the phone to Sergio ..."

"Who isn't in Italy," I said, looking at Gwynn and Mason.

JET continued, "I had already called 911, and it didn't take long for Mr. Gwynn and Mr. Mason to show up with those two SWAT guys."

I was just staring at him blankly but said, "You did good, kid."

"Again," Fred added.

CONFESSION IN CHARACTER

F red had contacted the Art Institute of Chicago from the lead we received in Antwerp regarding Abel's sheet of Chinese characters. Through a series of telephone handoffs, Fred sent the document to a Paul Kit-Wen Tso, who was the curator of the Asian Art exhibit at AIC, which included calligraphy and logograms. Fred explained our predicament and that we were having a difficult time having this logogram containing Buddhist and spiritual content translated in a meaningful way.

Fred explained to Mr. Tso that we knew little about the paper except that it was a personal epistle involved in a possible suicide. There were no aspersions cast that the document had any historic, artistic, or Holy Grail-like significance or value. Tso was very gracious and said he would be willing to look at it and render an opinion as to its meaning. He claimed there would be no fee involved if the translation was fairly straightforward, but if others needed to research or review in depth, he would be pleased with a donation to his department at the museum.

Of course Fred said, "No problem," *Abel's got this one.*

We had scanned the page and sent it to Mr. Tso with hopes of gaining yet more insight into the multilayered reaches of Abel's cranium. We received a five-page letter back from Tso stating that two other experts had also reviewed the sheet of characters and rendered an opinion. It was obvious from the depth of the translation that we would be sending a generous donation to the Art Institute.

Tso explained that the message within was disturbing, alarming, sinister, worrisome, and very personal and that they had no interest in who had authored the document but had another question if it might be answered. I thought, *Yikes!* This was a scary lead-in. Tso and his associates were curious as to the expert that so poignantly transcribed this to Chinese. It had been done so provocatively and intellectually that they would be interested in making the acquaintance of this individual for their own future reference and research. Of course we had no answer to that question. We did not know who transcribed the document even if we knew the author of the contents.

The author was a person who was very troubled and in a great deal of pain. The characters intimated the pain was both physical and emotional. Tso stated that the author, whom he referred to as he, lived a life of discontent, never at peace or at one with himself. He felt a cloud of gloom hanging never far from his head, which caused great anxiety to his being.

This person was a paradox inasmuch as he referred to his spiritual life as being agnostic, yet he studied many types of religions and various gods in an effort to find peace within. He settled on Buddhism, not so much that he believed with all his heart in this one direction, but more that Buddhist beliefs and ideology made the most sense to him. Ideology itself is a system of ideals that form the basis for real conditions of existence.

Generally practitioners of Buddhism strive to be awakened from the sleep of ignorance, seeing things as they really are, free from faults and mental obstruction. Further, references to pantheism were a common thread through the writing. Pantheism is a belief in the universe, although it is subject to interpretation just as Darwinism versus a Supreme Being theory is.

It sounded like Abel consciously wanted to separate mind from body or, as Fred cleverly put it, religion from state. The paper was a combination of confession, seeking redemption, and ridding oneself of the materialism of this world. (Wow—that didn't sound like Abel!) Tso pointed out that didn't necessarily mean simply material possessions but the physical sensation of one's life also. Tso could only say that there was not a specific character for suicide, as most religions shun that act, but death by personal choice was definitely an option being considered. The author paradoxically mentioned Christianity and Catholicism in his early life, even though suicide is considered a mortal sin in those religions and thus they had no bearing on his beliefs.

He didn't believe his soul would be separated by spiritual means from his earthly being, but darkness was entering his life. (*Darkness from the walls of his skull squeezing light from his brain? Or referring to Daleka as darkness?* I wondered.)

He claimed he knew right from wrong, not that he practiced either as a habit; he made no excuses for living opportunistically and gluttonously, in particular enjoying pleasures of the flesh. He felt he was being surrounded by evil. (*Daleka again?*) There was an evil one wandering the earth with his blood. (*His love child from his postcollege days in Europe? Perhaps he was cranked on drugs, delusional with thoughts he was somehow responsible, and decided to off himself and Daleka?*) Through the devil's trickery, his relationship was almost consummated. A reference to a dark or evil child again but not sown by his own seed but another source (they claimed there was no word for it). He saw the mother's eyes in this child of darkness, yet it was not his, this one. (*Oh no! Daleka is his stepdaughter?*)

In general, Tso went on, although Buddhists strive to be free from mental obstructions, this person seemed to acknowledge his faults and was trying to escape his demons. Problems and suffering arise from a confused and negative state of mind, with confusion and negativity perhaps caused by his pain. He was looking to transcend to a peaceful state of mind.

He did not make amends to anyone for a life he believed was poorly lived, but for some reason he wanted to go on record cleaning and clearing his mind. He felt he had no one to tell but must declare something of his life, or it would have been fully without meaning. (*So he was declaring he was a diamond smuggler, a sex addict, and a murderer, but other than that, not a bad guy?*)

Tso mentioned that, just as in the English language, many characters have different meanings, and to become thoroughly familiar with the nuances of character writing takes many years of study and research. Likewise, it is advantageous to be familiar with the person who is composing. This becomes easier if the body of work you are reading, translating, or trying to understand belongs to a published author's style you are already familiar with. Therefore a single letter, such as Abel's, can still be subject to various interpretations.

We had a handle on that point and reasoned Tso was allowing himself a wide breadth as far as deducing the exact meanings of the content. Had he known Abel and his personality, maybe he could've read further into it. How would you even attempt to explain Abel to an outsider like Tso? He said he had done the best he could, and that was all we expected and hoped for.

THE EXIT INTERVIEW

F red and I had been waiting, not necessarily patiently, for an interrogatory from the authorities. We got the usual "Don't leave town" and one I hadn't heard in the movies: "Your major assets have been frozen pending an FBI interview and investigation," which conjured up visions of sitting on uncomfortable chairs under sunlamps during a deposition. Would the two police factions play out like a TV show? Would Gwynn kowtow to the fastidious and superior FBI, like Andy Griffith and Barney told to step aside when the state police came in to solve a crime? Mason had taken the lead on the case, and it seemed Gwynn and the IRS became peripheral players.

The good news was no one had died in several weeks. Since the Hatch incident, there was an eerie uncertainty waiting for things to get back to normal, though I felt nothing would ever be normal again. My day-to-day life was fraught with an uneasiness I couldn't shake. And if I felt like I had butterflies on opening night, Fred seemed just as rattled trying to maintain a level of composure and sardonic humor.

At one point he asked, "Just curious—do you think anyone will violently die around you this week?" If he thought that was funny, it wasn't, but frankly I couldn't blame him. At least he wasn't pulling another stunt like his fantasy story.

I couldn't help myself as long as he was being a wiseass. "Besides Elisa, Abel, Daleka, Simon, the Secret Man, Bora, and Hatch? The day isn't over yet."

It was plain creepy going in and out of my office. The carpet had been replaced, but I found myself stepping around where Hatch's body had been shot. By the way, contents insurance does not cover bloodstains. Our greatest concern was what the FBI, Gwynn, and IRS had uncovered and how it would impact us, or more to the point, me. What would happen to the bond money and diamonds now that they had been discovered? There would be no alibi or fabrication on my part. I would simply plead ignorance. Abel's body jewelry and the bonds were taken as evidence after the office shoot-out, and imagine our relief that we hadn't sold or tried to fence anything. That was by design, however; we thought it premature to sell the bonds or fence the jewels because there had been no resolution to the case.

Now…enter the human mind and greed at work. Whether the diamonds were stolen or not, they belonged to Abel unless, in this order, someone claimed them, such as next of kin, or they sat long enough and I was able to abscond with them. The bonds, however, unless proven purchased with stolen money, technically belonged to me because they belonged to La Ventana and I owned La Ventana. But we were sure the FBI had their own ideas about the disposition of the assets.

The restaurant was back operating, and although there was a general vibe that "another something" had happened, the patrons came back with very few questions. The Abel and

Daleka crash-and-burn event received much more publicity for obvious reasons. Anyone would admit that two kinkily clad weirdos crashing eighteen stories to their handcuffed deaths through the window of a restaurant named "The Window" and smashing like bugs on the sidewalk made a pretty good story for the news at eleven. Even though Fred, JET, and I were witness to a mind-numbing, gory, and ear-deafening shoot-out/takedown of an international jewel thief, with warm blood splashed on my face, it hadn't hit the media as such.

I knew the investigation wasn't over, but when Mason scheduled an appointment with Fred and me, I was expecting something akin to an exit interview. In what I considered a brilliant tactical maneuver by the FBI, it was not mentioned that JET, poor Mrs. Alba Tratorio aka Nonna Bella, and Jessica were interviewed separately and simultaneously in different corners of Chez Neo.

On an early Monday morning, designed for the FBI's advantage, I presumed, Agent Mason Parker, another suit, and a flaming redheaded stenographer came into the office. Mason and the other FBI agent pulled up the only two chairs in the office as I sat at my desk, and Fred and Red, the stenographer, in a black pantsuit with a lime-green blouse, sat on the couch. I wasn't sure if dogs were allowed in such meetings, but Kellogg insisted on attending. He lay in a dignified position on the windowsill sporting a fresh Stars and Stripes bandana.

Mason introduced everyone, including me—as Agatha Lantana, my given name. He gave a general purpose for the meeting as Lucille Ball's fingers fluidly massaged her digital steno machine with that stern and classic emotionless face that all stenographers have in the movies. Mason recited legalese from his well-worn notes, covering formalities and disclaimers should anything go to trial, and then looked up, fixing a gaze on Kellogg's perfect sphinxlike pose.

Intending a slight icebreaker, I said, "Not to worry; he won't talk."

Mason was not amused. "Commendable you didn't try to cash any of the bonds. Not only would you have implicated yourselves, but selling would've been impossible; the serial numbers would have shown as stolen. It helped also that you didn't sell the diamond jewelry from Abel's evidence envelope," he said as his eyes darted between Fred and myself. There was a long pause. Mason broke his own silence. "You *didn't* sell any of the diamonds, did you?"

"No," I said, thinking Mason was bluffing to see if we had more diamonds.

Why wouldn't or didn't I expect this? What kind of dream world was I living in thinking he didn't know about everything, including the La Ventana ownership? Yet he did not mention the stray rocks in Abel's desk. Furthermore, and unbeknownst to Larry the lawyer, Gloria the accountant, Fred and me, Mason told us Abel and "the boys" had an international corporation that the FBI and IRS seized that was not associated with La Ventana. It was called Satchland Inc., a clever acronym for our three favorite felons: Sable, Hatch, and Cleveland. Within Satchland was Salus Inc., which owned a couple of boats, an airplane, a few high-end cars, and other assets.

"Crap, what did this mean to my ownership of La Ventana?" I wanted to ask before being slapped across the face with more bad news. Mason explained that La Ventana actually had a clean history and I did in fact own it. I owned La Ventana, but the bonds had vaporized. They were purchased with illegal funds, as Satchland was listed on the bonds in addition to La Ventana.

Mason said, "Off the record," as Lucy's fingers stopped as if she had just been unplugged, "I didn't think you guys would find the bonds in the desk, but that's where they were and the 'uppers,' my superiors, said to leave them there. Even with Abel dead, they figured someone knew where to find them."

I glanced at Fred; his eyes were already on me. If there were cartoon balloons above our heads, we would have had an image of Kellogg exuberantly pointing under the desk, with a hand drawn in place of a paw. This while we were engaged in sexual gymnastics on top of the desk.

"Back on," Mason said as Lucy's mannequin-like body came back to life, "the good news is you are not implicated in the long list of counts against Abel Connelly, William W. Rice aka Hatch, and Anthony Morrison aka Cleveland."

Ah, I thought again, with a quick glance to Fred: the Secret Man, "Morris" for Morrison.

"The bad news is you can't keep any of the goods. They are being appropriated by the FBI and IRS, part of a larger cache of stolen items and implicated securities."

Fred interjected, "I know I don't have anything to do with this, but I have a question. We were under the impression there was a 'Mr. Big' running the operation or a larger organization?"

Mason answered, "You actually are involved in this, Fred. Just because you're an independent contractor and not a direct employee of La Ventana doesn't mean you couldn't be complicit in any of these crimes."

The "this guy knows everything" look on my face must've been as transparent as glass.

"Off the record," *unplugged,* "you know, Ms. Lantana, we do get out of the doughnut shop occasionally.

"There was not a Mr. Big per se, but the FBI considered this operation a ring, although independent from a larger organization. Rice, Morrison, and Connelly worked together as partners. If there was a Mr. Big, it was Abel."

I looked at Fred. *Aha! Boris's boss wasn't in Pardubice because his boss was Abel and his boss was dead!*

"Abel was the only one with a business large enough to launder money. There were a couple other players in Colorado and California that we already have, mostly fences, and Interpol is cleaning up some European contacts and connections. Just like mining for gold, there are probably hidden jewels, cash, and certificates that we may or may not find. Back on." *Plugged in.*

"So now what?" I asked.

"We'll still have some questions, but for now you can get back to running your business. It's only supposition on our part, but we have logically concluded that the La Ventana ownership was not transferred to you, Ms. Lantana, as a goodwill gesture. Had the rest of Abel and his partners' plot panned out in their best interest, you would certainly not be reaping the benefit of this asset."

Wow! Fred nailed that scenario on the head.

Mason kept going. "We imagine their plan, or Abel's plan, was predicated on getting rid of you," he said with a cold stare directly into my face. "Your nickname was 'Squab,'" Mason remarked.

"Squab? I always wondered if Abel had a nickname for me."

"Yes, squab as in a pigeon, and if you're the pigeon, you're someone to get swindled or stung. You were the pigeon who was going to be used or duped. All the players, except you, ended up dead, including Elisa Zielinski, sunk knee-deep in cans full of concrete in the Hudson River bed. It was very ugly. The drag hooks brought up only the top half of Ms. Zielinski's torso, severing her at the knees. She was cast in five-gallon pails of concrete that were later retrieved.

"We haven't found any documentation as to how the rest of Abel's plan would have worked. After your body was found, Abel would have probably feigned surprise, discovering you were the clever embezzler who forged documents showing your La Ventana ownership and evidence you were going to murder him! Abel, shocked and dismayed, would be beside himself in utter disbelief that you were a monster almost getting away with this hideous plot to kill him and take over the restaurant. You were also a built-in scapegoat had the diamond-smuggling operation, or any part of it, been exposed or discovered during your embezzlement scheme.

"But you wouldn't get in trouble; you couldn't talk— remember, you're dead. The treasure of pilfered money along with other evidence, if found, would rightfully belong to him. We traced the purchase of another Sharp ER-A-347 electronic cash register in Abel's office closet to just before you were hired. That unit was supposedly a backup or extra. But he was printing up phony profits or 'pretend skimming,' with the fourth register as insurance.

"He would probably blame that on you also. If additional spending sent up a flag with the IRS after you were gone, Abel could say it was money you had embezzled. He could say he found it, and no one would know it had come from diamond smuggling. It's confusing, but a clever and creative way to put a whole new spin on skimming."

Smacked with this on the spur of the moment, Fred and I simply shook our heads in confusion. My next question of course was, what was the disposition of the money between registers, how would it be accounted for, and so on?

Before I could ask, Mason declared, "Technically there's no trace on where the other funds went.

"That wraps it up, at least for this morning. I'm not sure what this does for your future plans in Salerno. But best of luck to you with that venture. We'd appreciate, at least for now, if you tell us if you have immediate plans to leave the country. Also, it may take a day or so, but all your funds and accounts will be released and available."

Crap. I looked at Fred, thinking, *does this guy have a camera in our bedroom?*

Now What?

Our silky-smooth machine, labored on for four months, suddenly had a bag of bolts dumped in, bringing it to a frozen halt.

*We still had a deposit on the space that was to become Restaurante Tavola Cinque in Salerno, Italy.

*We had a cancellation clause in our lease that was nothing more than losing the deposit that was Abel's gift in cash from the Swiss bank box. Was the project still feasible now that the money balloon of comfort had suffered a serious leak?

*The bond certificates and genital gems had been returned to the FBI. The "rhinestone" gems from the desk had not been mentioned, and we certainly weren't going to pop up and say, "Hey, Mason! Did you guys forget these?" Furthermore, we weren't about to sell them only to find they were on an inventory and had yet to be mentioned.

Or worse yet, Mason would sneak up behind us and blurt, "*Aha!*"

No, we would sit on them for a rainy day. That was fine, but they would not be helping us fund the restaurant.

*The 1.4 million in bonds went poof!

*The sale of La Ventana, which would have put us over the top for the Italian T5 build-out, went poof when banker boyfriend ceased to be Jess's boyfriend!

We still had the stock certificates found in Abel's Pardubice Czech Republic office, which were valued at €20,000 or about $21,000 US. That was better than a pointy stick in the eye but not enough to build out a restaurant. We also had the cashier's check for €8000, but it was two years old so we weren't sure if, number one, it would still be honored, and number two, we could even cash it without skyrockets exploding under Interpol's scrutiny. We were in the same predicament wondering if Mason or Interpol would drop a bomb as soon as we tried to liquidate the stocks.

I felt like my neck and shoulders were in a plow-horse collar and being sent to the field for a long day in the sun. Not only was my dream going down the drain, but Fred felt an awful responsibility for planting the initial seed and pushing to get as far along as we had. Compounding that was the guilt and disappointment I felt for Nonna Bella and JET, let alone Sergio, who would probably still strike out as a lone wolf. Sergio's chance of success was a double-edged sword. He would have a tougher time making it without our backing; however, he had credibility, coming from a highly rated restaurant in a major market, with a professional portfolio and plenty of references.

Nerve-frazzling anxiety doesn't describe the mental and emotional strain that building out a new restaurant on a good day is, which includes dealing with several contractors, their subs, deadlines, and construction schedules—and waiting for the next thing to go wrong. Now try to do that all in Italian. *Wake up, Lantana; maybe this is the way it's supposed to be.* Bottom line: it might have been a fun gig in a nerve-racking way, but I couldn't take care of everyone.

Fred did the only logical thing: he collected Kellogg and me, a Papa's Tapas gyro, some Roditys, and a Nonna Bella oatmeal cookie, and we headed to Hamilton Preserve in the Taurus. He packed light, with a single backpack and a bottle of water and biscuit for Kellogg.

We drove in silence, not somber but thoughtful. Parked and unloaded, we marched off into a cloudless sunny blue November afternoon. It was very peaceful and one of those last rare days where bright sunshine flooded through the treetops, which would hold in heat for a few more waning hours. The colors were late this year, and the dying leaves were offering their most spectacular colors. Still in silence, even Kellogg realized this walk was strictly business as he stayed right with us, his little paws crunching twigs and leaves double time to our feet. Fred had led us into the hall of pines, where we would inhale deeply with relief and resolve. Fred decided to sit on a fallen pine just off the path as he slipped out of his backpack. He snapped off a piece of oatmeal cookie for Kellogg in lieu of the biscuit and poured some water in the paper bowl. The *look* was on Fred's face; wheels were spinning.

"I think we should still do it. We'll have to watch things closer, money, that is. We will need an appraisal of La Ventana, the equipment and business, in order to borrow against, and business loans on restaurants are high risk in the eyes of a bank and very difficult, let alone borrowing for a business in another country. We no longer have a built-in buyer, so I don't know how long it will take to sell the place. Certainly longer than the deposit will hold Tavola Cinque. I think we should go back there and open a bank and brokerage account, depositing some of our cash, the stocks, and the cashier's check. It can cool, establishing some credibility for us. It's a start."

I paused for some time, shaking my head. "Let me guess: you're suggesting we keep La Ventana with Jess operating it, somehow watchdog her, and forge ahead with Tavola Cinque?"

"Yep!"

Norway's Dr. Helgeson

I don't think anyone downplayed Abel's intelligence. It is well-documented that many of the greatest criminals are bona fide geniuses, not that anyone was putting Abel in that category. His undated epistle took my impression of Abel to new depths. The irony of a *character* like Abel writing his own *character* assassination in Chinese *characters*! This certainly piqued our interest into more of Abel's medical protocol and treatments before his death.

We knew Larry Feinstein not only had power of attorney for Abel but also medical power of attorney. Fred and I shared the Mr. Tso letter with Larry and discussed Abel's character confession and the "to whom it may concern" attempt at atonement as well. Larry was aware no one had required closure over Abel's bizarre and violent death, but we were curious to more fully understand his condition. We began kicking around ideas as to how to get this information. Larry went to work composing an outline.

Through Abel's medical files, we knew he had traveled to Norway regularly but did not know the extent or type of his treatments. Larry had the Norway file from Abel's cabinet and began drafting a letter to a doctor Barbara Helgeson, team leader apparent for Abel's cranium overhaul. With a dossier of documentation that included death certificates, coroner's report, and international HIPAA red tape docs for Larry's legal right to information, he asked the good doctor for a report leading up to prognosis and Abel's last visits to the Norwegian Neurological Sanatorium.

After back-and-forth correspondence, including phone calls, Dr. Helgeson was convinced Larry's intentions were legitimate. She had conferred with the American FBI about Abel's medical files and had actually spoken with the FBI coroner, in real time, during the autopsy he was performing on Abel. Larry signed waivers assuring his line of questioning had nothing to do with the authorities, piracy of medical research, or initiating legal action of international malpractice in the case of Abel Connelly. Larry satisfied Helgeson he was not interested in specific or clinical treatment but instead behavioral case study and direction of Abel's thought patterns/ processes, piecing together clues as to motivation for the deaths. His research was an effort to reach a reasonable conclusion to determine the likelihood or probability as to whether the deaths were accidental, murder or murder/suicide, or double suicide. Unless Abel had exposed personal information about Daleka, Dr. Helgeson wouldn't know if Daleka was a wacky sex addict, a suicide wannabe along for the ride, or a greedy diamond-smuggling bitch working her own con for monetary gain.

Satisfied that she did not have to give trade secrets on how to drill a brain, Dr. Helgeson proceeded to give a brief history of Abel's migraines as reported from his childhood, leading up to treatments at the sanatorium, which had begun about two years ago. Abel declined a surgical procedure skewed too negatively for Abel's liking. The likelihood of leaving him with the mentality of a teenager did not thrill him, although he was to be a happy and headache-free teenager. I told Fred he already had the mentality of a teenager. Joking aside, we agreed that would not be our personal first choice either. That left experimental drugs, which ranged from a regimen of oral drugs taken over a long period, perhaps the rest of his life, to a more radical approach.

That other option was pinpoint injections of lysergic acid diethylamide, good old-fashioned tripping acid from the days of Timothy Leary. LSD25 was developed in the 1930s, legalized in the 40s, experimented with by the CIA during the Cold War as a truth serum and mind control agent, with the possibility of future chemical warfare. It was made illegal in 1970 and classified as a schedule one dangerous drug, basically with no medicinal benefit. It has since been clinically proven that taken in low doses, 90 percent of claims it is dangerous have been proven false, in addition to the fact that it is nonaddictive.

With a lack of watchdog organizations like the US FDA, Norway in particular has been conducting experiments for over fifteen years, specifically for certain types of neurosis cluster headaches, debilitating headaches that can cycle as long as three months without any response to medication. Several cluster headache patients were sent into remission from small injections of LSD, with "simply astounding results," said Dr. Helgeson.

We were under the assumption Abel's condition was terminal. Having exhausted treatments in the United States, how desperate, isolated, and frightened Abel must have felt facing an unknown inoperable disease with no one to comfort, console, or even talk with except Norwegian physicians. I wondered how much Hatch or Cleveland knew about this. If they did, would they be sympathetic or already calculating splitting Abel's third of the loot?

Our understanding was Abel had been diagnosed with a cephalic disorder, a congenital condition that stems from damage during abnormal development of the nervous system of the brain. Cephalic conditions are not necessarily caused by a single factor but can be heredity or environmental, involving the mother during pregnancy and medication she might have been taking. Slits or clefts in the cerebral hemispheres misfire, creating cognitive impairment in judgmental areas yet are hyperactive in others.

But we were informed, *"Mr. Connelly's prognosis was indeed dire but by no means a death sentence. He was aware of, and we had discussed, a new regimen of injections we felt had a very high percentage success rate. He would however have to stay in-house for the first four weeks, being monitored heavily. He had already sent a deposit for the first round of treatments, a team was being assembled, and scheduling had already begun when he expired."*

That conflicted with our suicide theory, or at least challenged it. Unless he had lost the will to live, why would he not want to go through with the treatments? Regardless of what his long-term plan was, with me running the store, he would not have to worry about the workaday stress of operating a restaurant. After his initial in-house stay, in order to become normalized, he would be free to move about. Sure, he would be tied to the clinic or his treatments or injections, but lots of people have medical issues that require ongoing maintenance.

It was hard to fathom that Abel felt a strong moral conviction to do himself in on the merit of cleansing the earth of two evil individuals. Considering the murderous mischief he, Cleveland, and Hatch had already engineered, it seemed improbable they couldn't conjure a different way to get rid of Daleka. Abel never gave the impression of being selfless. In our sarcastic summation, we guessed Abel was simply a diamond-smuggling, sex-addicted, smooth-talking, successful businessman with migraines, whose world was basically crumbling at the foundation. End result? The question was still clinically unanswered.

SAFE!

I decided to once again look through Abel's file cabinets in the office to see if there was anything relative to start-up information for a new store. There were two files in the bottom drawer, farthest back, labeled restaurant. I had never paid much attention to them, figuring they were old news from the California store. The lunch crowd had thinned, and I thought it a good time to take a look. Maybe there was a stray doc illuminating some fabulous unknown trick. I chuckled, thinking I might find an errant diamond.

Taking a break from bookwork, I began looking at the two legal-size filing cabinets in the corner. Although investigators had taken Abel's computer and returned it, they had not removed the desk or file cabinets. An investigator spent the better part of a day copying files.

Setting a cup of coffee on top to restart my investigation, I promptly spilled it between the two cabinets. I slid the cabinets apart, forming a 'V' to sponge up the mess. I noticed a patch of irregular carpet going against the grain. Sliding the cabinets farther apart, I peeled the carpet back—oh look, a floor safe! Abel never told me about the safe, and I had no idea where the combination might be. *Wait till Fred sees this.* I mopped up the coffee and pushed the cabinets back together, not wanting anyone else to see what I had found. I went back to inspecting the files, mostly finding equipment brochures, suppliers' names, and old menus.

Fred was equally tickled with this discovery; he quickly pulled out his phone. The number on the safe was for the Oyster Lock Co. Oyster didn't have the combination on file; in fact, they had no record of this safe. They said they could probably open it but had to wait until tomorrow for Clark, a semiretired old-timer, who came in on certain days to do bench-work.

About nine thirty the following morning, JET escorted into my office an older man wearing a blue work shirt. It had "Oyster Lock" in white block letters on the back, and "Clark" in white script over the pen pocket on the front.

Fred immediately engaged Clark in small talk and found out he was not only a locksmith but a safecracker who had done ten years at San Quentin about twenty-five years ago. That put him at about seventy by our estimation. He told Fred embellished old-time stories about safes that he had opened, including ones he had robbed. The ones he opened like ours usually had nothing but old *Playboys* or maybe a bag of brittle marijuana.

Clark had an electronic stethoscope on the safe as he continued spinning the dial back and forth. We weren't so sure paying by the hour was the most cost-effective way to get the thing open inasmuch as Clark was wearing dual hearing aids and thick readers. Having been lying on the floor, face over the safe, for over an hour, suddenly he yanked the earphones from his head as he rolled to one side, exposing less than a full complement of teeth in a lovely shade of mahogany. "Y'all mind if'en ah pull the door first? I won'e look inside; jus' make me feel like tha ol' days."

"Sure," said Fred.

Clark rolled up to his knees, straining to open the small but heavy door. The door creaked open, and struggling from there, JET helped Clark up to his feet. He wrote the ticket for one hour—ninety-five dollars. I wrote a check, Fred gave him a twenty dollar tip, and we dismissed Clark and JET, much to JET's disappointment.

Fred rolled his arm in a grandiose "take it away" gesture to me. I knelt over the safe, wondering if I should use surgical gloves to remove the contents. Not for evidential reasons but for sanitary ones. The safe was small, only the size of a gardening bucket, but deep. Clark struck out, sort of. There was no smut or dried-out weed, but there was an array of sex toys. I recognized dildos as such; the others I wasn't completely sure about.

I pulled out a legal pad curled around the wall of the safe. Flipping through the pages, I realized there were full sentences in my handwriting cut from other documents and taped to the pages. They were worksheets and test forgeries for "my" La Ventana ownership documents. Line after countless line of my signature. You could see the progression until they were so fluid I couldn't tell Abel's forgery from my own signature. Every detective show tells you there are no two signatures alike. Short of doing an overlay against a bright light on glass, it was obvious

Abel was painstaking in his practice so as not to copy individual signatures but to make each signature original, duplicating the cursive shape of my letters.

Next was a thin brown zippered leatherette case that had "Prudential Insurance" embossed on it. I didn't bother unzipping the case but handed it to Fred as he was walking back from locking the office door. He sat at the desk and began perusing.

In the bottom center of the safe sat a midnight-blue velvet pouch, from Crown Royal whiskey, with a gold pull string. Feeling the sheer weight, I could feel my ears flushing with blood and beginning to ring as I fished it out. Rising from the floor, I looked at Fred, almost in a hypnotic state, staring at him at the desk, my mouth slightly agape. He was intent reading whatever documents were in the attaché. I slowly opened the mouth of the pouch and began pouring a jumble of dirty gray, mixed with shiny, rocks on the desk in a long line. We sat silently across from one another for what seemed to be an eternity.

Fred laid out a long line of stones according to size to inspect. There were at least three dozen, the largest being approximately ten millimeters wide.

CONTENTEZZA

Fred cupped my hand as we sat quietly in the first-class lounge at Leonardo da Vinci International Airport in Rome waiting to board Delta flight 782 nonstop to Bali. As the hostess came by, I held my other hand up and smiled, indicating we needed nothing. I held onto my smile, thinking that truly we needed nothing. Agatha Lantana, the Nebraska farm girl and unlikely multimillionaire in the first-class lounge.

Besides packing for our trip, we had a late night making sure everything was in order at Tavola Cinque, our lovely and, more importantly, profitable restaurant in Salerno, Italy. So much had revolved around Table Five at La Ventana that we named the new restaurant Tavola Cinque, Table Five in Italian. Instead of Table Five being showcased deep inside for the elite, as it was at La Ventana, Tavola Cinque was prominently placed in the front window overlooking Via Nizza Street in downtown. It could seat six to sixteen, depending upon how we expanded it. It had been eighteen months since Abel's safe and its contents had been discovered beneath the file cabinets.

The blue velvet bag in the safe had over $1.5 million in partially processed and uncut diamonds. They were probably worth up to twice that much after evaluating, cutting, polishing, and distributing.

The Prudential leatherette case did not contain stocks, bonds, or cash, but two term life insurance policies. Each policy had a two million dollar face value, and Abel and I co-owned each. One was on my life with Abel as the beneficiary, and the other was on Abel's life with me as the beneficiary. What difference would it make if Abel willed the world to me as long as he knew I wouldn't be around to collect on it? Both were in effect at the time of Abel's death, and we presumed the policy on his life would have been an illusion for the authorities, showing his generosity and consideration, that I would be well taken care of if some tragedy befell him. The guise would also be a buffer to maintain and continue operating his beloved La Ventana if the restaurant fell on bad times with me as the sole proprietor. Abel was a great guy.

Fred and I further guessed in the event of my untimely death, which had no doubt been thoroughly planned and calculated, Abel, Hatch, and Cleveland had plans for an extra two million with evidence of my corpse. Two million more dollars in insurance would have rounded out their fortune of millions in diamonds and international funds to divvy up in some faraway place over a case of Cristal champagne and half-naked beauties. Perhaps my murder would have played into Abel's scheme of me being an embezzler. The extra two million would come with the dilemma of producing my body for proof after murdering me. The thought so utterly creeped me out that any channeling of serendipity in the deaths of the Satchland boys did not offset my revulsion.

In an effort to make me feel better, Fred surmised, "They probably did realize a lost opportunity when they murdered Elisa. It would take a bit more thought than dumping you in the Hudson. But well worth the two million dollar effort, say, snapping *your* neck if you slipped down the back kitchen steps."

The way things turned out, Abel was quite generous to insure himself. The insurance company tried to nullify the policy as suicide, but the deaths were ultimately declared accidental and therefore the company had to pay. I decided to use some of the funds to provide for my family, Kellogg's relatives via the national Humane Society, and social services for battered and abused women in Nebraska and nationally. That wouldn't help the road hookers my grandfather had dealt with, but if it helped someone in that position in the future, it made me feel better.

Through arm's-length communication from the United States with Bora's father, Boris Lazarof, in Pardubice, under the guise of sympathy for his barbaric daughter, the throwback to Attila the Hun, we found that Daleka was in fact Abel's stepdaughter. Abel did have a love child with his foreign flame on the post-college vacation to Europe where he met Boris, but that child married at seventeen, supposedly moved to Romania, and was never heard of again. Her half-sister, Daleka, entered the picture at some point, becoming friends with Bora when they were quite young. We didn't expect Boris to admit any of the illicit dealings he had with Abel nor how the girls got involved.

It was inferred that, at least initially, Abel knew nothing of his relationship to Daleka. Although not blood relatives, the whole situation dripped with taboo creepiness. If Boris's daughter Bora was the "good one," it didn't matter; we didn't care—we didn't plan on exchanging Christmas cards with Boris, Mikael, or Geoff in Antwerp. Nor did I plan to send a new tennis shoe to the London Fog trench coat mugger.

Analyzing Dr. Helgeson's information of Abel's condition, combined with his suicidal tendencies, provided numerous scenarios. In conjunction with whatever high-powered nitromethane was coursing through Abel's veins, along with Mr. Tso's profound translation of Abel's commitment to rid the aura of evil surrounding his reality, it was possible he had no intention of releasing himself from the physical and emotional bondage of the Dark One's muscular wrist. Killing two birds, so to speak. Or maybe Hatch was right, and the handcuffs would not unlock or release. Maybe Daleka, downed out on barbiturates or not, was still too much for Abel to handle physically. The dining room had looked like the Little Bighorn after the battle. Perhaps Abel himself did not know his ultimate intention until the final millisecond. Bottom line? It was still classified as an accident by the Troy Police Department and therefore, reluctantly, Prudential Insurance Company. Score one for the good guys, if you can call us that.

My tax-free life insurance money was a well-known fact to the IRS and FBI and was plenty to build out Tavola Cinque. The other assets seamlessly blended in. This helped distance us further from the likelihood we were carrying on the diamond business from Abel and the boys. The FBI and IRS could go about their business catching bigger fish, which would hopefully misdirect their attention from our future activities when it came time to liquidate our diamonds.

Everyone was excited for the new store, perhaps knowing how closely we came to losing everything. Jessica seemed to fully understand that this was *her* chance of a lifetime. And there was plenty of time to get laid and keep La Ventana her priority with a needle-sharp pencil. Sergio was on his best behavior, because although he believed he could launch as a lone wolf, he had the foresight to recognize his long-term prospects were much better if he persevered with us. He began interviewing and training apprentice chefs at La Ventana as soon as Fred and I left in earnest to build out the new store.

The first eight months of the transition were exhausting. We were occasionally commuting individually back to Troy making sure nothing was amiss. Setting up the financial organization took a great deal of time on Fred's part. As Fred did that, I was establishing connections with the invaluable help of Guillermo, Nonna Bella's nephew. Fred and I rented two small apartments, initially attempting to keep some sort of normalcy of living like we had in the United States. That didn't last long as we realized we had a brand-new normalcy. We dropped the month-to-month leases and found a house to rent, large enough for the three of us. Kellogg seemed to revel in the spaciousness of a house and the unbelievable size of his fenced and grass-covered litter box.

Za was employed part-time to help at Chez Neo. This was met with favor from Jessica and a few bartenders. Some felt she was set up as a watchdog, yet others liked the security and presence of one more person sitting quietly with a cell phone. Za kept an eye on things, summoning a busboy if the bartender needed help or having a quick trigger finger for 911 if there was a boisterous situation.

The Chez Playboys were never to be seen again.

On occasion Fred and I went back to the States together to check on La Ventana in Troy, and Touhy Nebraska to visit family and friends. Za and Series 7 took us up on an invitation to stay in our Italian house when we went back home. Because they were good friends, especially Za, the Tratorios treated them as if they were movie stars, probably because of their high fashion dress. Also Series 7 insisted on driving himself around in a rented, black $140,000 Maserati Quattroporte sedan.

We relied on JET in the same capacity at the Italian store, but he was no longer a busboy, although his Aunt Veronica was the general manager and hostess. That was as far as the family affair went with the restaurant. Occasionally for parties and holidays, Nonna Bella contributed as a baker but was not in a chef's capacity.

One afternoon JET came into Tavola Cinque with a mongrel rat hamster much like Kellogg first appeared, except female and black. He claimed it was a stray that followed him home, the same BS Fred tried to pull. I just giggled. We assisted naming the mutt—Nabisco. Nabisco and Kellogg got along famously, and she learned rules quickly from him, including how to use the yard that Kellogg insisted was a litter box. It didn't take long for Nabisco to start bossing Kellogg around. Good girl.

JET, although old enough to have his own apartment and making good money, stayed at Grandma Alba's bungalow, but often with his Russian girlfriend named Zoreen, who had a roommate and an apartment. My sweet innocent JET was all grown up, and the thought of him having sex was disconcerting to me. Fred rolled his eyes at my overly protective mother act. My mouth dropped when he told me JET had been introduced to manhood in the States. Fred claimed he had never seen me blush before. Zoreen was an exchange student; she seemed sweet enough and was planning on staying in Italy.

I told Fred, "My biggest concern is she will break my little JET's heart and I will have to sink her in the Hudson."

"No! Nobody's died in almost two years!" Fred said.

Fred, with the help of Larry and Gloria, had created a corporation in addition to Table Five called Tavola Cinque Inc. for the Salerno store, which had been up and running for almost a year now. Per our agreement, Sergio came to Tavola Cinque to cook and boss kitchen staff around from under Italian code-approved stainless cooking hoods. Once things had leveled out to organized chaos, Fred, Sergio, and I took some jaunts to Barcelona, exploring the restaurant scene there.

Sergio quickly re-upped with old friends in the food industry to the point that he garnered some temporary jobs as a chef. He began dividing his time between Barcelona and Salerno as he had already trained some chefs at Tavola Cinque. Fred and I visited Barcelona when Sergio was cooking. We admired his menu, combining the New York and Salerno cuisines. Fred and I came up with a long-term idea: open another T-5 in Barcelona, making Sergio the master chef at both locations. Sergio beamed at the idea.

Fred was contemplating a third corporation, Restaurants International Inc., for leasing this future store from an owner who was considering retirement. Sergio began cooking there, and although he was an excellent chef, his overzealous chutzpah created a problem: he lacked self-restraint in operating his own store. He came to this conclusion after Fred had to bail him out of the Barcelona city jail on a pugilism charge. He was arrested for beating the crap out of a customer who, perhaps drunk and disorderly or maybe just being a flamboyant Spaniard, complained and insulted loudly about Sergio's sea bass.

Sergio still entertained thoughts of owning his own place but came to the realization he would not have enough of his own money in the foreseeable future for that to happen. We future dreamed, to Sergio's delight, that a place could one day be his operation within Restaurants International, appropriately named "Sergio's T Cinco."

Larry got along well with Fred in understanding our objectives and goals, as did Gloria, our accountant, who continued to work on her need-to-know basis, being well-paid for her significant knowledge in tax-related matters. She added international accounting services to her business card.

It was easier, at least in my mind, to break assets down into three parts: the two corporations with two restaurants, the insurance money, and the diamonds. Fred transferred funds in as confusing a way as possible, opening a bank line of credit for La Ventana and separate bank accounts in Rome and Salerno. He thrived on the action of keeping it all straight.

Diamonds are not traded on commodities markets, but profits from our restaurant and diamond sales funded a commodity account Fred opened. I was concerned about commodity trading from Fred's explanation of the risk involved. He worked with his own self-imposed limits for losses. Further adding to the restaurant-based illusion, his trading was mostly done in pork bellies, beans, and corn.

Jerry the jeweler carefully expanded his horizons, networking with high-end, long-time associates and branching into international diamond marketing and selling. We had ample time to decide and slowly sell the large batch of diamonds.

Before our vacation to Bali, our checklist was complete. Kellogg was in the canine-capable hands of Nonna Bella, still sturdy and competent. The next forty-five hundred miles and seventeen hours would provide almost too much time for cocktails, naps, food, hand-holding, relaxation, and work, but we enjoyed the work. In four short years, after I first arrived at La Ventana in Carlita, my rusting Toyota Corolla, first-class travel was now the norm, not the exception, for Fred and me. I had planned on being a restaurant owner by forty. A lot of luck played into making it by thirty-seven years of age, but I did not take any of it for granted. Most mornings I woke with Kellogg's smiling face staring at me and imagined him saying, "Dorothy, you're definitely not in Kansas anymore."

A driver would be collecting us at Ngurah Rai International and delivering us to a condo in Denpasar Bali, a posh rental where we would stay for ten days.

Fred was dozing in his window seat as we started pushing back from the Jetway. Looking past him to the overcast sky above the tarmac, I lightly brushed back the graying hair on his temple, which had begun to show up about a year ago. He didn't care about it, and I thought it was sexy. I smiled at the thought of so much time spent analyzing my relationship with him. The anxious hours wondering about trust, commitment, and love. We were definitely partners, committed to each other at many levels, caring for each other in a way that symbolic rings weren't necessary. Marriage had never been revisited since our walk in the park. It only mattered in the place Aggie Lantana came from.

We pulled from the taxiway onto the runway, next in line. For that brief moment in time, you could see most of the airport and the jets inching along, waiting their turn. Our bodies sank into the wide, soft-leather, first-class seats as I felt Fred's hand roll up on top of my thigh, eyes still closed. I put my hand atop his and then returned to my view. I thought back to my dinner with Nonna Bella in her little apartment on East Seventh Street in Troy. I remembered as she beamed at her wedding picture with Antonio, the love of her life.

She said simply, "Contentezza"—contentment.

In a few minutes we broke through the overcast, and the Italian sun bathed my face with warmth. Fred's hand twitched gently beneath mine as I closed my eyes, a soft smile curling the edges of my lips. Contentezza.

Printed in the United States
By Bookmasters